JAMES HOLMES'

B O D Y   S H O P

PREMONITIONS, REVELATIONS
AND THE PREDICTION

JAMES HOLMES'

BODY SHOP

PREMONITIONS, REVELATIONS AND THE PREDICTION

STEVEN JOURNEY

Contents

Prologue

James Holmes' Body Shop is the true story of the considerably unusual life of Anthony Marchant, a businessman and property developer who was born with an unusual apparent gift of precognitive foresight. Throughout his life, his gift has placed him around certain people and situations, from which he has surmised that the "End Times" are truly upon us and are immediately imminent.

Anthony, along with his wife and family, resides in the mountains of northern Georgia, USA. Anthony's character is based on the true life of the author, Steven Journey, which is a pen name.

In early 1981, Anthony was given the opportunity to travel to New York City to help construct Trump Tower on Fifth Avenue. He was 38 years old and approaching what he considered to be a midlife crisis in his career when he was given the opportunity. At the time, Anthony had twenty years of well-rounded experience in his field. He was college-educated with degrees in accounting and economics, and he was also naturally talented and professionally trained as an accomplished artist and musician. However, he felt that he could better provide for his family—which consisted of his wife Marie,

1

his son Mark, and his daughter Jen—by temporarily moving to New York for the project.

Anthony was extraordinarily gifted in another manner that he never shared with anyone except Marie. On rare occasions, he would tell her of an occasional "feeling" that he would be made aware of concerning a world event or even a family matter. More often than not, his foreshadowings came true. Anthony was, and still is, very aware of what God has shown him in an astounding manner on two specific occasions. Those events occurred thirteen years apart. Furthermore, they were even related to a third revelation that occurred sixteen years later.

It was the "similarly connected" relationships of all three revelations that prompts Anthony to make a dire prediction for the near future of the world.

Anthony temporally moved to New York City and, after a brief stay in Manhattan, found his way to Rockaway, Long Island, where he leased a beachfront efficiency apartment. He traveled back home to Georgia for a visit approximately every six weeks. On one particular late-night return trip to New York, he met the very attractive 26-year-old Dr. Andrea Ranier, a child psychologist and professor who asked to join him while they were seated on an almost empty Boeing L-1011. Andrea and Anthony conversed extensively and later exchanged information about themselves, including contact information.

Andrea explained to Anthony that she was writing a paper to publish on early childhood memory recollection capabilities.

Anthony laughs and explains that she is talking to the right guy when it comes to childhood memories. He surmised that, because of the strenuous circumstances of his birth, he can recall the details of his birth immediately after having been born. Not only that, but he had also verified the circumstances with members of the family who attended at the time.

However, no one believes his recollections.

Andrea is taken aback in disbelief and promptly digs for her professional card. Anthony is that guy she had always wanted to interview.

Anthony agrees to connect with the doctor at a future time, and much to his amusement, Andrea then promptly falls asleep on Anthony's shoulder for the remainder of the three-hour flight. In a while, the plane approaches JFK and flies over the beach at Rockaway on the moonlit night. Andrea leans over Anthony to see the Atlantic reflecting the moonlight, and he tells her that he lives on the beach at Rockaway. She looks at him in surprise, but she doesn't tell him that she also lives there.

They say their goodbyes at the airport, and Anthony thinks later—in the weeks afterward—that it would be better not to contact Andrea. He felt that he didn't want to divulge his memories from his infancy. He didn't want to get involved with Andrea. She was extremely intelligent and absolutely beautiful besides. He loved Marie and didn't want anything to disrupt his family.

The Fourth of July 1982 was approaching, and Anthony didn't want to fight the holiday crowds by traveling, so he remained at his apartment at Beach 131st in Rockaway for the holiday. On the Fourth, he ventured out to the surf line for a beach stroll. There were tens of thousands of people on the Rockaway beach, so that it was difficult to walk and maneuver the crowds. On his return to his apartment, he faintly heard a voice calling his name over and over. It was Andrea. Anthony was astonished that the two of them had connected up in such a crowd.

She explained that she owned her parents' house at Beach 140st, and she had not told him. Later that weekend, Andrea invited him to a late dinner. They became much more closely acquainted, and the evening that began with dinner and conversation stretched into the wee morning hours with a long walk on the beach.

THEN IT HAPPENS!

Anthony walked Andrea the ten blocks home on the beach, and they held both hands, facing each other. They were strongly attracted to each other, and as they mutually started to kiss, suddenly they were visibly and forcibly separated from each other by an unseen force that physically pushed Anthony across the sand.

Both Andrea and Anthony were completely sober at the time.

They were both stunned, to say the least. After fifteen or twenty minutes of attempting to discern what had just occurred, Andrea then leaped toward Anthony and planted a deep and aggressive forever kiss smack on his lips. It was obvious to Anthony that Andrea was demonstrating a defiance to whatever had caused them to be violently separated a few minutes earlier. Anthony was smitten to say the least, since Andrea was—in all probability—the aggressive type whom he had searched for in his youth but had never found.

That moment, and that kiss, stirred a deep reevaluation of himself at a time when he was apparently having a crisis of confidence in his own life. It would be a fierce inner battle that would last for years as their lives kept crossing and Anthony's precognitive senses kept guiding him in ways that he didn't want follow.

The relationship between the two continued and develops as she introduces Anthony to her sister Sam, a professor, and her brother Eric, an investment counselor.

In time, Anthony is called back to Georgia for a position that he had applied for in the past months.

The mystique of the incident that occurred on the beach that late evening was the glue that actually held their relationship together over time, as Anthony eventually had to return to Georgia.

Upon returning to Georgia, Anthony and Marie sold their home and changed careers. As the difficulties and related issues arose, they both began to question the decisions and directions that they had taken at midlife. Then, on what seemed to be a normal weekday morning after Marie had departed for work, Anthony suddenly had an epiphany!

He was stunned, to say the least, and he was also changed in a way that was clearly noticeable to Marie. However, he never shared the event with Marie for several years. That which he saw on that occasion would later be of critical importance in making an identification for a coming future event. However, he did reconnect with Andrea simply to tell her what he saw and to question his own sanity.

As time passed, life got easier and Anthony's career change was beginning to pay off. Anthony and Marie were finally able to construct a new home. The lot was situated on or near an old ancestral Indian ceremonial site and near a cliff and cave.

Anthony was a Christian, and he had prayed about the construction and the safety of the men who would build the house.

After a few years, in 1996, Anthony had yet another epiphany. This one was not of Heaven, to say the least. It was of two unidentified men, and the scene was at the opposite end of the spectrum from the epiphany of Heaven that he had been introduced to thirteen years earlier. Anthony, surprisingly, was not frightened. He maturely observed and, when he had seen enough, he dismissed the pair with a hearty, "Get thee behind me, Satan!" The epiphany dissipated.

After more discussions with Andrea, she invites him back to New York for an audience with her associate friends and her Rabbi. A family trip is planned, and meetings were held. Anthony detailed his past thirteen years of strange occurrences to Andrea's friends. It is Christmas 1996.

After months of discussions and consideration, Dr. Andrea and friends simply can't bring themselves to believe Anthony. Several other unusual incidents occur in Anthony's life. Among those, he had also casually predicted the bombing at the Summer Olympics in Atlanta in 1996 before his daughter traveled there with her friends. Anthony is still steadfast in believing what had been revealed to him in two related epiphanies. His recollection of the explicit details of each epiphany were so impressed upon his mind that he could see them through all of his waking hours.

He continued to maintain friendships and contacts with Andrea and her New York friends, as he shares his experiences to them again and again at their requests.

Years pass and on a July evening in 2012, James Holmes murders 12 people in Colorado at the precise minute that Anthony emailed Andrea with the name of James Holmes in the subject line. Anthony had made up the name of a business out of the blue pertaining to the email subject matter.

Anthony had no knowledge of the James Holmes murders until the following morning, and he did not know any other James Holmes.

Andrea was stunned at the email and informed all of her associates and friends.

Finally, they believed! They were finally convinced that Anthony did indeed have a God-given gift. Now the $64,000 question was: who was the man standing with Satan in Anthony's second epiphany? That revelation was also presented to Anthony in a strange way, and all are later shocked by the identity of the Antichrist that is alive and walking the world today.

The man is currently in his seventies and currently walking the Earth. Logic should then have it that if the Antichrist is alive and walking the Earth as I write this, then the end—as described in Revelations—must be very near.

This fictitious story was set where the author actually lived in New York while he actually helped to build the Trump Tower. His friends there were used as characters who were created to present the factual incidents that he experienced over his life. Even though the story is based on real characters, it is written with a purpose to deliver the "Message." His predictions for the very near future are factual, as are his predictions of the nearness of the End Times.

By Steven Journey

Introduction

The Marchants, Anthony and Marie

This is a fictional story based on the numerous true incidents and actual revelations in the life of Anthony Marchant. His predictions for the very near future are derived from those revelations.

DISCLAIMER: All characters are fictional and nonexistent and any resemblance to any organization, event, or events is purely coincidental.

Furthermore, any resemblance to any person or personalities, living or dead, is purely coincidental.

However, various eminent revelations, events, and predictions for the future described within are true as witnessed by the author who, for the purpose of this book, will go by the name of Anthony Marchant.

CHAPTER ONE:

The Midlife Thing

ATLANTA INTERNATIONAL, awaiting a plane.

I was scheduled to fly back to NYC on a late Monday evening flight. It was Memorial Day weekend in 1985. I had left my family in Atlanta at the gate, and I was going back to my job in Manhattan. I always took the latest possible flight so that I could spend every minute with my family. My wife Marie and I have two children, a boy and a girl who were ten and three at the time. My trips home were usually six weeks apart, but with the 4th of July coming up, I had decided not to return home until Labor Day. This was going to be more of a difficult time away from home.

Nevertheless, I longed for the day when I would never have to be separated from them again, or see those departing tears. At least they weren't tears of hunger. The salary was considerably higher in Manhattan and the expenses weren't all that unmanageable, so the time spent away from home would be worth it in the long run.

My usual Delta Flight 0984 departed Atlanta at around 10 p.m. and would arrive in NYC at 1 a.m. The flight was never crowded and was usually open seating.

I was looking forward to this particular flight. It was always uneventful, but this time, it was scheduled at a time when the moon was going to be full and low over the Atlantic as we arrived at JFK. With clear weather, I would be able see the reflection of the moon off the Atlantic as the plane made its final approach to JFK. I had seen it many times. There is little to compare when you are able see the lights of Manhattan cast against the full moon and its reflection off of the Atlantic Ocean.

Other than that, there was nothing much to look forward to except work in the big city.

They announced the call for boarding, and I found a right-side window seat in the forward cabin and settled in for the flight.

The plane was virtually empty, but an attractive young lady—whom I had carried on a short casual conversation with in the coffee shop earlier—walked in and asked if she could join me for the flight.

"Certainly, be my guest," I said.

My row was empty, but she chose to sit in the center seat next to me and I thought it curious, but I certainly didn't object at all. As I said, I had noticed her in the coffee shop while awaiting the flight.

We exchanged pleasantries, and then we struck up a brief conversation. She was an attractive professional and appeared to be in her late twenties or early thirties.

She simply asked, "New York?"

"Yes, going back to my job," I said. "Yourself?"

She told me that she lived there and was a professor. She taught college at NYU.

She asked me about my employment, so I told her that I worked for a company that was constructing Trump Tower on Fifth Avenue. She said, "That's interesting! You work for the Donald?" I laughed. "Indirectly," I said. "I work for a subcontractor, installing various systems in the Tower—among other things."

I really didn't care to converse about work, but she continued. "Do you like him?"

I asked her, "Who, Trump? I'm curious as to why you would ask."

"I mean, what is he like?"

"He is very nice! He always speaks and seems most appreciative of our work and is amazed at the fact that we travel such a distance to work for him. He brings his children on the job occasionally. They are very cute kids. They are definitely well-behaved kids. They even wear little overcoats to match their dad's."

I asked her why she had asked that question about Donald. She answered that she was simply curious. New Yorkers gossip a lot.

"What do you teach?" I asked.

"I teach psychology and I do research."

"Okay, not being too nosy, but what type of research?"

I laughed and reminded her that I was from the South. We have a natural need to know other people's business.

She laughed and explained that, currently, she was researching the human capacity for early life memory.

I said, "Such as childhood memories?"

"Well yes, but more than that. I am searching for those children or adults who have locked away not only early childhood memories, but possible traumatic childhood experiences, or those who have issues dealing with traumatic events."

"Straightforward memories of childhood, dreams, or what?"

"All of the above! Especially the very young. The younger, the more I am interested in researching their past." She commented, "You seem to be fairly perceptive about the subject."

I laughed. "I took the required Psych 101 in college, and that was all I could handle."

"I suppose everyone has an ability to recall events from the past, whether pleasant or not," she said. "But then again, I suppose there might be a recollection that pops up from out of nowhere—like a recollection of a memory, although you have no idea where it possibly could fit into your past." Then she commented, "You do have some idea of my scope of study."

She said that was the area that she was concentrating on—the "mysterious locked-away memory" that most of us seem to have.

I laughed and told her that I'd had that ability all my life, even from when I was an infant.

She smiled and said nothing. Then I placed my headset on, turned over with a pillow against the window, and went to sleep.

She had no idea that I was serious. She was talking with a guy who remembers the actual trauma of being born—or so I had been told by leading psychologists.

It was 2 a.m. when I felt the plane slow a bit as the engines decreased their thrust. That woke me up.

I looked out the window and saw the incredible full moon as it was rising in eastern sky. Miles ahead, in the distance below, was the island of Manhattan and all its boroughs with millions of shimmering lights—a beautiful sight, as I had expected.

The doctor had been asleep also, and she awoke at about the same time that I did. As a matter of fact, she had been pleasantly sleeping on my shoulder, and she apologized as she awoke.

I laughed and said that it was certainly no bother. I had found it comforting, and—to be quite frank—I had rather enjoyed it.

I asked her if she cared to look out my window and see the full moon reflecting on the Atlantic as we made our approach. The scene was incredible, and she leaned over and took a long view. At that point, her face was only inches from mine as she looked out the window. She was every bit as attractive as the scene down below, or even more so.

I was thinking, "Did I brush my teeth?"

We glided over the tip of Long Island, slowing further as the flaps cranked out on our approach, and I made the comment that I could almost see my apartment along the shoreline of Neponset.

She acted surprised and asked if I lived there. and I told her that I did.

"Nice area," she commented. "On the beach?"

I said yes, but then she said nothing else.

I still had my headset on and smiled as we made our final approach. I took one more look at the moon and told her that the song that was playing on the headset was, "When you get caught between the moon and New York City."

She said, "Now that is amusing! Perfect timing!" As we were about reach the terminal, she looked at me and added, "My name is Andrea. You mentioned memories relating to your early childhood?"

"Well, yes," I said.

"Were you serious?"

I said, "Yes, very!"

"Would you be willing to discuss it in my office? Perhaps contribute a bit to my work?"

Jokingly, I said, "How much does it pay? I could think of several memories if the pay were good!"

She didn't react to the joke. "No, I'm very serious, and I would only want information if it truly occurred and if you have had clear repetitive recollections about them."

I gave an effort at a slight smile and expressed that perhaps I would, if I could find the time.

She said that she was available anytime but that I should call and schedule an appointment for a private talk at her office. She also told me that it would be preferable if it were on a weekend, if I didn't mind, as she would have more time to converse.

I laughed and said, "Well, if you think that it would be that interesting of a topic, I just might call you."

She asked my name, and I told her that it was Anthony Marchant. She then she reached into her purse and pulled out her card. It read: *Andrea M. Ranier, PHD. Professor of Psychology, New York University.*

I told her that I was sorry that I didn't have a card, and we walked to baggage claim together and waved goodbye.

"Nice meeting you! See ya!"

"See ya back!"

It was 3 a.m. by the time I got my luggage and flagged a taxi.

It was a hot night in Queens as we drove the ten miles or so to Far Rockaway and then on out to Neponset. It was certainly no place to be in the middle of the night, even in a taxi. Every time we stopped at a traffic light, the prostitutes would start toward the taxi. To make things worse, the air conditioning was busted and the windows were rolled down.

I sure was lonely, thinking about Marie and the kids back home in Georgia. My son was playing summer league soccer and my daughter had just finished her first grade in grammar school. My wife worked as a paralegal and the children stayed with their grandmother during work hours.

I had come to New York because there was little work for me in the South. Jimmy Carter had gotten the economy into such bad shape and the interest rates were as high as 19%. No one could afford to build anything because of the mortgage rates.

It was always at these times, during the worst economic conditions, that the tower cranes went up in New York City and investors started building buildings.

Trump Tower was being constructed, along with the IBM building next door, and the AT&T down the street was almost finished when the Feds broke them apart as a monopoly. That construction came to a grinding halt.

I was simply happy to have a place on the primo job in the city: Trump Tower.

The taxi continued along until we reached my street at Beach 131st in Rockaway. My apartment was right on the beach with a great ocean view. I never told Marie about the killer apartment being right on the beach. When my buddies decided to go back to Georgia, I chose to stay and work all the overtime that I could. The pay was great, compared to back home.

Also, it wasn't like I was a stranger to the situation in New York. In the 1960's, when I was in high school, my dad worked on an Empire State Building remodel for a year and Mom and I came up and lived for the summer in the famous Old Chelsea Hotel. It was old even then, and it was a fabulous old hotel with an impressive list of famous people among its previous clientele. What a fantastic history. During my summer there, I even was able to see the red and black USS United States ocean liner. It was gliding under full lights, surrounded by tugboats, with black oil smoke pouring from its stacks. It was 3 a.m. one summer morning as it docked on the Hudson River.

My brother had even helped build the North Tower of the World Trade Center in 1969. I was not a stranger to New York. As a matter of fact, I loved it and I loved its people. There was ever a dull moment in New York City.

I was fortunate enough to find a single-room apartment in an old brick WWII officer's residence there right on the beach at Beach 131st.

As the taxi pulled into my drive on the dead-end street, the moon was high overhead and the Atlantic was black but sparkling like diamonds over a slightly heavy sea. The salty air that blew in was refreshing after the long flight and the smelly taxi ride.

I paid and tipped my driver. He said something like "thank you" in broken English that was heavily tainted with a Russian accent as he pulled away. I could barely understand him, but I had great sympathy and admiration for him, as he had told me that he loved living in New York but was very lonely. He had previously won an immigration lottery and had come to America a couple of years past; then he had saved money and sent for his family. They had been en route by way of Moscow when their Aeroflot flight crashed and killed everyone aboard, including five members of his family. How could I complain about missing my family when compared with his tragic story? I told him how sorry I felt for him, and I stopped and thanked God for His blessing again in every situation.

It was almost 4 a.m. when I started into the apartment, but I stopped and set the luggage down on the stoop and decided to walk out on the beach. My room offered a view that looked out directly to the east and over the ocean, and it was only 50 yards from my doorstep to the surf. The beach was totally void of any humans as far as I could see, so I decided to take a walk. I was not working that day anyway. I thought that I might as well enjoy the early morning and catch a sunrise.

I had walked the beach dozens of times, but not under a full moon—as it was that night. As I reached the surf, I pulled my loafers off and started to walk slowly northeast along the surf toward Jones Beach.

The sea breeze was knocking the tops of the waves and carrying a light spray through the air. Distant lights trailed off to northeast

Long Island. Then they continued toward Long Beach and to Jones Beach into the curving distance, twinkling until they disappeared. Suddenly, I was stunned! My mouth flew open in surprise as I realized that I had walked that very same beach before, at least 25 years in the past. As a young twelve-year-old Boy Scout, I had played on that beach for three days with my fellow Scouts, and all my life, I could never remember where it was. I had even painted a commissioned oil painting that depicted an old 1800s-era sailing ship that was sitting just offshore.

I realized then that I had actually leased an apartment exactly where I had spent a week with the Scouts after the 1957 National Jamboree in Valley Forge, Pennsylvania.

It was simply a coincidence, but it gave me an uplifting feeling to realize that I had been there as a young child. Pleasant memories flooded my walk along the ocean for the rest of that early morning.

Looking back on my life was beginning to be more pleasant than looking forward. At the time, I was thirty-eight, a college graduate who was still searching for the genuine purpose that I felt I was born for. I couldn't begin to imagine the scope of that purpose, at the time, because it was certainly not visible in the not-too-distant future. It would be slow to materialize, but it would be almost overwhelming once it manifested itself.

CHAPTER TWO:

An Unseen Escort

It actually felt good to fall back into the work routine. The project was going well, and my enjoyment of the general excitement of being on the streets of New York dulled my longing for home. The word was sent out to all the men on the project that the "topping out ceremony" would be taking place in another week. Donald had invited all the workers on the project to the 50th floor celebration, and I had that to look forward to. I thought that perhaps it would help to get my mind off of missing the wife and kids. I had decided to postpone the trip home for a couple of weeks. It was difficult getting flights around the Fourth of July.

Going home every six weeks was fun, but seeing the tears of my wife and children when I left to return to New York was always tough.

The Fourth of July was coming up, and with it, a four-day weekend. My friends were headed to Bar Harbor for sightseeing, but I had already been there and done that trip, so I opted to stay at the beach for local fireworks and planned to just grab a hot dog and lay out on the sand. The beaches were not what I had been accustomed to in the northern Gulf of Mexico in Panama City, Florida, and Gulf Shores,

Alabama. The sugary white sands of the northern Gulf of Mexico spoil beachgoers from around the world.

Walking on the dirty gray New York City beach was taking your life and your health into your own hands. The sand was a shade of gray, and there were the beginnings of litter along the beach being sprinkled with used syringes that collected at the tide line. Everybody was shooting up with used needles everywhere you walked. Not a fun thing to walk on.

The best place in the sand was right in front of my apartment at Beach 131st.

I was 15 blocks away from the crowd at 116th Street; however, on the Fourth of July, almost all the beach looked like an anthill that was crawling with so many people.

On the morning of July Fourth, I stretched out under an umbrella for a day of sun while I also waited for the weekly arrival of the British Concord SST. It always fun to watch as it landed at JFK. The flight path, both going and coming, was directly over my apartment.

It was my first Fourth of July on the beach, and the crowds didn't disappoint. I had always seen photos of New York beaches during holidays. Tens of thousands came and sat wall-to-wall for miles with lily-white skin reflecting in the sun.

People wall-to-wall. Temperatures in the nineties and boom boxes blaring Latino music. On the beach were old people, people with children, fat people, skinny people, people who were arguing, inebriated people, and people making out.

There were lots of souls making out—right in the open, and they didn't care.

It was maddening, and I certainly wasn't used to that. Back home, we went to Panama City or Destin or Gulf Shores, which was over in Alabama. With the quiet, sugary white beaches with white gulls and white pelicans flying over cottages that were also white, you always felt like you were in church when you went to those crystal clear waters of the Gulf.

High overhead at Rockaway, the airplanes with banners advertising Seruchi designer jackets flew up and down the coast all day long. Everybody had a Seruchi! Finally, after a while, I simply couldn't stay out any longer. I gathered my beach towel and cooler and headed for the apartment.

Halfway up the beach, as I was stepping through the bodies, I heard someone calling, "Anthony! Anthony!"

I looked, but I didn't see anyone I knew until I saw a girl waving a towel at me. I certainly didn't recognize her—at least, not immediately, and certainly not in that black bikini.

What a surprise! She got closer, and I realized that it was Dr. Ranier from the flight out of Atlanta.

"Hello! I thought professors all went to the Caribbean on holidays—or at least to the Adirondacks."

"Not all of them," I managed to say. "What a pleasant surprise! How are you?"

"I'm good," she said. "It's good to see you again, and so soon."

I said, "It's a strange coincidence, I suppose."

She said, "Actually I had thought you were going back to Georgia, and I didn't tell you that I live just down the beach at 140th." I stood back on my heels as she continued, digesting the reality that she and I were practically neighbors. "I was hoping to see you. You haven't called me about our little talk, and I had no way of getting in touch. I was hoping that you would. I thought perhaps you had changed your mind."

I said, "Well, it has been a month. I haven't forgotten you. I'm a bit lazy, I suppose—or I suppose that, in reality and considering the subject matter, I'm a bit more reluctant about sharing the story."

She replied, "I understand that, but your sharing would never be divulged to the public. There would be protective legal documents signed with the legal department and University backing."

I offered to think about it some more, and she countered with a dinner offer for the following weekend. "I'll pick you up and we can go up to the Hamptons for a private dinner," she said. "I know a great little seaside bistro. Would you do that? We could break the ice a bit."

I really didn't hesitate at the offer. "I suppose so. You set the date and time, and then we will go."

"Wonderful! Would next Friday be agreeable? Around 4:30? We can get there by 9 p.m."

I agreed, reluctantly. I had promised to share my story, and I felt that few people—if any—had ever had my life's experiences. That was especially true, considering one unusual gift in particular that I would eventually come to share with her.

She suddenly hugged my neck and walked off, turning only to confirm and voice my address. "Beach 131st at 4:30 p.m. next Friday?" I smiled and nodded yes, still feeling her hug. Besides, she left suntan lotion all over me.

Still, I was reluctant about going. Within five minutes after she left, I felt a bit depressed about agreeing to go. I have an inner personal protective instinct that has always kept me above water and away from snakes during my life. I suppose that I acquired that instinct while growing up in the deep woods of Georgia.

It wasn't so much that I didn't want to share my past and my memories; the fact was that I was married and I intended to stay that way. I loved my wife and I loved my family and I was a very long way from home.

Dr. Ranier, or Andrea, was a very beautiful, intelligent, talented, young, brown-eyed Jewish beauty. I was taken aback by the bikini version of her. She was stunningly attractive.

I couldn't deny being attracted to her. I still remembered her sleeping on my shoulder on the plane. She had thought I was asleep, but I suppose that I wasn't. I had sensed that she was there.

I could never reveal my attraction to her—to the point of hiding it. Semper Fi! That was me. I intended to stay that way. And I had a family awaiting back in Georgia.

Why was I even thinking in such a way? Nature's beast?

I suppose it was. Nothing new about lusting for a brown-eyed, dark, brown-haired beauty. David and Bathsheba's example was duly noted in my mind, along with all the consequences thereof.

I thought: *Be careful, Anthony! Marie is your "everything!" You have told her as much for twenty years.*

However, as Andrea walked away and headed off the beach, I still could feel her hug and almost taste her scent.

Back to work!

The holiday was over. It was a milestone week at the Tower. It was topping out week. I had never realized it before, but all the men in my family had helped celebrate "topping outs" on buildings in New York City. I would be the third in the family with this celebration on top of Trump Tower.

I really didn't know what to expect. It was 5 a.m. and the 15 short blocks to the subway were like an early morning walk. And they went by quickly. The salty onshore breeze was brisk and cool, and it felt refreshing as it awakened me for the day. It was also a welcome relief; it had been very hot the day before.

The regular commute route from Rockaway crossed Broad Channel, then traveled about ten miles through Queens before going underground just before we reached the East River. Twenty rocking clackity-clack blocks more, and then I was off at 53rd Street. and Fifth Avenue. That was followed by a short three-block walk to the Tower. It was the same, day in and day out, always accompanied by the same people and always on time in those days.

There was one thing I enjoyed about the job, and that was the subway ride: to be among so many people while never seeing anyone whom you knew personally.

I always mused about the same guy in drag with the bright blue eyeshadow and the fake beauty spot. He always winked at me.

Then there were the little Jewish Holocaust survivors with their wrist tattoos. Loved them! They always smiled at me.

So every morning, I could always look forward to at least a wink and a smile.

On the afternoon commute, I could look forward to seeing Angelina. She was a street person who wore nine dresses and skirts at the same time. I always smiled a big smile at her, and one day, she finally smiled back.

This day was to be a different experience. It was topping out day. We would work for half a day, then assemble on the 59th floor and have lunch. 11 a.m. came and we worked our way up the Tower to the 59th floor.

All of New York's dignitaries were there. Mayor Koch, Rudy Giuliani, the governor, and every super-wealthy Wall Street magnate along with Donald, Ivanka, and the rest of the Trump family—including his dad.

Donald then made a short speech. He introduced and congratulated his project contractors and subcontractors, and then he introduced his project superintendent, who was the first woman to build a skyscraper in New York City.

Yes! I was truly impressed. After a nice French cuisine buffet lunch that was served by waiters in white chef's hats, photographs were recorded and we disassembled, and that was that.

I think that it is considered bad luck *not* to have a topping out ceremony. It's a celebration of sorts, and it gets major publicity.

Just before that ceremony, I had the opportunity to actually purchase a single-bedroom condo on a lower floor. The newspaper advertised it as a "once in a lifetime" opportunity. It was certainly that! There was a $100,000 price tag for the unit.

That sale lasted six weeks. Then Donald stopped the sale as interest in the building picked up.

After he halted sales and six weeks later, he offered all those buyers $200,000 in order to repurchase their units. The offer was for six weeks only. Then, another six weeks later, he was selling those same units for $500,000.

My fanny is still sore from kicking myself for not buying one of those $100,000 units. They are worth $3 million each today.

The week passed quickly and Friday rolled around before I knew it. I reached the apartment that day and went for a quick fifteen-minute swim in the Atlantic. The cold saltwater was truly refreshing and medicinal.

I took a quick shower and dressed for the evening. At least I would sample some nice restaurant cuisine and enjoy an enlightened conversation. That, in and of itself, would have been a pleasant respite from the daily chatter around my construction site.

I loved my New York friends, but I suppose it was the continual attempts at interpreting their conversations that was a challenge for me. I was from Georgia and I was accustomed to Southern accents, not New York jargon, and that certainly didn't help. When there were crews of Jews, crews of Irishmen, crews of Italians, and crews of African Americans who were all from the Bronx, it seemed impossible to understand their lingo. My crew happened to be full of Southerners. It seemed that, for the most part, we were the only ones who were working and knew what we were 'doin''—as they say in the Bronx.

I frequently played the role of interpreter for my Southern buddies.

I was living in my own apartment. I chose to get away from my friends, along with the city noise, and find a quiet place on the beach. As I previously mentioned, I thought it odd that I had chosen an apartment in the exact same place that I enjoyed 25 years previously as a youth.

I keep trying to convince myself that it was a coincidence and not some weird stop on an even stranger path for my life. As it turns out, that is exactly what it was: a weird stop. Upon looking back, I find that the rear view mirror may suggest that it was also Divine providence. Once I was able to connect all the coincidences of my past with those that would occur in the near future, I was almost certain of that.

The time was moving toward 7:30, so I went out on the ocean deck to wait for our evening to begin.

I remember that I was actually a bit nervous. Would she show up or decide against coming? It really didn't matter, but I might have felt sort of "stood up"—had she not shown. I didn't have a phone or any way of contacting her.

Just then, I saw a car approaching the dead end at my street and after a bit, I saw that it was her. I guess, with all my mixed emotions, I was rather relieved as she drove up smiling.

"Hello! Are you ready for some great seafood?"

I said yes and smiled back. I offered to drive, but she insisted that the evening was her treat and that she would also provide the transportation. A Duster? A 1972 Plymouth Duster!

"Do you like it?"

"Certainly! I love it," I responded with genuine enthusiasm. Nevertheless, I offered to drive my red 67 P-1800 Volvo that I had driven up to New York when I moved into my apartment, but she waved me off.

"Next time we will," she assured me. "But for now, crawl in!"

"Yes ma'am," I said, and crawled in. Then I asked her, "Where do I have the pleasure of being taken?"

She replied, "To my favorite restaurant in the whole world."

"Wow, I'm honored! Mine is the 'Pic-A-Burger' back home," I admitted, tongue-in-cheek.

She managed a smile at my humor.

As we pulled away, those mixed emotions of going to dinner with an attractive female—who was also a semi-stranger—made themselves known to me. I decided to suppress my misgivings and go with the flow.

Enjoy the evening! I finally said to myself. To behave myself and act like a proper guest was paramount for the evening.

I asked, "Am I properly dressed?" A casual sport coat and slacks and loafers were all I had.

She said, "You look fine. It's a nice place, but it's casual dress in the summer."

"Where is this place?"

"Montauk. Or at least it is close to there. It's about two hours away."

"Really? That's fine. I like midnight snacks."

She laughed and said, "It's on the bay and they have great seafood. They seat guests until midnight on the weekends. We have reservations at 11:15 p.m."

"11:15? That is when Wendy's closes back home."

She tried to reassure me. "It's a summertime-only open-air bistro, and it stays packed on the weekends."

"I am in no hurry. I'm off for the weekend with nothing to do except see Montauk."

"Who is Wendy?" she asked.

I said, "Never mind. Just good burgers down home."

She drove us to the Long Island Expressway and headed north.

I asked her how her classes were going, and she said that they were off until the fall semester.

"That is one reason I wanted to get acquainted so we could possibly do an interview or two in before classes commenced," she explained. "I thought it would be nice to go out for a fun evening."

I told her that I would have called her office later in the summer for the interview that I had promised her during our chance meeting on the flight, but our having bumped into each other on the beach worked out just as well.

She said, "If you feel uncomfortable going through with it, you are certainly not obligated in any way to proceed. We will just have a fun dinner and let that be it."

"I suppose I should have brought notes and we could have proceeded with the interviewing process," I remarked, wondering why I hadn't thought of it sooner.

"No!" she replied immediately. "This evening is all about the two of us getting acquainted and having fun."

"Well, I'm a man of my word and besides, I've always wanted to tell someone with a PhD in psychology about my youth and perhaps find out what the heck occurred during those adolescent years."

She said. "Actually, I didn't want to work tonight, but I will ask that you give me a bit of insight into where we will be going when we start our meeting or meetings."

"Insight? Can you be more specific?"

Then she asked," Could you give me a small hint about the subject matter of your thoughts or remembrances that we might discuss during interviews? If you do, then maybe I can relax and enjoy my meal and your company this evening."

Jokingly, I argued, "No, I want to eat first. That way, I'll at least get a free meal out of this."

She laughed easily, and the knowledge that she appreciated my sense of humor warmed me. I suggested that we should get to the restaurant first and then I would give her a brief idea about my past—just an overview, I decided. I would take small, calculated risks with revelations about myself.

Then I changed the subject and mentioned the Plymouth again.

"This little Duster runs rather well," I said. In reality, I was stalling her. I didn't want to start the evening with her thinking that I was completely off my rocker. I might have had to walk home.

She said, "It's my beater."

"Your what?"

"My beater. It's an old car that I don't mind getting banged up in the traffic. We have a lot of crazy drivers in New York City."

"I have a nice little Volvo at my apartment, but I don't want to drive it in these potholes," I countered.

"Yes, I did notice your Volvo."

"Yes it is a 67 P-1800 coupe. Red!"

She said, "I'll trade titles with you."

Immediately I grew possessive. "No! We won't be 'doin'' that."

She laughed again. Just then we arrived at the restaurant—*Nemo's Bistro on the Bay.*

It was 9 p.m. as she turned off the engine. "We have a couple of hours to kill. We could walk through the local shops, if you like."

I was glad to accompany her. We walked along the docks and found a park bench that faced straight out to the harbor.

"Curiosity has the best of me," she finally said as we sat down together, overlooking the dark waters. "Are you going to give me a hint? Please?"

A sudden fear came over me—that I wasn't going to get fed at the bistro if I didn't tell. With the ominous way my stomach was rumbling, I wasn't going to survive the trip back to Rockaway unless I had a decent seafood dinner. She had me over a barrel.

Reluctantly, I said, "Very well, I'll give you a big hint. And only if you promise not to laugh!"

"I promise! I'll even buy extra dessert tonight."

I smiled, secretly enjoying the playful challenges she presented. "I was born in a house that we moved away from when I was three years old."

She interrupted, "And you can remember as a three-year-old?"

"Actually, much more than that," I answered ruefully.

"What else do you remember?"

"You want me to tell you *before* we eat?"

She gave me an adorable look of faux exasperation. "Come on! I've already promised extra dessert. What else do you want?"

Some inner instinct must have told her that I couldn't resist her prodding, and she was right. I capitulated at last. "Fine, here goes. But don't laugh!"

"I promise I won't laugh! Please? Tell me!"

I started at the very beginning. "I was born at home in my great-grandma's house. It was a farmhouse. My mother's five sisters, my dad, and my nine-year-old sister—along with our family physician, Dr. Rowe—were in attendance for my birth. I've had flashbacks since I was nine years old, and I remember everything in my life—including most conversations. But I guess the most curious thing, which you may think impossible, is the fact that I can remember everything—even from a few seconds after being born!"

"What?!" That nearly brought her off the park bench. "No way. You must be imagining things! A baby can't focus its eyes until twenty or so days after birth! No way!"

With a shrug, I leaned back against the bench. "I didn't think for a moment that you would believe me, but it is true nonetheless. There is much more to the explanation and plenty of detailed memories, I assure you. And there is one other thing for you to consider."

"What is that?" she wondered, ignoring the ocean view and giving me her undivided attention.

"The fact that I was a breech birth, requiring hours in labor and causing extreme blood pressure to my head. I have spoken to only one other person in my lifetime who underwent a similar circumstance."

She was awed and completely intrigued. "What did that person share with you?"

I shook my head. "That is all I want to tell you for right now. I want to enjoy the rest of the evening." I softened the remark with a sideways grin. "This evening is my bribe, and I want to enjoy it. But I will say this: Mom was in labor with me for almost ten hours. I have thought about so many details over the years—about the circumstances around my birth—and as time went forward and witnesses were questioned in the family, they realized that I knew what I was talking about. Now, do you still want to have dinner with me?"

"Of course!" she answered promptly. "And with crème' brulée for dessert!"

"Very well, but no more questions tonight. Please, Andrea?" I was in earnest about that.

"Okay, but I have a thousand questions already! This will be very interesting." Then she made an effort to curb her excitement and said, "I promise. I will set up a meeting."

I offered my hand, and she shook it. "Agreed!" I said. "Set up the meeting, and I will tell you much more in time. Much, much more."

The prospect seemed to make her a little giddy.

We went in to eat. The meal was fantastic! The food and the music were mesmerizing. Kudos to *Nemo's Bistro on the Bay.* There is no better place to drift into the evening after the sun goes down.

Just after eleven that evening, Andrea suggested we get started back to Rockaway.

It was a magnificent evening, but I agreed that it eventually had to come to an end. It was a long way back.

We didn't talk very much on the way back. I had asked Andrea to hold off with the questions in order to let me gather my thoughts. Based upon the fact that she couldn't come up with much in the way of other conversational material, I guessed that my preliminary revelations were already dominating her thoughts as well.

Now and then, we made trivial small talk as she popped the Duster up onto the Long Island Expressway and we headed south. To divert attention away from me, I asked Andrea about her family, and she told me that she had made an early life mistake and married very young. The marriage lasted only a short while and there were no children.

Then I asked her if she attended Synagogue.

She laughed and said, "Well, I am Jewish, but I only attend around the holidays of Rosh Hashanahs." That was to keep her family from disowning her. Then she glanced sideways at me. "Are you religious?"

I said, "Everybody is religious, at something. However, not everybody believes in God. I am a Christian. I believe in Jesus!"

She nodded, her eyes on the road. "I thought as much. I just don't talk about it. I'm Jewish and I am of the Chosen Race."

I let it go at that and asked instead, "What about the wedding? Did you have a traditional Jewish wedding?"

"Absolutely! Smashed the wine glasses and was whirled around in a chair above all my big cousin's heads for like what seemed forever. It was fun! Dizzying, but fun. Three hundred people attended, flying out of California on two chartered 737s, and there was lots and lots of food. And then it was over. Just like that! $60,000 bucks later!"

"And so, I guess the marriage lasted about the same length of time as the wedding," I remarked. "No children?"

"No children," she confirmed.

"I am truly sorry," I offered.

She shrugged. "It's okay, but that's sweet of you. I would have expected that sympathy from a Georgia boy."

I grinned at her. "Aw shucks," I drawled.

She ran off the road, laughing. I suspended my Southern jokes until she got control of her vehicle, but it was nice to end the evening with some levity. I said as much, and she heartily agreed.

By 2:30 a.m., we pulled into Rockaway and drove by a local popular hangout called *The Wharf.* It was always popping until daybreak, and that night was no different. There was a crowd there.

"Wanna stop?" she asked impulsively.

I wasn't feeling it. "No, I think you can run me on to the apartment. Do you mind?"

"Absolutely not! Please do call me next week, and we will set up a time to sort some of those old memories."

We turned up Beach 131st, and she pulled over to the curb outside my apartment and turned off the engine. As I exited the Duster, I looked around my apartment entrance and noticed that the beachside of the apartment and the deck was clear. No one was out sitting in the lounge chairs.

Andrea was sitting in the car with the window down, so I turned back to her and said, "I know it's late, but there is nobody out there. Would you want to sit out a while? The breeze is nice," I added by way of persuasion.

She shut off the car. "Sure, why not?"

The deck was situated behind the house, and it was level with the sand. There was a nice place to sit for an elevated view of the ocean. That night, there was an endless stream of freighters and cruise ships pouring out of the New York Harbor. All of the ships were lighted and headed in different directions. It was a beautiful sight. Andrea and I walked out on the beach, and when she stumbled a bit in the heavy sand, I instinctively caught her hand to balance her. She laughed and grabbed onto mine with both hands, and that stopped her fall.

Neither one of us had had anything to drink that night, but we both felt a bit lightheaded and tipsy anyway. The light was dim in the wee hours, and I was feeling mixed emotions—just as I had previously with all of the hand touching.

I wanted to hold her. I wanted what every other red-blooded 38-year-old Southern male wanted. But being true to my convictions, I couldn't act on it. I knew that I was in dangerous territory. No doubt that it was her scent that I loved, along with the touching; and the dimly lit beach was the perfect time to hold her then gently kiss her.

I sensed that she felt the same way! She wanted to hold my 6'2" 212-pound frame. She was beautiful and I was not an unhandsome guy.

I gently turned her toward me, with my hand in hers. Then I reached for her other hand and pulled them both close to my chest.

I could feel the excitement rise in her breath, matching mine as well as our lips touched for the first time. Her kiss was everything that I had expected and more, making me lightheaded; and then I felt her breast lightly touching me through my shirt.

With all the sense of pleasure that God ever created welling up inside of me, I knew that I was going against all rational and better judgment and failing. Everybody always remembers the very second when they fall from grace.

It was at this exact moment that *it* happened.

It was this moment that neither of us would ever forget for the rest of our lives. We would subsequently talk about its mystery almost every time we met from then on, and we still discuss it to this day. But the memory was not centered around the moment of pleasure, but rather what happened when we kissed.

The jolt!

As I kissed her, the only way to describe it would be that I was hit by what seemed to be a jolting force that drove me away from Andrea and across the sand backwards, flailing my arms and trying to regain my balance.

I flew backwards fifty or sixty feet, and then even further back. It pushed me with a force like a giant invisible pillow.

Andrea was screaming and crying over and over, "What the hell is that! What the hell was that!"

I was stunned and at a total loss for any words. My breath was taken away. Of course, my first and utmost concern was for Andrea. She was scared by what had just happened, but otherwise, she seemed alright.

We were yelling loud enough to be heard above the surf in our fright! We also didn't need the attention of the beach patrol. Some lights were beginning to come on from the nearby beach houses. We had done nothing, by ourselves, to cause the commotion—except perhaps spiritually.

Surely not! That just doesn't happen in the real world, and when I voiced that opinion later on, Andrea could only nod wordlessly in agreement.

However, she was Jewish and I was a Christian. And I was always supposed to be devoted in my faith, at that. Andrea was the first kiss that I had shared with another woman, other than Marie, in twenty years.

Not knowing what else to say, I told her, "I must have stepped into a hole or something, and it threw me backwards."

But she replied emphatically, "Oh no, you didn't step into any hole. There was no hole there!"

She and I both stood across from each other, physically exhausted from shock. That was strange and otherworldly!

I totally agreed—the hole theory held no water. It was a lame attempt to explain away what had happened. It was definitely a frightening experience.

After that invisible pushing incident occurred, I didn't bother to tell Andrea that, as a child, it had happened to me before. As I was walking across our church parking lot in broad daylight, I had been pushed down to the ground by some unseen force.

It was a strange feeling. It was like an invisible pillow fight, and it certainly seemed to have a life all its own. The pressure was invisible.

Then, as Andrea gathered her wits, she walked up threw her arms around me and kissed me very long, deeply, and passionately—as if to boldly defy whatever force had interrupted us. It was an incredible kiss full of powerful feelings, yet it was frightening at the same time.

She then turned and walked toward her car, saying she would be awaiting my call.

I stammered, "Soon! Very…soon!"

I stood there, rooted to the spot as I watched her go. Good grief, what had just happened?

CHAPTER THREE:

Down A Rabbit Hole

Andrea drove away, and I turned for my apartment, stumbling as I tried to unlock the door. It finally opened, and I grabbed a blanket and pillow from my bed and took a seat in the deck chair under the covered area of the deck. There was lightning in the distance, and the wind was picking up as a summer storm approached.

It was time for contemplation.

Perhaps what greater storm did I stir, if any, to cause that frightening incident? It was not something I had imagined, and Andrea was certainly witness to that. It frightened us both so very much only few moments earlier, but the nerves would be unsettled for days and we would remember if for a lifetime.

The approaching storm was soon blowing, with rain coming down in sheets. A fitting end to the tumultuous evening, I suppose.

I questioned myself at that very moment: *What on Earth just happened?*

I had been forcefully thrown fifty or sixty feet across the sand. Andrea was screaming in terror as a witness to the strange event. I wasn't injured, and Andrea was not harmed either, but the weight of the invisible force had still been issued with a definite purpose: to throw the two of us apart. That was the only conclusion that I could draw.

It was just a simple kiss, but what a kiss it was! Such a beautiful Jewish creature! It was my first kiss shared with a woman other than Marie in twenty years.

I was immediately reminded of my beliefs and what they teach as warnings. Was that force a physical warning? I knew that what I was doing with Andrea went against my beliefs, but such an astounding reaction? Surely not!

I asked myself: *Did that force come from without, or perhaps from within myself?*

Did I think about asking forgiveness that very evening for kissing Andrea and playing a dangerous game with her? I have to say that I did. But then I dismissed my concerns as being a silly overreaction to some natural phenomenon. It was simply unbelievable, and I was thinking—even hoping—that would be the end of the subject.

I know there was a reason that the devil was portrayed as a serpent in the Bible. The spirit is willing, but the body is weak.

I tried to mentally picture how the incident might have appeared to a third party, had anyone else been present and revisited the episode. The thought was just as frightening.

I don't know why I chose to sleep outside that first night, but I didn't want to go inside. I curled up with my blanket and pillows in the beach chair and shivered. It started to rain—a steady gentle rain on the tin roof as I fell asleep with those conflicting thoughts.

In a few short hours, the rising sun reflected off a glassy smooth Atlantic and awakened me. It was a very bright morning, and I was hungry. I could smell the aroma of fresh bread in an oven wafting from Mrs. Julliard's kitchen. Mrs. Julliard was my landlord. She had actually selected me over two other prospects to live in the apartment that I leased. My former neighbor had recommended me to her.

Months before, during the spring, I had been living at Beach 115th Street with fellow technicians. They were going to leave for nuclear plant jobs scattered throughout the South. I didn't want to spend the summer in that Southern heat, so I opted to remain in New York at the Tower. I had wanted to move from my first apartment to a place further out on the beach, so I began the search for a room.

We were riding the A-train back out to Rockaway after work one day and discussing the upcoming summer and our rentals. I got up to look out the front car as we approached Broad Channel, and a very attractive Puerto Rican girl approached me and introduced herself.

"Hi, my name is Flora, and I see you often on the train. I couldn't help but overhear you discussing a room for the summer."

"Yes. Got any suggestions?"

"I do, I do!" Then she told me about the house where she and her boyfriend had lived on Beach 131st. She instructed me to come out around 6 p.m., and she would speak with the landlady, Mrs. Julliard.

"Thank you, Flora," I said. "I'll check that out."

That same day, I rushed over for my appointment and got there early at 5:45 p.m. There, standing on Mrs. Julliard's doorstep, were two other local people who were also wanting the room.

I introduced myself, and she said, "Oh, Flora's friend."

I answered yes, even though—at the time—I didn't know that I was Flora's friend.

"Come on in," she invited me. I followed her, leaving the other two applicants on the doorstep.

I immediately leased the room. New York had rent control in those days. A room on the Atlantic was $250 per month with all utilities included. What a deal.

I thought: *Thanks, beautiful Flora—wherever you are.*

I found out later that she actually lived downstairs in the daylight basement with her Puerto Rican transit cop boyfriend. I could hear them almost every night. They would fight one night and make up the next. One week they would fight more, and the next week they would make up more.

I had a great room with a view of the Atlantic in the old red brick WWII officer's quarters. It had a kitchenette, a private bath, and a parking space for the P-1800—along with its own private entrance. Amazingly, it was directly on the beach in New York City!

I was on the deck, stretching the early morning stiff muscles while constantly thinking about the previous evening with Andrea. What great fun with a beautiful person! But what a very strange and memorable ending.

Mrs. Julliard interrupted my train of thought with a shout. "Anthony! How do you want your eggs?"

Wow! My first morning here, and she was offering to cook breakfast.

"Please don't bother! I can go to the local grille until I buy cooking utensils."

She then insisted—at least until I got settled in.

I finally asked for eggs over-easy or scrambled. It didn't matter. She invited me in for a great Saturday morning breakfast.

Mrs. Juilliard was almost 80 years old. As I ate, of course I was obligated to listen to her family history with all of its personal triumphs and tragedies, but it was a fun morning and I enjoyed hearing her share her stories. She said that she always loved Southern boys, and she was absolutely crazy about the music group *Alabama* that was topping every chart at about that time.

I told her that they were a favorite group of mine also, but I didn't tell her that I had previously lived only about ten miles from them on Lookout Mountain. As I later found out, she had all of their tapes and albums, and I heard her play every one of them again and again.

Later that afternoon, Dr. Christopher—a dentist who also lived in Mrs. Julliard's house—came out to the deck for a rest. He introduced himself, and we had a pleasant discussion about Trump and the tower that he was building. Dr. Christopher seemed interested about the process that was required to build skyscrapers, and even though he was a lifelong resident of the city, he had never spoken to anyone who actually helped to construct one.

After a while, I told him that our landlady had cooked my breakfast that morning and served it out on the deck. I suggested that he should have been there, because she was a great cook.

He said, "She no longer speaks to me."

I was surprised. "Why not?"

He said that about two years earlier, he and another tenant had found her outside the front entrance of the house, sprawled in the sand. She was ultimately diagnosed as having had a heart attack. He said that he performed CPR resuscitation on her and brought her back to having a stable pulse with normal breathing. She then later fully recovered in the hospital.

I was perplexed. "So?"

"I don't know. All I know is that I did save her life, as anyone would expect me to try and do, and now she ignores me." He shrugged. "Go figure."

"Maybe she was in bliss or about to enter Heaven and you brought her back," I suggested. "What do you think?

He laughed, his complacent gaze on the waves that were rolling in to shore. "I will never believe anything like that."

"Why would she harbor disdain toward you if you resuscitated her from being dead?"

He said that he didn't try to think about those things.

Not being Christian enough—as I should have been at that time in my life—to explain Heaven, I simply said, "Someday you will."

He looked at me then. "You seem emphatic about there being an afterlife."

I answered, "I know that I know! Heaven is real only through Jesus Christ. And so is Hell by rejecting Him! As I understand it, it's our choice as individuals."

He smiled and shrugged again, then said that he didn't waste time thinking of those things.

Another week or two passed. I decided that it was time to give Andrea a call to schedule my appointment, as promised. I reiterate that my interview was not really going to be subject matter that I wanted to share. It had always depressed me to speak about it. And if I did speak of it, people would roll their eyes. No one ever believed me anyway. Never!

I needed to call Andrea. Mrs. Julliard had a phone that I was welcome to use, but instead I drove to a booth for privacy.

I had never dialed Andrea's office, and I didn't know if she had a secretary, so I thought that I might be able to leave a message. I dialed the number and there was no answer at first, so I hung up the phone.

I started to leave. I thought that, since I had dialed the number and no one answered, I had made an honest effort. I started to walk away, but then I had second thoughts.

I turned back and redialed. I had made a promise.

Andrea's secretary finally answered and told me that Andrea was not in. She asked for a message, so I just left my name and nothing else. The secretary asked if I was certain that I didn't want to leave a further message. I said no—only my name, Anthony. She said that she would relay my name to Andrea.

It was Thursday and the weekend was coming up. I went back to my apartment and got some gear ready to head out to the beach. As I was walking out the door, I saw the Duster roaring down 131st toward the apartment.

Andrea had been off from work and had been at home when I called. Her secretary had relayed the message, so she immediately simply drove the ten blocks or so to my apartment. She knew that I wouldn't answer Mrs. Julliard's phone.

She blew the horn and waved. "Hi Anthony! I just received your message. Can we talk?"

I said, "Sure. When?"

"Right now! We can go to my office or my home office up the beach. It doesn't matter."

"Let me get my notes."

"Great! You have notes?"

"Yes. I've been writing them down since you first mentioned that you were going to ask me questions."

I grabbed my notebook and climbed in the Duster, and Andrea drove us up the beach to Neponset where she lived. She radiated bridled enthusiasm. I, on the other hand, was nervous.

Neponset, I found out, was a very upscale section of the neighborhood with many celebrities and corporate people living along the beach. It was certainly an idyllic lifestyle. Five minutes later, we were turning into her drive. The house was situated right at the end of the street, just the same as the old officer's quarters that I was living in—only her house was much nicer and very well-appointed.

Andrea invited me in, and I was taken aback by the craftsmanship. The interior was Frank Lloyd Wright and the exterior was Craftsman. Simply beautiful and expertly crafted!

Andrea invited me into her office, which was a converted covered porch right on the beach and overlooking the seawall that ran along the beach. It was a million-dollar view through large windows.

I told her that I designed homes and had constructed a few, and that I was totally impressed with hers.

She said that it was her childhood home and that it was also her inheritance from her parents. Her siblings shared other real estate, but Andrea got the home. She asked me to have a seat and suggested that we talk awhile before we got started.

We sat in two large leather chairs in the sunroom, facing out to the beach and turned slightly toward each other. All I could think was how comfortable those chairs were and how I was feeling a bit too tired. I was hoping that I wouldn't fall asleep.

About that time, a maid surprised me and walked in with two glasses of white wine.

I laughed and said, "I really don't drink, especially when I need to retain my cognitive skills. How about a cup of coffee instead?"

She apologized and returned with a cup of coffee. Then Andrea picked up a notepad and asked if I was ready to start.

"Sure," I said. "What do you need to know first?"

She asked if I cared to share a bit of family history. "Would you share a snippet of your mother's childhood and how she met your dad? Then we will move to your dad's history. You can give details or be brief. I just want an idea of the family unit and how it may have affected you as a child."

"Certainly," I agreed. "First of all, you would think that we would have been dysfunctional as a family when you consider my parents' individual histories. However, we were not dysfunctional at all." I took a sip of coffee before I continued. "I will be brief. My parents were as cordial as any two people could be under their respective circumstances. They met in Alabama when Dad was 19 and Mom was 14. Two years later, they were married.

"Mom's mother died of appendicitis when Mom was only 9, leaving behind six children—five girls and a boy. My mom was the oldest. Her youngest sister was two at the time. Her dad remarried and had 5 more kids. He couldn't feed them all, so he would eat at a restaurant before he came home from work and let the kids fend for themselves."

"What a jerk!" Andrea interjected.

I shrugged. "It was the 1920s, and a similar situation was taking place in Harlan, Kentucky. Up there, Dad's mom left both him and her husband in 1918, when Dad was only 6 years old. But she took his little 2-year-old brother with her. The night that she left him with his dad, they had only a single potato in the pantry.

"Dad grew up on his resolve to be as responsible a parent as existed anywhere. He never blamed his mom, nor did he ever have a cross thing to say about her or his father. He loved her without reservation, even though she had taken his little brother and left him virtually alone.

"Currently my dad is still living and taking care of Mom, who is in the final stages of Alzheimer's and living in a nursing home. It is currently a very sad period of time in the Marchant family household."

I looked directly at Andrea. "Andrea, I will tell you about this, and then we can move on."

Her gaze was just as even. "Tell me anything you want, Anthony."

"I love my parents more than life itself," I continued. "We are three siblings in the household and we are each eight years apart. I am the youngest. My sister is eight years older. I hardly know my brother. He is eighteen years older than I am. We were all raised differently, and we are all pretty normal. By the time I was born, Dad knew a bit more what he was doing—as far as love goes. I am crazy about my dad.

"I may divulge more about my parents and siblings later, but if you don't mind, I would rather cut to the chase and tell you as much as I feel like telling you while I am still in the mood."

Andrea leaned back in her chair. "Anthony, we can stop at any point. If you feel like continuing, why don't you tell me first the story about being nine years old and having had flashbacks that you didn't understand?"

"Sure. I never, ever remember having nightmares—or even dreams. Occasionally, I would remember something out of the blue, and I didn't really know quite where to fit it into my past or present life. The memories never really bothered me. They were not frightening. Well, except one that I used to have flashbacks about," I amended.

"What was that memory in particular, Anthony?"

"Well, if you don't mind, just mark it down that I mentioned it and we can come back to it. I may recall several. But moving on to an important issue: as late as when my children were adolescents, strange incidents would occur, or I would receive a phone call from a past friend, and I knew—when the phone first rang—who would be calling before I answered it."

"What?" Andrea almost dropped her pen. "You're psychic?"

"No, I don't call it being psychic—just very highly aware. Perhaps even clairvoyant. If a person is dishonest or up to nefarious deeds, I can seem to sense it. I'm aware of people, places, and things. I get feelings that I can't explain, and they often come true. I am probably a good case study for being precognizant!"

Andrea couldn't seem to say anything. For several minutes, she just sat there, looking at me. What was left of my coffee had grown cold, so I set down the mug and waited for her to digest my revelations.

Finally she spoke. "Has anything occurred since you've been an adult?"

"Well, dozens of incidents, simply dozens. I first began to notice when my wife and I built our first home. I was twenty-six. That was the age when I felt as if I was instructed to write a book someday. Our home was new, and we were sitting outside in the afternoon shade as the kitchen phone rang.

"I told Marie I must answer that. 'That's Greg!' I said.

"She said, 'Greg who?'

"'Greg Alford! I haven't heard from him in ten years.'

"As I ran for the phone, she said, 'Anthony, how do you know it's Greg?'

"I answered, 'I don't know, but I think it's Greg calling.'

"I ran in and grabbed the wall phone and answered. The voice on the other end said, 'Anthony! Long time no see, man!'

"I laughed and told Greg what I had told Marie. He said, 'Still at it, Anthony?'

"'At what, Greg?'

"Greg said, 'Don't you remember, when we were kids, that you always knew where things were and told us things that were going to happen, and they usually did?'

"I told Greg, 'No, not really!'

"Greg said, 'It sure left a funny feeling when those things did happen.'"

Andrea was quiet for a moment, scribbling down notes. Then she looked up at me and offered a rational explanation: oftentimes, when we haven't seen someone in a long time, we will think of them, and coincidently they could be in the area.

"I understand that," I said. "But another time, when I was taking my two-year-old son to Atlanta, we were on I-75 going to the ski shop one Saturday. Simply making playful conversation, I asked if he had ever seen a red Ferrari. Naturally, he said no and asked me what that was. I told him that it was a rare and beautiful sports car.

"I didn't tell him the model or describe it. I simply told him to look along the Interstate for a red Ferrari, just in case one went by. A few minutes later, a red Testarossa passed us.

"I was as totally shocked as anyone could imagine! The car was very rare because it was 1972, and that was the first year of production. I called the car name and model, along with its color, less than five minutes before it came by. Of course, my little Mark was thrilled! How did I do that?"

Andrea seemed so absorbed by my stories that she had temporarily given up scratching down notes. "Perhaps you may have seen it previously and subconsciously remembered it as it drove by?"

I explained that from where we entered the Interstate, that scenario was impossible.

"Were any other occurrences that were similar?"

"Actually, there are dozens," I said, growing a little more comfortable with sharing such personal information. "A most surprising one was a weekend trip through the Great Smokey Mountains, and we were rounding curves on a crooked road.

"My son Mark was driving, and he said, 'Dad, it sure would be fun to have a sports car on these roads.'

"I agreed. 'What if we had a white 911 Porsche Cabriolet with the top down?'

"My son said that would be totally cool—just as that very car that I had described immediately came around a blind curve a mile ahead, going the other direction, and met us as we drove by.

"He said, 'Dad! That's weird! How do you do that?!'

"I laughed and gave him a high five. I agreed that it was indeed weird. Then I explained that seemingly out of nowhere, a thought will enter my mind and when it does, I either verbalize it or 'go with it'—whichever suits the situation that I am in. It has been that way with me all my life. Only a few know about it."

Andrea agreed that was definitely out of the ordinary.

I told her, "My dad and his mother were the same way: they were able to tell things in advance. How do we do it? I haven't a clue. We are all Christians, and thus we are not believers in—or users of—unholy things. My dad always had forbidden me to even touch tarot cards or Ouija boards as a child.

"But my dad did have a nightmare that awakened my mom one night. It was during WWII, and at the time, he was working long hours at a steel mill. He came home for a rest and had a dream that the crane in the blooming mill had run off its rails and out the end of the mill.

"Mom told him that he was only dreaming about wild things from being so tired. But later, when he went to work, the overhead crane was out the end of the building and sitting in the mill yard."

"Wow, that is unusual," Andrea remarked. "What do you suppose enables these premonitions to occur?"

"I have no idea."

She said, "There must be several more instances regarding that unusual ability in your family."

I told her that there were. Also, we never thought about it much, because it was normal. We just accepted it as a part of our existence. We never acted on it, or gambled, or warned anyone about anything. Andrea then asked me what I would consider the most interesting, or perhaps even frightening or most unusual, incident.

"There is one where I simply scratch my head, trying to figure out how it occurred," I said.

"Do you care to tell me about it?"

"Why not?" I said. "Once, I had to make a trip to Birmingham and traveled near to my dad's hometown of Fort Payne, Alabama. Your favorite group, 'Alabama,' was from there.

"Also, a friend of mine named Steve Trammel lived near there. I met Steve at college, and we became friends. He was a very accomplished professional portrait artist, and I was a watercolor hobbyist. We were friends for almost ten years, and after we each got married, we went our separate ways. He moved to the Chesapeake Bay area and made a nice living as a portrait artist, and I settled in South Georgia.

"As I drove through the Fort Payne area, I happened to think of Steve and wondered how he was doing. I thought that I would like very much to see him again. Just like my friend Greg, it had been more than ten years since I had seen Steve.

"Anyway, it was just a passing thought as I drove, and I didn't dwell on it. I continued to Birmingham on business, and then later that evening, I stopped by a mall that I hadn't been to in years. I only stopped there because we previously shopped there at a nice ski shop. I am always searching for the latest in snow skis.

"I found out that the ski shop was no longer there, so I wandered around the mall without any real purpose—except to window shop. I was about to leave, and then I decided—for some reason—to go into the basement of Rich's Department Store. I had never been there before, so I was simply feeling like I wanted to check the place out.

"There was a certain 'drawing' sense that I can never explain that was keeping me from leaving the building. I decided to ride the escalator down to the basement, where I noticed the furniture department. I looked inside, and across the room, there stood Steve."

Andrea uttered another, "Wow!"

I chuckled. "I totally agree—wow! As I said, it had been ten years, and the two of us lived 1,000 miles apart from each other. I was totally stunned. It gave me weak knees and cold chills. I asked myself, 'How did I do that?'

"That incident occurred at a time in my life where I was beginning to take notice that I was blessed with an ability that was unexplainable to the common man. But I definitely had it.

"Seeing Steve utterly frightened me to the point that I didn't even bother to speak or even garner his attention. It actually upset me so much that I turned around and left. Somehow I had been 'drawn' to his location. What in God's creation gives me that ability, and for what purpose?"

I sat there for a few minutes, looking at Andrea without saying anything. She just shrugged a little and shook her head. She didn't have the answers any more than I did.

Finally I said, "I suppose that was one of the most unusual incidents. But there are others—many others that have occurred during my life. But that one where I met Steve in a random mall really let me know that something was going on, and that there was something very unusual about me. I had a gift that I couldn't explain, so I learned not to discard those 'intuitive inclinations' as they came along.

"As I mentioned, there are many more. I started listing them, and then I just stopped because there were so many."

Andrea interrupted then. "Anthony, do you ever hear voices?"

"Absolutely not," I replied. "I never heard any voices, other than from live people who were in my presence."

"I see," she said, her brow furrowed in thought. "Sorry—please continue."

I told Andrea later about one incident that took place when I was twenty-six and working with a coworker on the roof of a school. We were installing equipment and Mike, my coworker, started a discussion about who I was and how I came about my career.

"He said, 'Anthony, you don't look like the type of guy who would follow this line of work. You look more like a professor or an executive or somebody like that. I know you are intelligent enough to achieve your college degree. What are your plans for the future?'

"I told him, 'Mike, I really don't know. I have no idea, except that I know I'm going to write a book someday.'

'A book?'

"'Yes, a book. I have always had this gut feeling that I am supposed to write a book. I don't know the subject matter or the type of book, but I'm going to write an important book.'

"'How do you know? What kind of feeling is it?'

"'It's more like an intuition, but it is a 'driving' feeling within me.' Then I asked him, 'Are you a hunter or a fisherman?'

"'No, not really.'

"'Great, Mike, you are not helping. A hunter stalking a deer, or a fisherman who is about to catch a big fish, simply *knows* what will happen shortly before it occurs. Many a golfer has said that they *knew* that they were going to hit a hole-in-one right before it happened. This type of instinct is very similar to the sportsman's unexplainable intuition.'

"'Fine, then let me ask you a few questions. How did you know you were going to marry the girl you married?'

"'Well, for one thing, she told me and that was that!' When Mike laughed, I chided him, 'Be serious for a minute!'

"Nevertheless, he was determined to grill me. 'Ha! Are you still married?'

"'Yes.'

"'Kids?'

"'Yes, three.'

"'Do you know their wants and needs before they do?'

"'Yes.'

"'How?'

"'Just a feeling. With me, it's always 'just a feeling.' I think that it is intuition mostly. Everybody has it to some degree, and some have more than others. You can't pin it down or quantify it. I have a feeling that God will let me know when and what to write, and when and how to get it published.'

"Mike looked up and spoke directly to the late October sky. 'That's interesting, Lord; now He is going to write a book.'

"I said, 'I know it's crazy, but I also feel that I will write and publish it only when the timing is right. I feel that timing and the information that I will have will be of utmost importance with whatever I write. The timing must be right for publication of the book. I simply have that feeling.'

"Andrea, I don't know about writing any book. I don't have anything interesting to say or to teach—at least, not yet. Perhaps someday, I will. But I will tell you this: I truly feel that I am supposed to write a book—perhaps to inform or even warn people with its content. Who knows?"

At that point, Andrea suggested that we take a break and come back in a couple of hours to talk about my early memories as a small child. Her housekeeper tapped on the door to say that she was leaving. She mentioned that there was pizza in the oven, if we wanted a bite to snack on.

Andrea invited me back to the kitchen, and we sat at a small antique metal table that looked very similar to my parents' breakfast table. There was a new curiosity in her gaze when she looked at me, but as we settled in to eat, she steered the conversation away from the past and focused instead on current events.

"How long are you planning to work in New York?"

I swallowed down a mouthful of pizza. "I can't really say with any certainty. Perhaps six to nine months—I don't know. I suppose I will be here as long as I can stand it. There is much more work here for years to come, but I will go back as soon as I can connect with a project that is closer to home."

Then I asked Andrea about her family. "This is a large house," I prompted.

"Yes, we have a large family."

"I don't want to pry, but do you live here alone?"

"Actually, yes," she said. "All my siblings have married and moved. I share a mortgage on an apartment in Manhattan with them. My brother works his investment business out of the Manhattan apartment. As a family, we just gather there occasionally, and then we gather here on an occasional weekend or holiday. All my nieces and nephews do love that beach. As the years go by, it's more and more difficult to get everyone together. But I enjoy the quietness of the beach year-round, and my office is nearby in Queens."

I finished my pizza and suggested that I needed to get back to my apartment. It was getting late. We would have to reschedule a time when I could finish divulging my recollections.

Andrea seemed a bit disappointed.

"I am going to return," I assured her. "I promise to tell you everything that I can remember. We haven't even begun to get to the really weird parts. Besides, I am very anxious to hear your opinions on those events and recollections."

I was walking to the door when Andrea suddenly realized that she had driven me to her house. "Oh, I forgot," she said, laughing as she went to get her car keys.

"I can walk; you don't have to bother taking me back."

"No, I insist," she said, and she apologized.

As we left the porch and walked to the car, it had gotten dark finally. The sun didn't set until eight o'clock in the summer there.

She drove the ten blocks to my house, then pulled over and cut the engine.

"Would you care to sit with me on the deck?" I invited her.

"No; I'll take a rain check though."

I nodded. "When should we have another session?"

"Maybe next weekend," she answered. "I'll have more time then. I need to contemplate my next questions and how I want to ask them."

"Very well, suit yourself," I said. "I would like to continue whenever you're ready."

"May I call your landlady and set the next appointment?"

"Sure. She will take a message, as long as it isn't after 8 p.m."

"Got it. See you, and thanks."

"You are welcome."

CHAPTER FOUR:

A Child Of Wonder

The summer was passing quickly. August arrived, and Manhattan was stifling. The island does hold its heat.

The scent of the city, which emanates from the streets and the subways, often changes. More unidentified things were sticking to the soles of my boots than I could imagine. Storefronts and displays are being changed; street banners are being installed, which were advertising fall festivals and new theatre venues.

When the banners for *The Feast of San Gennaro* festival in Little Italy go up, that signals the beginning of autumn in NYC. I wanted to be there for that celebration one more time before I moved back home. Maybe some of the crew would be interested in going with me. My crew was mostly Italians, and they were always looking for a party. The *San Gennaro* down on Mott Street was one big street party that lasted all week. It would give me something to look forward to, once I returned from the trip home.

It was a good year for Old Broadway. It was the summer of *Cats*, *Best Little Whorehouse, Back to the Five and Dime, Jimmy Dean*—and a great list of many others.

Progress on the Tower was going well. The main levels were being leased at a record pace. King Juan Carlos paid a visit and cut the ribbon on a new Spanish Leather Shop in a primo Trump Tower retail ground location.

Trump cut another ribbon and turned on his famous six-story waterfall inside the Atrium Mall.

It wouldn't be long before the Tower construction was going to top out. I had a feeling that it also wouldn't be that much longer before I would be leaving for Georgia.

Donald was on the Tower site daily, directing traffic. That's the way it always was with Donald. He never missed a beat. He always knew the solutions, no matter how great or how trivial. We called him the "Answer Man" on the job. He always had the answer.

On Labor Day weekend, I was flying home to Georgia for a week. Andrea had called and left a message to invite me up to Narragansett for a lighthouse tour, but I needed to see my family instead. I suggested that we go in October for a couple of days, and she agreed to plan for it.

I also suggested that, when I returned from Georgia, we should schedule another session, and I would finish the tale about my recollection of my infancy for her—if she cared to listen. I needed to give her all the details of that strange snippet of my childhood. My ability for awareness from such an early age would play a great part in the revelations that were yet to come.

I was anxious to hear her opinion. I still had not divulged details about the infancy of my life to Andrea, even though we had visited and dined a few times. I had shared it several times in the past with others, and each time, I always was looked upon in disbelief. It was not that I minded sharing the story that much, but I always got the same response when I did.

Andrea did not push me to talk, and I respected that about her. I was definitely going to share the memories with her. I had grown to enjoy her clear understanding and opinions.

I found that every time I had ever discussed any subject matter or issue with a person who happened to be Jewish, I had always received the clearest logic pertaining to the subject. Andrea was first Jewish girl I had ever known, and I valued her opinion. I didn't want her—or anyone else—to think that I had been delusional with my flashbacks as a child, much less as an adult.

Those people whom I had shared with in the past, including a few family members, couldn't grasp what I was telling them. For them, it was beyond the realm of possibility—it was rolling your eyes time.

However, much later in my life, I heard an evangelist describing his life and the trauma he had received from a serious accident. He began his speech with a topic that concerned the trouble he had caused his mother at birth. He was a large child physically, and he weighed a whopping fifteen pounds at birth. His mother was many hours in labor until she finally delivered him as a healthy child. He said that it was the strangest thing that he was later able to recall the events very shortly after his birth. No one ever believed him. Nor did they ever believe me. The evangelist and I had that in common.

I know that the brain is a mysterious organ. It is complex beyond imagination. I have often thought of its mystic capabilities—especially when I think of events, either before they happen or as they are happening. At that moment, there is something going on with the brain that no one can explain. It is a strange ability to have, but for me, it is also strange to be subjected to.

It was late August, and I made flight reservations to Atlanta for a week's stay at the end of the month. Marie wanted to go to the beach in Destin before the children returned to school for the fall semester. Summers were longer for kids back then; usually summer vacation lasted at least twelve or thirteen weeks.

It would be my daughter's first year in school. I wanted to be there to see her first day. I could hardly believe she was growing up so quickly, and I was unable to be there every moment for her and my family. She was a very bright child.

I had a purchased new single-lens reflex camera, and I photographed her often—as any parent would. One afternoon, as I was photographing her, and she said, "Daddy, your camera is broken."

"What?" I asked, and I told her that I didn't think it was. When she insisted, I looked the camera over for several minutes and didn't find any issues. Later that evening, I examined the camera over and over. Finally, I looked inside the lens at the iris shutter and snapped it. One of the leaves of the iris flopped down unattached and retreated to a normal position after I released it inside the lens. Yes, there was a defect in the shutter. I apologized to her, and she seemed to understand that she was indeed correct. She was a smart three-year-old!

As my children grew and matured, I constantly looked for any sign that they might have inherited the unusual mental abilities or anomalies that I possessed. They were both very talented and extraordinarily intelligent. I discussed it many times with Marie as they matured, but neither of our children seemed otherwise out of the ordinary. The only exception that I ever considered was the one time when my eighteen-month-old son asked me about something that he could not have possibly known.

I was leaving for home the following day—on Friday. Later that Thursday afternoon, Andrea called and asked to come over.

"Sure!" I said. "And bring your swimsuit. I am going in the surf for a while."

She laughed and said, "Sure!"

I didn't think that she would, but at least I had extended the invitation.

I had cleaned up a bit and was sitting out on the deck in the breeze, listening to the surf and watching the seagulls. After a few minutes, her Plymouth Duster pulled up. Andrea popped out in a beach jacket and her swimsuit, carrying her change bag.

"Well," I said, "you surprised me by wearing your swimsuit."

I wanted to go for one last summer-ending swim, so we headed for the surf. As usual, as we hit the salty Atlantic, it was so cold that it thoroughly took our breaths away. The surf was up, but not too rough. After we acclimated ourselves, we spent a pleasant hour or so riding the waves while bodysurfing. Andrea was a great swimmer. She grew up swimming and surfing every summer day during her youth.

After a while, a guy whom she knew came along with his surfboard, and she asked to borrow it for a curl or two as the waves were picking up. I sat on the shore with him as we watched. She was amazing to watch, catching curls and kicking up spray. She could certainly ride a board.

If there was anything I could have changed about my existence on Earth, it would have been to live either in the western mountains or along the coast. Any coast would do, as long as there were harbors, surf, lighthouses, and sailboats. I loved them all.

Andrea made several more runs, displaying her surfing talents. She was in total control of the board and the wave. She caught one more spectacular wave and rode it into shore.

"Wow!" She laughed. "I'm glad Jeff came along with the board. That was unexpected and total fun! It was like old times!"

As I sat on the beach, I thought to myself: *I can only imagine.*

Marie asked me out for dinner, since I was going to leave the next day, and I had agreed to go. We went into the apartment and cleaned up over the next hour or so. Andrea had brought a change of clothes. I showed her where the towels were located and how to fix the hot water.

"I'll be out in a flash," she said with a gracious smile. Thirty or forty minutes later, she stuck her head out and said, "Your turn."

I laughed and took a cold shower—I needed a cold one anyway. We left for Jones Beach as it was growing dark. We found a beachside seafood bar, and anywhere we went, we found great food and great atmosphere. There were mostly locals frequenting that area of the shore, and the bands were local, but they were unusually talented cover bands. It also seemed as though everybody knew everyone else personally along that stretch of the NYC sand. They all knew Andrea, and they loved her.

We ate a leisurely meal, then walked along on the seawall while dodging spray and watching the lights. As we walked, she asked if I minded holding hands.

"Not at all!" I agreed. "I certainly don't want to go flying uncontrollably across the sand again though."

She laughed and asked, "What do you suppose that was all about that night?"

"I have no idea," I answered—but then again, perhaps I did have an idea. I didn't elaborate or give any hint as to what I really thought.

"Honestly, what do you think that was?" she asked again. "It was certainly not a figment of either of our imaginations. I mean, I am a highly trained professional, and it truly happened. I saw and experienced it with my own eyes!"

"You're right!" I said. "It did happen. We saw it, and I experienced it, and it was as strange a thing that has ever happened to me."

Andrea also agreed that it was as strange an incident as she had ever witnessed, ever!

"I have given it much thought, and I believe that the explanation may be much simpler than we expect," I said.

"Please elaborate, Dr. Marchant," she said, smiling.

"Very well!" I said. "But don't make fun of my analogy. Do you promise?"

She smiled and said, "I promise! Sorry."

"Here goes," I said coyly. "Strange or not, perhaps it was meant to protect one or both of us—and, in doing so, it was also meant to keep us apart. Perhaps we are being watched over, and we are not destined to become a couple. And perhaps we were never meant to be together, even for a moment. Whaddaya think about them apples?"

"Oh, I never thought that." She laughed. "I really don't think that God gets personally involved on an individual basis such as that."

"Well," I said, "that is all that I have thought about since it happened. Andrea, I am a spiritual person, and I am attuned as much as I can be to the Holy Spirit. He is my guiding light, and I follow His will for my life. When Jesus said, 'I go, and I will send the Holy Spirit'—that is precisely what He did on the moment that He passed from this Earth. That is Scriptural, and therefore it is not only for my protection, but for your protection as well."

"Oh, Anthony! Are you serious?" she said in disbelief. "I don't believe any of that. I admit, people get together all the time, legal or not."

"Andrea," I said, "Please listen carefully. I do have feelings for you—deep feelings. But they are feelings that—as I see it—can never be. You are all that a man could ever dream of or want. But I feel that it would be terribly destructive to both of us beyond our imagination."

"Anthony, I know you love your family, I know that!" she proclaimed.

"Let's just not go there. Let's not go into the relationship thing, and let's just enjoy the time we have together," I pleaded with her.

"I know that you will be going home, and I don't want to think about it or discuss it!"

"As weird as it may sound," I continued, "I think that what actually happened was that I was being physically separated from you by either your guardian angel or mine. Or maybe it was some strange entity that just didn't appreciate us being close together. Whatever it was, it was definitely not natural, and it was not of this physical Earth. It was all-powerful, whatever it was. You and I both are witness to it having happened. Does that make any mature sense?"

"So?" she retorted.

"Andrea?" I asked her cautiously.

"What?"

"What about you?"

"I have feelings for you as well," she admitted. "I tried to push them off, but they have become deeply seeded and they creep back during my unguarded moments. I have never felt this way in my life," she said as squeezed my hand ever tighter.

"Can we table this conversation?" I asked her. "Please? Besides, you didn't answer my thoughts on the event." I paused for a moment, then continued with my thought pattern. "Anyway, I want to tell you about my crazy entrance into this world at birth. I need to discuss it soon. If a job were to open up near home soon, I'll be going back to Georgia. I want to describe what I remember to you in person and not over a phone on a long-distance conference call. I have a feeling that, when I do return home, I'm going to be spending a fortune on long-distance calls to New York anyway."

"Well, I hope to me?" she asked. Then she added, "I would like that."

"Let's go back to the deck, and if it is empty, I'll tell you a bit about what I can recall," I offered.

"Great." She reached for my waist and arm and squeezed them.

An hour later, we were back at the apartment. It was late, and the deck was clear and darkened. All the lights were out at the house.

The starry night was cool, and in the background, the surf rushed and ebbed upon the beach in a timeless rhythm.

"I brought some merlot. Would you care for a glass this time?" Andrea invited as we took our seats.

"Yes, I would, but I'll have to decline, thank you. I'll need to think with a clear mind. It's needed for what I'm about to tell you."

And with that, I began. "Before I was born, I had two other siblings: a brother who was seventeen and a sister who was nine. My dad had purchased a small home and was making monthly payments of thirty-five dollars on the mortgage. He had not owned the home very long when suddenly he was out of work. He missed one payment and the local bank foreclosed on him in thirty days. Along with the embarrassment of having to lose the house, there was the fact that my mother was pregnant with me at the time, and they had two other children to feed. That placed untold pressure on my parents.

"My dad was able to purchase the old family farmhouse to repair and remodel it. He built windows and doors, then insulated the walls and finished them. After a period of hard work, the house was habitable, and we moved in about the time that I was due to be born. Word went out, and the doctor was summoned—along with mother's five sisters. Her brother and brothers-in-law were all fighting with General Patton in Sicily. Mother's labor started on a Saturday and I was born twelve hours later, on a Sunday. That was me—a Sunday's child. Are you bored yet?" I asked, glancing toward her.

"Not at all. I'm making mental notes," she replied, seated comfortably across from me.

I nodded and continued with my tale. "Twelve difficult hours later, I was born. It was a breech birth. My aunt Margaret turned to my dad and said, 'Thank the Lord that is over!' Then she added, 'No damned man is worth all that!' And that certainly endeared the two of them for the rest of their lives."

"Were you alright after all that?" Andrea interjected.

"I was fine, I suppose—considering the trauma. This is where it may interest you," I continued. "When I was about nine years old, I started having flashbacks or memories that I certainly didn't understand. Occasionally, I would have a remembrance of that particular period of time in my life. It didn't seem to fit anything in my existence. At least, I didn't know of anything. I never told anyone, and I carried it well into my adulthood."

"How would you come to recall the time? What would trigger the thoughts?" she asked.

"Many things, I suppose. The casual quip I made to you on the airplane about old memories and seeing you react with that curious but pretty smile caused me to suddenly begin recalling it all." I smiled.

"Please tell me what you remember," she urged.

"Okay, here goes. I remember seeing a tall, glowing, rectangular-shaped yellowish light in a darkened or blacked-out room. It was a large room—or, at least, it seemed so. Of course, nothing was in focus. Nothing! Almost everything was black. Between me and the tall lighted rectangle shape was a black-shaped figure, which I later was led to believe was Dr. Rowe, my doctor."

"Why did you believe that it was your Dr. Rowe?" she asked, curiously.

"Well, simple logic," I replied.

"Logic?" she countered.

"He was standing between me and the window. He needed all the light that was possible to see to deliver me. It was a dark farmhouse room with twelve-foot-high ceilings and few windows. I actually remember the figure as having what I later realized were glasses on the end of his nose, with his head tilted back and his chin protruding—like someone looking through his bifocals. Of course, at birth, I had no idea what I was seeing. I just saw objects that were blurred and unidentifiable to me. As I grew up, I later realized that it was definitely Dr. Rowe's profile."

"What else did you see?" She asked.

"I recall seeing five or six other thin, blackened figures moving around the scene. They were all moving around. I certainly couldn't focus. I don't recall hearing any sound, and I also know that a baby's eyes can't focus for several hours or days."

"What was it that you thought this scene actually was?" Andrea asked me.

"In later years, another acquaintance of mine who works in the medical field made an emphatic statement about it."

"What was it?" she asked.

"I told my lifelong dentist about it, and he said that I had remembered things from the moment that I was born. What do you think?" I asked her.

Andrea said, "I think that your dentist friend was right. The darkened figures were your mother's sisters, or nurses, and maybe your dad."

"Wow, inquiring minds come together," I said thoughtfully.

"How very unusual, and how exciting! Tell me more, please!"

"I also later recalled my sister carrying me into a cold room that also had a tall rectangle of yellowish light. I don't know if this was immediately after I was born or days later, but I remember that the room turned out to have a long tall window that had a shade half-drawn. I was wrapped in a pink cotton blanket like a papoose, and the blanket was wrapped around the top of my forehead and tucked in. My sister laid me in the corner of a deep purple velour couch with my head against the corner of the armrest, and I remember that the couch was warm. There was a heater nearby that I felt warmth from. The very strange thing that I vividly remember was that, as she carried me to lay me down on the couch, I was actually looking down on my sister as she carried me. I could see both of our faces as if I were looking down from above. She let me down to the corner of that dark purple velour couch. It was as if I were having an out-of-body experience and looking down."

"Goodness, do you recall any thoughts as you watched this procession?" she wondered curiously.

"Yes!" I exclaimed. "As absurd as it sounds, I remember being wrapped in a *pink* blanket. Through the years, and as I grew older, I pondered and worried about why it was a *pink* baby blanket! I was a boy!" I said, exasperated. "Andrea, I actually was truly concerned about the color of that blanket until I grew into my adolescence. Much later in life, I asked my sister about it."

"What did she say?" Andrea asked.

"She laughed and said, 'How on Earth did you know or even remember that? Anthony, tell me exactly how you knew the blanket was pink?'

I told her that I remembered seeing myself wrapped in it, and she said that it wasn't possible. And I said to her, 'Well, you tell me how I knew it was pink then! You aren't disagreeing with me, so you know that I know that it was PINK!'"

I sighed, recalling the story. "She then told me *why* it was pink. She said that all my aunts, along with Grandma Pruitt, had told mom that she was having another girl, so they gave her all pink baby clothes and blankets for my birth. There were no blue gifts available."

Andrea laughed and said, "That happened a lot in those days."

"Andrea, I remember that like it was yesterday," I said.

"Anthony, listening to this, I am ecstatic. You are the person I've been looking for as I research this subject—I mean, with your experiences," Andrea said enthusiastically, leaving her chair and crossing the deck to hug me around the neck. Then, a little embarrassed by her own excitement, she sat back in her seat and made a gesture. "I'm sorry, please continue. Tell me all that you can remember."

I continued, of course. "After my sister laid me on the couch, the sun was at a low angle and the rays were shining under the shade on that end of the couch. The shade was not drawn completely, and it was allowing the sun to shine into the room. It was not shining in my eyes, so as I lay there, I could see dust particles floating through light. It was *very* cold in the room, as my birth date fell on the last Sunday in November. Therefore, dust particles were rising and falling in the heat of the sunlight and the heat of the nearby oil heater. I could feel the pleasant warmth of that heater. I know that babies aren't supposed to be able focus eyesight for long periods of time, but not only did I see the dust particles, I knew what they were. I seemed to know what they actually were," I emphasized, so that she would understand the significance of this detail before I went on.

"Also, I saw the knick-knack quarter moon mounted high above on the wall by the window. The wallpaper was torn slightly beneath it. On the knick-knack moon were tiny steps that led to the top, and there were small white porcelain figurines on the steps. There were small children and one cow."

"What else? My goodness, I'm amazed."

"Well I suggested to you that I probably wouldn't disappoint," I said pointedly. "Is that all?"

"Anthony, I'll have to say that it certainly does not seem possible, or even probable from a professional standpoint, that what you are telling me is all true," she answered directly.

"I know," I said. "I would have probably questioned your credentials, had you totally agreed that all of what I just said was true. However, consider this: I remember all that I have described, and I have verified it with my slightly astounded sister, who is now forty-seven years old. She also remembers the event vividly. She was nine at the time. She was amazed and did remember wrapping me in that pink cotton baby blanket like a papoose and laying me on that couch shortly after I was born," I pointed out to her, then thought for a moment.

"Andrea, if you use this information in your research as more than a mention, or if even that, I am willing to sit for a test of any available sort to verify it—even hypnosis or a lie detector test. Something like that."

"Anthony, this is why I am doing the research paper," she said in a comforting tone. "There will certainly be a place set aside for this, and I may ask your permission for other experts to ask questions. What do you think?"

"I will consider that bridge whenever we get to it, but you may have to fly to Georgia for further info!" I said.

Andrea didn't look amused. "I don't want to think about your leaving."

"I am waiting on another position to open in South Georgia, but there is no telling when that will be. I may be around for the winter," I said, trying to soothe her.

"I hope so!" she replied in a small voice. "I want to hear about anything you recall as you grew older. How are your recollections pertaining to that time period?"

"Why don't we take a break for an hour, or maybe for a week or two?" I said, laughing.

"Alright, alright," she agreed with a smile, relaxing her rigid posture as she curbed her eagerness. "Why don't we go out for a pizza?"

"No," I said. "Let's just get a cup of coffee for now."

I stepped inside to make coffee, and I grabbed some cookies before I went back out. It was getting chilly, so I asked if she wanted to come in and snack. She agreed, and we sat inside on the couch as we drank the coffee and ate cookies.

I continued my story with the recollection about hearing very loud sirens and whistles on various days while living in the old house.

"What were they?" she asked curiously.

"May 8, 1945. VE-Day in Europe. I was 18 months old and the whistles were blowing for hours. People were running around the streets and dancing everywhere. I remember it as if it happened yesterday. Then, not long after that—on V-J Day—we bombed Japan. It was the same celebration all over again. The wars were over, and the celebrations went on for days. I remember the sirens again with people dancing in the streets."

I smiled at the memory, then continued. "Also, I remember sitting on the floor with a pencil and a piece of notebook paper, wanting to learn how to write cursive. I could only write several vertical T's that were connected with cursive, but I didn't know how to cross them. I kept asking my mother if that's what writing was, and she kept saying, 'No, that isn't writing, Anthony.' At two years of age, I said to her, 'Why aren't you teaching me?'

Andrea and I both laughed.

"Are you making mental notes?" I asked. "You aren't writing anything down."

"Believe me," she said, "I can remember all that you tell me."

We finished our coffee, and I turned off the light and opened the windows a bit for the sea breeze to come in. I sat down on the couch and looked out on the ambient-lighted beach.

"When I was three, my dad moved the family out of the farmhouse and into a new home on the east side of town. It was a pretty home on a hill. A couple of years after we moved in, all our relatives came from Chattanooga to visit for a weekend and see our new home. It was a traditional brick home located on a hill above the street and surrounded by very tall pine trees. On one side, there was a raised covered porch and a place to cook out.

Late one Sunday afternoon, I heard the large roar of an airplane flying off in the distance. I was five at the time, and I told my dad that an airplane was coming. He said, 'No, Anthony, it sounds more like a transfer truck on the nearby highway.' I argued with him and said, 'No, Pop. It's a big airplane!' He laughed and agreed, saying, 'Okay, Anthony, it's an airplane.'"

I mused on the memory for a moment, but continued with the story, "Immediately after I said it, a WWII-era Fairchild C-82 Packet Bomber flew fifty feet right over the top of the house, dripping molten metal from a burning left engine and setting the pine needles in our front yard on fire. My dad jumped up with all the family and exclaimed, 'Holy cow! It *was* a plane.'

"It crashed directly behind our house and set pine straw in our yard on fire, broke limbs out of the trees in our yard, and set the woods on fire. I was five, but I told my dad that it was an airplane. I simply had a certain feeling about it that I can't describe. I felt blessed, even at the age of five, because I had been taught early on and I knew God was watching over us."

"If the bomber had only been fifty feet lower, we would all have been consumed by fire. It happened on Friday the 13th in 1948. The pilots had bailed out over fifty miles away above a deserted farmland when the engine caught fire, and the plane flew around our town for over an hour before crashing. They had no idea that they were near a small city.

"We all went to watch the fire at the crash site over the rise. I wanted to go, but my mom said no. It was about that time that our neighbor, Mr. Gaines spoke up.

"'Come on, Anthony; let's go see that bugger!' He threw me onto his shoulder and off we went. Mr. Gaines was a Texas oil man, and he owned the Citi-Services Oil Company in town."

It was a great true story that I was telling Andrea, but I looked over and she was sound asleep. I smiled, thinking that she missed the best part. She was definitely asleep next to me on the couch. I gazed at the beach for a while, and then I also fell asleep.

It was 3 a.m. when I woke up, and she was lying with her head on my shoulder and her arms across my chest, still sound asleep. I eased upright, placed a pillow under her head, and then went back to sleep.

One more day, and then I was going home. I hadn't mentioned the many other memories of my early youth that I had suppressed in the past. I suppose that I had much more to tell her, if she wanted to hear it. I reached over and set the alarm for 6 a.m., and then I fell asleep again.

The alarm went off right on time. It was Friday morning. Andrea was still sleeping when a knock came to the door. I had no idea who had arrived at my apartment that early, but I answered it. I was surprised to find that it was Mrs. Julliard, the landlady.

"I knew you were going home today for a stay, so I baked you some bread for you to take to your wife!" she said with a smile.

"Oh, thanks! That's very nice of you." I politely accepted.

"And I cooked some blueberry muffins for breakfast. I thought that you two might be hungry," she added.

"Yes, ma'am. Thanks again."

Andrea was grinning as she woke up. "That was sweet of her to do that," she said.

"Right!" I scoffed. "More like being nosy, big time! She just wanted to check you out and see who you were."

"At least we got breakfast out of it." Andrea laughed, grabbing her beach bag. "I have to go. Have a safe trip, and give me a call when you get back."

On her way out, she quickly reached up and pulled me to her and gently kissed me high on the cheek. Another shock went through my mind and body, and as I settled down, she was out the door and gone before I could respond.

I drove the Volvo into the 116th Street train parking just in time to catch the A-Train. I always hummed that tune a bit as I rode the train. *A-Train* had been my favorite Big Band tune during my college days. I had played trumpet from the time I was in the third grade in Pittsburg through college at Auburn. It was a beautiful day in the neighborhood with a gentle sea breeze and clear skies, and I could tell that fall was in the air.

I rode the one-hour trip to Fifth Avenue and 53rd Street and got off the train, tipped my favorite panhandler a ten-spot, grabbed a Wall Street Journal, and walked three blocks to work. I had told Camerata, my boss, that I was going home early. That morning, he saw me come in.

"Hey Tony, whaddaya doing here? I thought you was goin' home!"

"Hi boss, I am!" I replied.

"Get outta here! Have a good weekend!" he said with a grin.

I laughed, but I had a few hours to kill. My plane didn't depart until six that evening. I thought perhaps I would do a bit of sightseeing before catching the JFK Express to the airport. I only had a carry-on bag for my trip home, after all. It was 8:30 a.m. and I had a lot of time to kill.

I finally decided that I would kill two birds with one stone and visit some of the mid-town sights, the Empire State Building, and the World Trade Center on the same day. So I rode the subway to 34th Street and arrived at the Empire State Building just in time for the Observation Deck to open. My dad had helped renovate the building in the sixties, and I had been there with the Boy Scouts. I remember calling my mom from a phone booth on the top in 1957 and yelling about where I was at the time.

I stayed on top of the Empire State Building for about an hour, then enjoyed walking the ten blocks or so on down to 23rd Street to the Chelsea Hotel. What a great six weeks that summer had been in 1960. My dad and friends lived in a twelfth-floor corner apartment suite while they were building a project at the Empire State Building. It was apartment number 1231. I heard that, in later years, a famous movie star or two had leased that same apartment. I mused on that as I walked.

I finished the morning at the World Trade Center. My brother had helped build the North Tower, but the observation deck was on the South Tower, so that is where I went. It seemed strange, but I always got an uneasy feeling about the Towers. For some reason, the times that I spent on the top of the World Trade Center were never comfortable for me. Could I have been strongly anticipating the future?

Probably not, but to go on top of them was intimidating—to say the least. I quickly snapped a few shots with my camera, the one that my three-year-old daughter had required me to repair. After that, I grabbed a sandwich and soda from the Observatory Restaurant and made my way down to the World Trade Center Terminal beneath the Towers. I caught the first available JFK Express and rode out to the airport.

It was good to be leaving for home, even though I had only been gone for a month. My stays away from home usually lasted between six to eight weeks. I was going to check on a project while I was at home and see what the starting date would be for transferring back to the South.

When I arrived at Delta's check-in, I was informed that I had received a page. I was given a local phone number. It was one that I didn't recognize, so I dialed it as soon as I found an empty phone booth.

I had unknowingly dialed Andrea's office directly. She answered and said, "Hi! I hope this call didn't inconvenience you."

I laughed and said, "Not at all, a complete surprise! What's up? Are you okay? Did you finally wake up?"

She laughed and said that she was fine, and she wanted me to know that she had heard everything that I had said—even though she was very sleepy at the time.

I laughed. "Ha! You didn't have to call me and tell me that!"

"I know," she said, the mirth fading from her voice. "But I wanted to say goodbye and tell you to please be careful and..."

After a long pause, I prompted curiously, "And what?"

"Please come back," she said, softly.

I was a bit taken aback. After a long minute or two, I simply said, "I'll be back, and then we will talk. And not just about my nutty memories. We will talk about other things, I promise."

"Please have a safe trip," she said again.

"I will, Andrea. I will be back! And I will have a safe trip, I assure you." After that, we hung up.

As my L-1011 flight lifted off, my thoughts drifted to the thought of Andrea and unrequited love. Everything I thought that I ever wanted was ahead—or maybe not. Only time would tell!

CHAPTER FIVE:

A Narragansett Weekend

When the plane landed in Atlanta, I retrieved the luggage and found a phone booth to call Marie. Thankfully she was at home, and she answered right away.

"Hi! Where are you?"

"I am in the Atlanta airport. I took an earlier flight, so I'm going to rent a car and you won't need to bother picking me up. Besides, I want to pick up a gift for the kids before I come in," I said, glancing around.

She agreed and asked me to also pick up milk and bread before I got home. It had been a long time since I had bought milk and bread. Even though it was only for a weekend, I was definitely back home.

We spent the weekend packed with a junior league football game. Mark was a wide receiver and a very talented pass catcher. He helped send the team to his junior league's national championship game in Gatlinburg, Tennessee. He did this by catching a winning pass against a very good, and undefeated, Louisiana team. There was thirty seconds on the clock when he jumped above the defenders and caught the pass on his fingertips. There was no time on the clock by the time he fell into the endzone for the winning touchdown. It was exciting to watch, but I was also sad that I was stuck in New York City and didn't get to see many of his games. Back then, they didn't take many videos of the games, so I had missed out.

For years before I left for New York, I used to spend every afternoon tossing the football to my son. He rarely missed a catch out of the twenty-five tosses every afternoon. I certainly was proud.

When I finally got home, Jen took me by the hand and led me to the living room and sat me down.

"Stay right there, Daddy!" she said as she went over to the piano and beautifully played a simple version of *Rondo*. I was amazed. I applauded, and then she wanted to play it again and then again and again. I loved every moment of it.

Later that weekend, we went hiking and canoeing up in the Little River Canyons of North Alabama. It was a great weekend. Marie and I went out for a late evening picnic on the nearby neighborhood lake. We had a long discussion about how much she missed me and about that uneasy feeling she got every single night when she laid down in bed alone. Her tears began to flow and continued to pour as she discussed my being away.

I explained the job situation and the time until it was scheduled so that I could return home. I explained it to her with the information I had from my agent. As it stood, it would be six months before I could return.

"I love the comfortable living that you provide, but I hate our situation," Marie said, tearfully.

"It will end soon," I assured her, but I didn't argue her point.

I kissed her, and we lay back on the blanket and looked at the incredible display of the heavens. There were even two beautiful shooting stars that night, which was highly unusual.

The next day was Sunday, the day that I had to leave. I kissed and hugged the family, then returned to Atlanta and caught my usual 10 p.m. flight. It was storming up the Atlantic Coast that evening, so the flight was a bit bouncy—even though it cleared as we approached JFK. I caught a cab and headed back on the bumpy ride to Belle Harbor. At 3 a.m., I arrived at 131st Street, unloaded my luggage, and entered the apartment. As I opened the door, I noticed a welcoming note slipped under the door.

The note simply read: *Hi Anthony, welcome back! Can hardly wait to see you! Please call this number tomorrow afternoon. I have a favor to ask. Thank you!*

Even though it was unsigned, I gathered that it was from Andrea, but I couldn't imagine what it could be about. I set the alarm clock, removed my shoes, and passed out on the bed—still fully clothed.

During the time I worked in the city, every time I returned from a visit home, it always felt good to be back in the apartment. This time was no exception, but I knew that—in a few short weeks or months—I would have to be leaving. And more than likely, I would never return to New York again—at least for work. As I returned to the Tower that Monday, we received word that there would be a project meeting at 11:00 a.m. in the basement floor area of the Atrium. The crews were to be reassigned to new projects as the complexity of the development entered the finishing stages. The commercial units on the basement and the first six floors were being leased, and the designers and architects for the new tenants were coming in.

I was assigned to an Italian interior designer who would instruct me as to where lighting and other technical issues should be resolved. Angelica, as I found out, was contracted to design several interiors for both the commercial units and at least three private residences in the Tower. That day, the work became both creative and enjoyable. Also that day, I was given an eye-opening window into the incredible wealth that permeated an undertaking such as the Tower.

When introduced to me, Angelica asked where I was from, and I told her Georgia. When she finished slamming her hands on her hips and rolling her eyes in that condescending manner that all of us Southerners know very well, she said, "I guess you will do!"

The other crews were all laughing at me. I shrugged my shoulders and winked at them. I told them that I could see that I was going to have some fun. As it turned out, Angelica and I got along very well after she found that I was a designer and also an artist.

Over the next few weeks, she would introduce me to her clients. One client to whom I was assigned was a thirty-year-old young lady whose grandfather had passed and left her with one hundred million dollars. I escorted her as we inspected the units, which were in the preconstruction shell and had not yet been configured. She settled on, and purchased, two units that were located on the 46th and 47th floor. The two units were situated on top of each other, and they each had a view of both North and South Fifth Avenue toward the

Statue of Liberty and north to Central Park. Incredible one hundred million-dollar views, for sure.

I could only imagine what it was going to look like, and Angelica's creative juices began to flow when we first saw it. Curiosity had the best of me, so I asked the young owner where the living room was going be constructed as we stood on the upper floor.

"Here?" I asked.

"Oh no, I purchased two units because I am installing a fifteen by thirty-foot lap pool to swim in on the top unit. Come back for our swim party when we get it finished," she said with a smile.

"I will place that date on my calendar," I cordially replied.

A few days later, Angelica invited me to inspect a unit that was being prepared for a very small and short gentleman. A contractor mentioned the expense of making the change. The gentleman jumped in the air and told him quickly to never mention money in their conversations again. Money seemed to be flowing everywhere, but no one was ever supposed to mention it. Strange!

It was a different world than ninety-eight percentile of the Earth's population could ever imagine. I knew that my window on such a world was to be short-lived, as I planned to return to Georgia in the near future. My thoughts turned to Andrea as I remembered the note that she had left for my return. It was time to head for the subway to return to my apartment.

I was a bit anxious to return to Belle Harbor that afternoon and perhaps see her. It had been quite a week. I even questioned why I was anxious. I would be departing soon to return to Georgia, and I was struck by the realization that once I left for home, I might never see her again.

I couldn't help but wonder what the note was about. I would find out soon enough, I assumed. I left the station at 116th and climbed in the Volvo, then drove to 131st Street. I reached the apartment and checked the mail before entering. I cleaned up for the evening and started to call Andrea, but I opted to make the call on the note first. I went to the hallway where Mrs. Julliard's public phone was located. I dialed the number and received no answer. It was late in the day, so I decided to wait until the next day and retry from work. Just then, the phone rang. I answered, and Andrea had called back from the number.

"Tony?" she asked.

"Yes?"

"Yes! You have returned home!"

I laughed and said, "Well, I'm back from home. How are you?"

"I'm great, now that you are back. I left you the note to call this number. It is my direct office number at the college, and I have a favor to ask of you."

"What's that?" I asked, curiously.

"Without giving any personal details about the things that you have shared with me, I told Dr. Phillip Landers about you. Please don't shoot me when you hear this, but I told him about you and some of the things that we have discussed."

"Andrea! Why? Good grief!" I retorted, shocked.

"He really wants to meet you. Anytime, anywhere. He is an associate of mine who has a PhD, and he is deeply involved in the same research," she explained.

"Very well, but please—not during this week. The meeting should be on the weekend, and it needs to happen soon. I may be leaving for a position back in Georgia or other points in the South very soon," I responded.

"Great! Are you home tonight?" she asked.

"Yes. I'll be here."

"Walk on the beach?" she asked, hopefully.

"Sure, I suppose. I'll bring a parachute just in case I go flying across the sand," I joked.

She laughed and said, "I can hardly wait to see you."

I turned on the oven and shoved in some leftover local upper-crust pizza. That was always my favorite Rockaway pizza because it tasted like Tony's Pizza in Detroit. When we lived there for a couple of years, we discovered pizza. My mom was a great cook and wouldn't eat "the stuff," as she called it. My dad found Tony's in an old storefront over on East Grand Boulevard. It was great. Every table had a single light bulb on a wire hanging over it, and the tablecloths were checkered red and white. Tony tossed each pizza by hand and cooked them to order. Mom grew to like them for a while, and then one night, she found a hair in her pizza. She never went back.

Anyway, I devoured my pizza and hit the shower. I had exactly three minutes of Mrs. Julliard's hot water to wash off the subway grime. There was not much hot water, but I couldn't complain about the rent. Mrs. Julliard was still under rent control, and my beachside apartment was only $250 a month. I didn't complain about hot water. I lathered up to shave just as Andrea knocked at the door.

I let her in, and she gave me a big hug and a kiss and got shaving cream all over her. She had a friend with her, whom I presumed was her associate, Dr. Landers. About that time, he spoke.

"Hi, Tony?"

"Yes?"

"I'm Phil Landers," he said.

"Nice meeting you. I thought we were going to meet on the weekend," I remarked, slightly irritated by the surprise meeting.

"Oh, we will. I dropped Andrea off here as we were coming from the campus," he replied.

"Have a seat," I invited. "I'm not doing anything this evening."

"No, but thank you. We will schedule a proper time as you requested, and we will do it soon. I must go now. Nice to meet you, and please have a nice evening."

"Sure thing, Doctor, and you as well," I said, seeing him out.

Andrea was left standing there. "I hope you aren't annoyed. He was bringing me home. I took the train this morning and didn't want to ride it back alone, as it was getting late."

"Not at all," I said, hoping to soothe her.

She gently hugged me again and said, "It's nice to see you again. You have shaving cream on your nose." With a smile, she wiped it away for me. "Are you still up for that walk?"

"Sure, let me throw on some sweats. Are we walking or going for a run?"

"I would prefer to walk, if you don't mind," she answered, smiling.

We walked from the deck straight out to the breakers and turned down the beach. New York City beaches are as hard as a parking lot at the water's edge, which is great for running. They are also studded with shells and sometimes used syringes from the druggies. I never walked on the beach late at night without a flashlight. So Andrea placed her arm around my elbow, and we walked together into the cool twilight.

"How was your week?" she finally asked.

"It was great seeing the family. We packed as much adventure as we could into one weekend, along with visiting Mom and Dad."

"How was your mom?" she asked, obviously concerned.

"Her Alzheimer's has worsened. It never gets better, as you are well aware. She still recognizes me, and everyone says that is exceptional because she recognizes few others. She is in her sixth year after diagnosis. I understand that it's an eight-year illness. No cure. It is really sad. However, if a college football game is on TV in the nursing home, you may as well not be in the room."

"Who is her team?" she asked, glancing toward me.

"Auburn, of course. She loves Auburn University and loves Shug Jordan."

Andrea laughed. "Then no Alabama? Right?"

"Exactly! She hates Bear Bryant with a passion. I just enjoy the rivalry. I don't know why, but Bear gets on her nerves at the nursing home so much that they have to turn channels."

We both laughed.

Andrea asked, "Can she still converse?"

"No," I replied, sadly. "She just makes a moaning sound. However, she can still write. They give her a new legal pad every day and a ballpoint pen, and she writes in cursive, *I LOVE YOU. I LOVE YOU. I LOVE YOU. I LOVE YOU.* Line after line, page after page, she writes it repeatedly. She still has the most beautiful handwriting of anyone I know, and well…" My voice trailed off and trembled as I thought of my mother.

Before I knew it, a few tears welled up and the sea breeze pulled them out. I let them dry on my cheeks.

Then I glanced apologetically at my companion. "Tough times in the family. Always tears when I think of Mom. Sorry."

Andrea tugged me closer and leaned her head against my shoulder as we walked.

"I'm alright," I assured her presently. "It happens every time I think of her repeatedly writing, *I LOVE YOU.*"

Changing the subject, I suggested to Andrea that both she and Dr. Phil may have been interested in the fact that my mother would tell me about her dreams as I was growing up.

"My dad never thought much about it, but my mom told me about a recurring dream that she had about being in an open casket at the final viewing. People thought she was dead, but she wasn't. She could hear and understand them. She said that she could not communicate to them, but that she was lucid, and she knew and understood every word they said around her. She said that she had the recurring dream for years, and that it was terrifying. My sister maintained that she could not understand what was said around her. I think that, with her lying in bed with Alzheimer's, her dream has actually come true, as it relates to her communicating to the world around her. What do you think about that, Doc?"

"Now that is interesting. I'll tell Phil and relay his response to that."

"I'd appreciate it. Anyway, when I visited Mom, I talked to her as if she were in a normal lucid state. I never did discuss anything that might upset her, and I forbade anyone else around her to say anything that might upset her."

Andrea remarked, "Your whole family seems to have that extra sense—or that sixth sense, as some call it."

I laughed. "Don't get me started on that again."

"So, when are we doing the lighthouse thing?" Andrea asked. "We need a long weekend away, and I want to explore as much of the coast as possible."

"I am game. I would enjoy seeing Point Judith, Narragansett, and Points North. Do you want to invite Phil?"

"I thought about asking him to come along. Would you mind?"

"Not at all! I think you two doctors make a cute couple. Andrea, please stop kicking sand on me! Besides, he seemed very interested when I mentioned the trip earlier. He also seemed very interested in *you*."

She scoffed. "Been there and done that, and I'm not ready to revisit that situation."

My natural Southern curiosity surfaced. "Oh? Tell me about that!"

"That, Mr. Marchant, is none of your business!" She smirked at me. When I laughed, she joined in. Then, as we returned to the apartment, she said that she would indulge me at some point in the future.

"Want to come in for a glass of milk?"

She laughed and said, "No thanks, got to go! I'll check with Phil about the trip, and I'll see you tomorrow—late. Is that alright?"

"Sure, just let me know."

Late the next day, Andrea called. She said that Phil would enjoy the trip very much, and he had asked her to thank me for the invitation. He also invited us to stay at his grandparents' summer cottage on Narragansett Bay, which we were welcome to use for the weekend. He said that it was only a modest place, but we could make do. We set the weekend trip to go on a Thursday, and that gave us ample time to enjoy a four-day, three-evening trip. Phil volunteered to drive his Chevy convertible. We were good to go.

It took only two and a half hours to drive up the freeway. Phil put the top of his convertible down, and the weather was perfect for the drive. As we neared Narragansett, Phil suggested a bayside restaurant, so we stopped and experienced a relaxing evening dinner. The venue was the type of place that had the character of the old days, so that I kept expecting Humphrey Bogart and Lauren Bacall to bounce in at any minute. There was a nice club band playing swing music. We enjoyed the atmosphere so much that we decided to stay and dance for a while. That turned into an unplanned four-hour meal and club dance.

Phil asked me about my plans to return to Georgia, and I told him that I would depart as soon as the positions became available. The last time I had checked, a position was opening at a nuclear plant in Eastern Georgia along the Savannah River. Once I got the call, then I would be gone within a week or so. I didn't think much of it at the time, but I later thought that he seemed a bit anxious for me to leave. I couldn't help but wonder why.

About that time, the band struck up, playing a familiar favorite: *Moonlight Serenade*. Andrea grabbed me by the hand and said, "Let's go!"

"Where?"

"Outside to the deck. The moon is coming up and they are playing my song," she invited, smiling.

We went through the double-glass French doors under the lighted trellis and walked out onto a raised, covered dance floor that was situated over the Bay. We danced the *Serenade*, then *Green Eyes*, and finally *You Go to My Head*.

The band was great, but it seemed that it was sure trying to get me in trouble with all those songs. We danced a fourth slow dance, and Andrea placed her head against my chest. I buried my face in her soft brown hair. As we danced, I thought I felt her whimpering a bit. Andrea didn't want to leave the dance floor, and neither did I, but it was getting late and Phil certainly must have thought that we had eloped.

As it was, Phil was totally preoccupied with a local female friend of his family, and he was enjoying the opportunity to reminisce about old times. I looked around and tried to imagine what it must have been like to have been brought up in the wealthy and privileged lifestyle that surrounded me.

Andrea excused herself to freshen up, and when she returned, we left the club for the cottage named Modest Bay. We drove along a high cliff road and came upon the bay. Across to the northeast, I could see the Point Judith Lighthouse with a full beacon flashing toward the bay and out to the open sea. It guarded the entrance to the bay, and every few seconds, it flashed its light toward Phil's house. I could imagine what it would have been like to be a mariner and to recognize that light as a hopeful beacon for a safe harbor.

We turned into the driveway, and the home was stunningly magnificent in its architecture and its condition. It stood with a two-story double porch, complete with a widow's walk on the roof. Phil's grandparents had purchased the home in the late 1940s from a sea captain's daughter. We retrieved our bags and gear and walked up the steps.

"Phil, I am totally impressed!" I said.

He smiled and said that he had wanted to invite us up earlier in the season, but the time had never convenient during the past summer. We walked to the door, and a maid met us. Wow, this guy had a maid too.

"Hi, Mr. Phil. We've been expecting you," the maid greeted him.

I looked at Andrea, and she looked down at her feet and smiled. I whispered to her, "Well, you also have a maid!"

"My maid isn't a live-in maid. This is like royalty," she whispered back.

"Whatever. I'll take it as long as she doesn't meet me with a towel as I exit the shower."

The maid explained that she had prepared the two front bedrooms upstairs—one for the lady and one for the gentleman. I found myself looking around for the gentleman in question. Also, she explained that she had prepared a late evening snack with wines, cheese, and crackers. It was certainly nicer than the Motel 6 that I was used to.

I carried our luggage up the stairs and dropped Andrea's in her room before opening my room. Both rooms had leaded glass French doors that led out onto the second-level covered porch, which offered a full view of the lighthouse and the bay. Each room also had a brick fireplace with small logs burning.

I thanked Phil graciously, and then Andrea announced, "I'm ready for snacks."

Snacks and wine were to be enjoyed along with a small fire, talks of architecture, storms, and sea captain adventures until the wee hours. I finally excused myself and went to my room, shaved, and took a shower. I threw on some sweats, picked up a deckchair blanket, and went out to curl up in a chaise lounge and watch the eventual sunrise. I promptly went to sleep.

I woke up at first light when a huge seagull landed on the banister right in front of me. It was still dark, and the seagull was silhouetted against the early light of day.

"Great seagull!" Andrea said. Startled, I looked over and found her sitting in the chaise next to me. She frightened me half to death. I wasn't expecting anyone to be out there with me. Before I could say anything, she held out a mug. "I brought you some cappuccino, if you like."

I gratefully accepted it. "Thanks! Breakfast in chaise lounge!"

Later that morning, we decided to eat all our meals out, so we packed a picnic lunch and headed out the door to explore the coastline. Point Judith Lighthouse, ferry rides to Block Island, rocky seashores with giant crashing waves: we missed nothing, it seemed, during our three carefree days. We were just three people having fun.

On the last evening, we dined as guests in Phil's home. Rene, his maid, had prepared an exceptional seafood meal using old original recipes from the captain's own kitchen locker, and she included a bottle of aged rum. One swallow, and my throat was on fire and my head was spinning. I told them that it was great stuff, as I complimented her in an old sea captain's hoarse voice! That was enough for me! I could barely speak.

On the way up the coast from Long Island, Phil had discussed some of the early memory information that I had shared with Andrea. He asked me if I minded sharing any other thoughts from my past that I may have recalled since my discussions with Andrea.

I didn't mind at all, so after dinner, we settled in the captain's library with a fire going and the distinctive smell of hundreds of old leather-bound nautical-themed literary works. Volumes of poetry, art, and drama lined the shelves from the walls to the ceiling. A huge model of the captain's ship and his huge ship's wheel were mounted on the library walls as well.

Again, I was reminded of the difference in our families' histories concerning privilege versus struggle. I couldn't help but compare. I had lived one and was visiting the other. I never envied the substance of privilege. Perhaps the wisdom that was inherent with the astute was what I envied most. It has been said that everyone is born with the same opportunities, but that simply isn't true. For every success, there are ten thousand failures, and those failures can be counted in people.

Phil came into the room with a notepad, while Andrea just sat and listened. Phil apologized and said he felt as if we should be out dancing, as it was our last evening in Narragansett. Both Andrea and I agreed that we were enjoying our time, and there was no need for an apology. In part, that was why I had actually come: to give Phil an opportunity to ask questions about my thoughts and revelations.

He then asked for any occurrences that were mental in nature, much like the Ferrari or similar episodes that I had earlier shared with Andrea. He told me that he had assembled extensive notes on most of that material. I expressed to him that those were the instincts I felt which I call "pre-thoughts." Those simply pop into my mind, as if I get the feeling to *turn here* when looking for direction or a location. Many people get those feelings.

Personally, as a layman who is totally uneducated on the psychology of the subject, I suspect that what I was blessed with is inherent in the survival instincts that we may have always had in early human development. Then I asked Phil and Andrea to tell me if they could explain how I learned of a solution to a project's electrical problem that I once had.

I explained that we were having problems with a system on a manufacturing project. After several failed attempts to remedy the situation, I dreamed—or saw—the solution in the middle of the night. Phil and Andrea grabbed their pads and awaited my story.

"I was working for an electrical contractor, installing emission control devices in various industrial facilities in the South. At that time, the systems involved a large array of control relays—each working in concert to operate various segments of the equipment. As the crews completed the installations, we tested the equipment for several days before we set it into operation. This system test had run successfully for several days and was ready to be integrated into the factory operation. On a Friday morning, we scheduled the last test at 8:00 a.m., but we turned it on and nothing happened. Hours of troubleshooting followed without success. The following Monday, we tried again, and still nothing."

I sighed, then continued. "I repeat that it had operated successfully several previous times. I sent the crew to other duties until I had the time to think about the installation process and the system failure. That night, I went to bed with the system on my mind. In the early hours of the morning, I was awakened, and in the darkness, I somehow saw the letters and numbers of a relay that we had installed. They were spelled out as white letters and numerals against a black background, as plain as day. They were: CR 1040-CR."

At that moment, Phil looked at Andrea and smiled, but he kept writing.

"What then?" Andrea asked.

"The next morning, I went to the plant, and the crew chief and asked if we were going assign a crew to look for the defect. I told him to open the control cabinet and look for the CR 1040-CR relay. He asked why, and just I told him to try it. I told him to please turn the system on and just climb up there and lightly tap the CR 1040-CR relay. He told me it was nonsense and that I was crazy. He wouldn't stop asking me why. I told him to just do it—please and thank you. He turned the system on and it did nothing. Then he tapped the relay CR 1040-CR, and suddenly the whole system of conveyors began working perfectly. That's when I smiled and walked out. The crew chief followed and asked me how I had managed to do that."

Smiling, I continued. "I told him that he didn't want to know, but I wasn't crazy. That's when he told me that I was certainly weird. I told him that I couldn't argue with him there, but he insisted that I tell him. So when I finally told him that the answer had come to me in a dream, he called it B.S. and walked off."

Phil and Andrea both were laughing by this point, but she encouraged me to continue. "What else? Please!"

"When I was six, the family was swimming at a place named Crystal Springs, and it was a bright sunny day. All my family—aunts and uncles included—were under a picnic pavilion when the weather turned stormy. I kept telling my mother that a tornado was on the way. They all laughed at my prediction. The sun was shining, and the family was enjoying the outing. They were relying on a 1949 weather report instead of relying on me. After all, I was small—only six years old. The sun was certainly out, but shortly thereafter, a tornado roared over the mountains and destroyed our picnic shelter. It threw the pavilion two hundred feet into the air and out into the lake as we ran for cover. I kept telling my mother, 'I told you so.'

"I admit that it is strange and seemingly unexplainable. I know that I have a special sense. It is undeniable. I have had it ever since I was born. I consider it to be a gift from God Almighty, the Creator of the universe. Why do I have it? Am I unique in the world? Not in the least, in my own estimation. The Bible clearly states that there are and will be prophets in the Last Days. Am I a prophet? I am not worthy in any respect to be special, nor do I claim that I am. But as I have said before, I've had foreknowledge of so many things before they happen that I don't have any doubt that I possess something that few others on this Earth have."

Andrea then spoke in a quiet voice. "Anthony, there is something—or, rather, many things about you that really are special. I noticed it when I first sat next to you on that plane from Atlanta. I believe that you have some special purpose in this life. Perhaps, at thirty-eight, you aren't anywhere near fulfilling that purpose. I would like to ask, whenever you go back home, that you keep in touch and let me know about your life and the things that are happening. They are definitely unique experiences. Perhaps God has plans for your *gift* that you can use in a way to help others."

Phil agreed. "I certainly don't understand it," he said. "Please do us both a favor. After you return home and as you continue with your life, if—or, I should say, when—anything unusual happens again, would you keep us apprised? Even the slightest unusual incident would be worthy of examination. We would simply enjoy keeping track. I would certainly like to compile a file on the events in your life—keeping them in the strictest of confidence, of course," he concluded.

I shrugged and told them both that I would consider it. After all, I supposed that this was the real purpose of our little getaway. Phil asked if there were any other dreams or epiphanies worthy of note. I told him that I knew of several, but a most depressing one that might have interested him was about Marie's Great-Uncle Walley.

"Uncle Walley?" he asked. "What about him?"

"I am of the belief that he murdered his wife, and no one will convince me otherwise!"

"What?!" he gasped. "Has he been arrested?"

"No, Dr. Phil, he has since passed on. This was several years ago."

"How do you know?" Phil asked.

"It's just the feeling that I get that I could always bet on. I am certain that he did. He thought that he got away with it, but I knew the truth from observing him on the day that she died. What he did to kill her, I don't know, even though I couldn't prove it now—that is, unless her body were to be exhumed."

Phil and Andrea almost talked on top of each other. "Please continue, tell us how you knew!"

"Walley was a bit strange, to say the least. He considered himself to be an itinerant preacher, and he would speak at one church for a while before moving on to another. He liked for me to occasionally visit the little hobby shop that he ran as a sideline business, and we would sit down and talk for hours about any subject. He had several enterprises and he liked to trade in the financial markets.

"One day, at a family gathering, he said to me: 'Anthony, did I tell you about the new project that I have been working on?' I bit and asked him what project. He told me that he thought that he was on to the secret of cold fusion."

I smirked, but I continued. "It was all that I could do to keep from laughing out loud. But Walley was a smart man, so I gave him the benefit of the doubt and encouraged him to continue with his explanation of his cold fusion theories. Then he said that there was a mixture of three chemicals that he used, along with a nickel-based conductor. He said that he had found the right mixture to produce and conduct an electrical current. Exactly how was a major mystery, so now I'm thinking: *either this guy has found the answer to all the world's energy problems or he is nuts. Or else he's up to something.* The most notable aspect of his experimentation was that he was telling everyone about it, from relatives to the postman to his preacher."

I shook my head with a sigh, but I continued with my tale. "As far as I know, he never was one to create a ruse to swindle an investor, so I went along with him; but I never inquired about how the invention he had come up with was supposed to create energy again. However, Walley kept talking about the invention for months and even years.

I had that *feeling* again, and I became suspicious, but said nothing. While all of this was going on, Walley's wife—poor aunt Debra, who was Marie's great-aunt—was afflicted with a progressive heart ailment and was continually going downhill. Her life was becoming a cycle of continual doctor visits for her heart problems, and she wasn't all that old either. Walley was a wealthy man by this stage of life, but he was so frugal that he lived in a run-down house and drove an old piece of junk for a car. He worshipped money and searched out ways to get more. Every time I visited him, he was studying his Bible. He had begun to preach at several churches, but I had this overwhelming sense that he was up to no good."

I couldn't help but smile to myself while reminiscing. "For a year or two—maybe longer—this pattern continued, until one day the phone rang and the news came that Aunt Debra had passed away from a heart attack. They lived just down the street from Marie's other aunt, so the call came for the family to gather at that particular aunt's nearby home. As I slowly drove by Walley's house, I noticed a very unusual sight, and I pointed it out to Marie. Marie asked me what was so unusual. I said that there was a man raking leaves in Uncle Walley's yard.

"She asked what was so special about that. In a hundred years, Uncle Walley had never ever hired anyone to rake his leaves. He had leaves in his yard that dated back to 1944. Why, on his wife's day of death, did he have a yardman working? Marie said that I shouldn't concern myself; she told me that it was his yard, so let him rake the leaves if he wanted to. Then, as I turned in to Marie's aunt's drive, I saw Walley leaving his garage with those same cans of chemicals that he had previously shown me for use in his cold fusion experiment. Why on Earth would he be cleaning out his garage and raking leaves when the hearse had just picked up Debra's body only thirty minutes before? Suddenly, I had that familiar feeling, and it struck me like that spark or jolt that I am familiar with. I said nothing to anyone, but I knew. Deep down, I knew.

A sigh left my lips at the tragedy of it all. "A few weeks later, I dropped in at the hobby shop and walked in on uncle Walley. We exchanged pleasantries. I asked him how it was going, and he said that he was fine. He asked about how Marie and I were—you know, the usual. I told him that we were doing well, and that I just stopped in to give him my further condolences and to check on him. I asked him about Debra and what type of emergency she'd had. He explained that it was her heart. He said that she had been going downhill for months and that the doctors couldn't get a handle on the problem. I visited with Walley for a while and, as an afterthought, I asked if he was going to continue with the great invention. He said no, that he just couldn't get it to work, so he gave up and threw away the chemicals.

He thanked me, but as we sat and continued talking, he smiled and said in a wistful tone of voice: 'You know, Anthony, I'm the smartest man in the world!'

I looked at him for a few quiet seconds, then told him: 'No, Walley, you are not. Not by a long shot!'"

I shrugged my shoulders slightly. "He had a look of shock on his face, and I got up and walked out. He knew that I knew! I knew that he had killed her. The chemicals either poisoned her over time or were interfering with her heart's electrical rhythm, causing her to have an arrythmia and a heart attack. All conniving thieves and murderers have a need to brag about what they did. We would never know the truth, but the odds were that my hunch would be found correct."

Phil and Andrea were both speechless for a moment. They still didn't have an educated clue as to how I was able to have a *feeling* about such matters, but I did! Just a strong hunch or a sense—maybe even a sixth sense—and I still have them all the time. I explained again that those feelings were only a gift if they were used beneficially. I left it at that.

Our trip resulted in our mutual agreement to confer on future events as they presented themselves. It was a friendly pact that would last for years to come.

Andrea then asked, "Anthony, can you think of anything else that has stayed with you from childhood and has reoccurred in your thoughts? Anything?" She added, "Maybe something that hasn't happened yet?"

I smiled and said, "Well, I cannot speculate much on future happenings. I only know that, when I get an immediate feeling or that strange sense about something, I feel confident to go with it."

CHAPTER SIX:

Southbound, Finally!

IT WAS A NICE WEEKEND!

Three nights away with friends in Narragansett and the unexpected pleasure of staying in an incredible historical sea captain's home was almost too much to take in. Andrea and Phil were each going to be away on fall seminars and lectures for the remaining two weeks of October. I had plans to either simply enjoy the beach or perhaps pass some quality time by sketching seascapes for future artwork. Otherwise, I would simply be lazy and enjoy my final days at the beach and relax. I had seen all of New York City, including its art museums, parks, bistros, and millions of its people.

I had been taking the usual A-train ride into the city. On this day, I drove Woodhaven into to Queens and parked in public parking to ride the short trip into the 59th Street station. I was going to shop for art supplies, and I needed the car to haul them. I decided that I would not waste my time by walking up and down the beach every afternoon. I could spend the time working on some watercolors of the surrounding Rockaway Beach and the bay area instead.

After work that day, I walked up west 57th Street to a nice art supply dealer near Carnegie Hall. I dropped $200 on brushes, paper, paint, and all the paraphernalia necessary to paint watercolors. I had all the same stuff in my studio at home, but I was doing what I thought was necessary to keep my mind occupied in a constructive manner.

I was feeling a bit down that day—more than usual—as I was really missing my Marie and the family. The weeks were rolling by with my children growing up. My son was playing junior football in his last season. My daughter was taking her first piano lesson, and I wasn't there for that either. Also, I suppose that I noticed the ever-changing angle of the sun. That always was a bit melancholy to me. Throughout my life, I had been affected ever so slightly by seasonal changes.

Getting all of my new art stuff onto the subway and across to Woodhaven Station was going to be a challenge, but it was better than riding the A-train all the way to Rockaway.

I never considered that an *artist* would garner as much attention as I did while lugging that load of paper and supplies. I paint with large format sheets of paper, so one could imagine getting onto the crowded train at rush hour with all of that. I stood at the station and let several trains pass until I saw a little standing room available on an approaching train. I got onto that train and was met with, "Oh, look, an artist! Are you an artist?" It didn't help that I also wore a beard at the time.

I simply smiled and nodded my head. A few years previously, I had pursued the business of art a bit. I traveled to art shows and participated in fundraisers. A few galleries had displayed my paintings, and others requested that I show. After a while, I simply allowed my passion to become an avocation rather than a full-time pursuit. Besides, it was an expensive hobby. One small tube of quality paint could cost fifteen bucks in those days.

After a short trip over the East River, I arrived at my parking lot. I took my car and traversed the fifteen miles to Rockaway. I loved that scenic drive to Broad Channel, which ran through seemingly every slice of New York City culture. Finally, I turned in at Beach 131st, parked, and unloaded. I was anxious to get set up and do some sketching of sea life and subjects that I had seen along the beach and at Breezy Point.

Breezy Point is located at the very entrance to New York Harbor on the Atlantic Ocean, and it was one of my favorite areas in the city. If you fell out of the sky and didn't know where you were, you would never believe that you had landed in New York City.

As I left the apartment to go there, Mrs. Julliard opened her main entrance door and waved at me to come over.

"Hello, Mrs. Julliard! How are you?" I greeted her.

"Oh, I'm fine, Anthony. There was a call for you this afternoon asking that you call your agent in Georgia." Smiling, she handed me a note. "She left this number and wanted you to call first thing in the morning after eight o'clock. If you use my phone, please reverse the charges."

I laughed. "Yes, ma'am, I promise."

I carried on with my plan to drive the seven miles out to Breezy Point and do my sketching and value studies. I wasn't going to let the time go to waste: the call might have been the one that I was waiting for—a call to inform me that the position had opened up in Georgia, and therefore, I would soon be leaving New York. The sketches would last, and they would provide subjects for future paintings. I didn't like to use photography. My art instructor and teacher had always suggested that, by using your value sketches, your eye could see details that are subtle, and your sketches will reveal those nuances—whereas a camera shot leaves absolutely nothing to your imagination.

I only had a couple hours of daylight remaining, so after about thirty minutes, I found this great snow fence with a few seagulls gliding and screaming overhead. I must have been near a nest because they were going crazy—even to the point of diving at me. After several swats at them with the sketchpad, they let me have some peace, and I quickly rendered my first sketch. It was the only sketch that I was able to draw, as the darkness was closing in.

As I was walking back to the car near the water's edge and along the harbor shore, I heard the faint chugging of a ship's engine. I turned around, and a freighter with all of its lights blazing was almost on top of me as it glided quietly by. I was both shocked and thrilled to see it so close, so I reached for the camera and ran up high on the shore to get away from the tremendous wall of water that it was pushing. I was only able to snap a few shots of the superstructure. There was no time to sketch that beauty. A photo would have to do. There were so many lovely facets to Rockaway and the area. I drove past Riis Park and on to my apartment.

I turned on the radio and heated a leftover slice of pizza. Then I took a quick shower, dried off, and climbed into bed. I lay back on the bed just in time to hear Toto's *Africa* playing on my Channel Master. With that and my imagination, I quickly fell asleep for the evening.

At 5 a.m. the next morning, I was awake and cooking breakfast. I ate and took a shower, then walked the beach for a few minutes to watch the sunrise. I was eagerly waiting until 8 a.m. to make that phone call before I went to work. I walked the beach for an hour, looking back at all the beach houses that were facing the sunrise. Thousands of gulls were screaming, and I soaked it all in. I had a certain feeling that this one adventure was about to end.

I had thought about calling Marie and telling her about the call, but I decided against it. I didn't want to disappoint her. I had missed her, and for the better part of the past year, she had not been in my life. Neither had the children. An occasional long weekend and holidays were all the time we'd had together. Our family was separated by time, space, and altitude. It was time to return home, mend fences, and change directions for the midlife that was bearing down upon me.

I returned to the apartment, made coffee, and sat on the deck to wait for 8 a.m. to make the call. I knew, even before I called, that the position had opened and I would be leaving New York. As with everything concerning my feelings about future things, this was no different. I thought about Andrea and our *non-relationship, fantastic relationship*. I had joked with her that the only reason she came around, or was attracted to me, was because she considered me to be her psychological guinea pig. She didn't care for my assessment of the situation, but her denial of it was a bit on the weak side.

It was a quarter after eight when I made the call. And yes, I did reverse the charges for Mrs. Julliard. The agency secretary patched me in to the district supervisor. The conversation was brief. I was offered a two-year position at a nuclear facility at the Savannah River Project as a supervisor. I accepted in short order—with the provision that I needed to check in with the management field director the following Wednesday at 7 a.m.

I agreed, and then she recorded my credentials and registration information, and that was that. I was going home.

I hung up the phone, and Mrs. Julliard walked into the vestibule and said rather sadly, "Oh, are we going to lose you, Tony?"

I smiled and placed my arm around her shoulder for a slight hug. "Yes, ma'am, I'm headed home. There is just something about the South."

"Well, I'm going to miss you, and I know someone else who will also," she said.

"Really? Who do you suppose that is?" I asked.

"That beautiful little Jewish girl, that's who," she said coyly.

I just glanced at her, bit my lower lip slightly, and nodded my head. "Yes, ma'am, but I can't really speak to that—except that my family is waiting."

I grabbed my gear and drove to the subway station at 116th. Then I caught the next A-train into Manhattan.

I got started two hours later than I normal. I was only going to say goodbye to my friends. They had grown to be like my fraternity brothers. We worked, laughed, partied, and enjoyed each other's company as we worked for The Donald. I had my ceremonial Trump Tower topping out mug and extra money in the bank. I was on my way home.

As the train rocked on toward Manhattan, I saw several more Jewish ladies who were Holocaust survivors with their left arm or wrist tattoos. Just seeing those long numbers, each about a quarter of an inch in height, I could not begin to imagine their experiences. It had been forty years since Germany surrendered, so the ladies I saw would have been in their teens, twenties, and thirties at the time of the war.

Also, I got to see Elsie. She was a young lady that always wore nine dresses at the same time. I never knew if she was homeless. She was always clean, always smiled pleasantly. I could count all the different skirt hems, and there were always nine every time I counted them, and I counted them every time that I saw her. One day, she had smiled and told me her name. Then I had told her mine, and we were friends from then on. She always smiled.

That day, I told her that I was leaving. She was standing, holding onto the center pole. She held on with one arm and twirled around the pole like a child at play. I told her to stay safe and to stay pretty.

She smiled. "May God bless you and keep you, Southern Boy."

I smiled back, because I knew that she was in good hands. As far as the Southern Boy nickname, I suppose that she had given it to me because of my Southern accent.

Finally, we reached 53rd and I left the train. Robert was my favorite panhandler. He was just inside the exit to the station, and I would give cash occasionally. One day, when no one was around, I asked him how well he did panhandling.

He said, "I do about twenty-five thousand a year, and with my benefits, I can do—well, about fifty thousand!"

I just laughed and told him that I was going home. He said to tell the family that he said hello to them.

I got to the Tower and flashed my badge to the guard as I walked in late. That particular construction guard had saved Mr. Trump from a harassing situation at a restaurant, and Donald hired him on the spot to guard the construction entrance to the Tower for fifty thousand a year.

I rode the elevator to the 40th floor contractor's office and turned in my badge. I said my goodbyes and rode to the top where Donald was constructing his condo. I photographed Central Park and all the nearby views from his unit, then rode the elevator to the ground. Except for my son's going-away wedding trip, I would never go back to Manhattan. I knew that this part of my life was over, and a new phase would soon begin.

I decided to grab a taxi for the ride out to Rockaway. I hailed the first cab I saw and asked him, "How much to Rockaway?"

"I live out there; climb in," the taxi driver said.

"How much?" I asked.

He asked where I was going, and I told him. He said ten bucks, since he was going that way anyway. I laughed and thanked him. He said that he had seen me at *The Wharf* a couple of times, and I replied enthusiastically, "It's possible. Great food and always somebody to talk to."

He knew I had worked at the Tower, and he was going home to Rockaway anyway, so he accommodated me. I sat back and watched the skyline fade over my shoulder as we left for the island, and then the multitude of neighborhoods passed by. I was very familiar with the city after the short time that I had been there. I was almost thirty-nine, and it was also as though life were passing me by. Where did I fit in? Was this it? Was I jumping from one thing to the next, like stitching a patchwork quilt together? Although no one could argue that my quilt would certainly be colorful.

I had heard that those questions would become more relevant at my age, but I had never really given it much thought. Now I was beginning to understand. If you have no plan for your life, then you usually have no life. I was very sad, almost to the point of depression. I couldn't believe that I still had no defined purpose in life. I seemed to be drifting, but then I had that certain feeling about things that I had become accustomed to. My life and its true purpose still lay ahead of me. God gives every life a purpose unto Himself. I had always believed that. He created us for Himself. What, then, was *my* purpose?

I was at midlife! I was thinking that He had better get started or I was going to be off the map! Little did I know what the future had in store, especially for me. The process would take years to manifest itself, but little by little, I was given tidbits of an astounding puzzle and its answers as the years meandered by. There were clues to my purpose, strung together with an outcome that I could never have imagined. These were some of the subjects that I had never discussed with Andrea, and I certainly didn't know Phil well enough to share. The timing of my departure would be unfortunate, as Andrea was to be away for another week. I would be gone by the time she returned, and I couldn't wait for her. It was bad timing, but everything has a reason.

I didn't know where her seminar was being held, nor did I have a contact number for her. I intended to call her office and leave a message before I left. Also, I was going to pen a letter and hand it to her maid if I could get her to the door. Those were my only options. I had to break camp and move on. I knew, from the time that I was nine years old, that God had a plan for me. He has a plan for everyone, but I imagine that a person must ask Him the plan and then develop it. I just never knew what it was at the outset. No matter how much I asked for direction, I kept having to change.

Had God forgotten me? Was this wandering through New York City supposed to be my wilderness? Was it some sort of test? Was it He Who separated me from Andrea that night? Was it a moment of rage, or a moment of protection? If I had committed to a relationship with Andrea, would God's plan for my life have simply fallen by the wayside? I could not allow myself to see and say goodbye to Andrea. That was all there was to it. I couldn't deny my feelings and the attraction between us. They were there hidden behind every thought. I had to pack and just leave as soon as possible.

What a coward I had become. If I left without seeing her, then I would most certainly be a coward. Still, I had an excuse. I had to be at the new project by Wednesday, and Andrea was another week from returning to the beach. Somehow it would work out—or, at least, I hoped that it would; otherwise I knew that it wouldn't be fair to her. A part of me thought that a few long-distance phone calls would do it, but deep down inside, I knew that it wouldn't be enough.

I could call her, and I wouldn't have to make eye contact. I wouldn't have to see her face or let her see mine, and then I wouldn't have to remember whether she cried or not. Then I thought to myself that all of this conjecture was stupid! I was telling myself right then to not be naive. I was ten years older than her, and I was married with children who were almost half her age.

My cab turned into 131st, and I gave him directions to the end house. I asked again about the fare, and he said ten bucks—a deal is a deal. I laughed and gave him a twenty. I ended our time together by telling him that maybe I would see him later at *The Wharf*, and he told me politely that it might be a sure thing and that I should have a safe trip. After that, he drove away.

I had no intentions of going to *The Wharf* that night. I had no business there, since I had only met a few people during the time that I had lived there. I would borrow a table from Mrs. Juilliard and attempt a watercolor for Andrea as a going-away remembrance gift. I also had that goodbye letter to write to Andrea, and I still had to take it to her maid.

I had been an artist since my sister had given me a nice set of watercolors at the age of five. It was also about the same time that the plane had crashed behind our house. I was left alone and, with the help of my dad's trusty World Book Encyclopedias, I painted a frameable

watercolor of an island in Spain. My family was shocked, and so was
I at their reaction. However, they weren't shocked enough to see that
I needed to be sent to art school. Anyway, I learned eventually from
the masters. I learned how to stretch wet paper, use a natural sponge,
and correctly apply paint. While doing all of that, I still built power
plants and skyscrapers. Art occupies my mind and takes me away to
where I want to be.

It was only Thursday, and I would be leaving the following Monday
for the trip home, so I had plenty of time to get two or three attempts in
and create a nice finished painting for Andrea's gift. Rarely did I ever
succeed at the first attempt. Mistakes are not allowed in watercolors.
I grabbed the sketchbook and drew the snow fence that I had found
and sketched on Breezy Point. Then I filled the tray and wet the paper.
When it was just moist enough, I stretched the paper and clamped
it to the table.

I filled the large sable flat brush and squeezed out the excess
moisture, then painted the sky with three broad strokes. With only those
three daring strokes, I had the sky finished. I filled the foreground,
detailed the snow fence, and later—when it dried—I cut in the weeds
and seagulls with a bit of color pigment and a broken razor blade.

It was fun, but nerve-racking. One mistake and it would go into the
trashcan. It lay stretched until it dried, and then I signed it as *Tony
the Artist*. It would give her a bit of insight into a part of my life that
I had sheltered her from. It was only a token of my affection to paint
her a seascape, but she would know that it represented the best part
of my talent—my skills as an artist—and my appreciation of beauty

and nature. It was all the things that she loved, and it was the best that I could give her. It was from Tony the Artist.

It was late in the afternoon, and I left to get a bite to eat. I saw Mrs. Julliard again as I left, and she asked if I was still planning to go home. I told her yes, but that I may return sometime for a visit or two. She told me that she had a free apartment upstairs that I could use, and she invited me to bring the family up and spend a week on the beach.

I thanked her and told her how amazing that was. "Wow! Thanks, Mrs. Julliard. I love you! You do know that, don't you?"

She pretended to get the broom after me as we laughed. She was serious, but I knew that I would probably never return. This was my time away and my special place at the beach, and I didn't want to share it. It was my own private part of my life.

I went for Chinese takeout that night. There was a huge Chinese kitchen takeout near the station with the best Chinese food that I have ever tasted. I returned to the deck, sat in the lounge chair, and enjoyed my meal as the sun went down. I began to relax for a change. It had been a long day, and the painting effort had taxed my nerves a bit. I walked the beach again. I was truly going to miss this aspect of my adventure. I was thirty-eight and my birthday was coming up in November. The big thirty-nine! At least I would celebrate it at home with the family.

I showered and turned on the radio, and as usual, Toto was singing *Africa* again. I didn't mind because it is a great song. Later, the group Alabama was in the mix, along with Springsteen. Their songs were all truly loved by the New Yorkers whom I knew. It was time to write that letter. I sat at the table for a half an hour before I finally began to write. I wrote for an hour or more, then tore it up and rewrote it. I signed it and placed it in an envelope. To say that I poured out my heart would be an understatement.

I was making some rather large assumptions by expressing my true feelings. They were very personal, and I hoped that she would understand. I certainly didn't want to jump to any conclusions about mutual feelings. I suppose that was precisely what I was doing. I was drawn to her like a magnet. There was no denying it. I didn't want to fight it, but I simply had to, and I had to succeed.

With that task completed, I lay back on the bed and drifted to sleep. I didn't have to get up the next morning. It was my last weekend in New York. My adventure was almost over, and I thought about the dull existence that stretched ahead of me.

The next morning, in addition to packing, I had only one task scheduled: to deliver that envelope to Andrea's maid or her mailbox. I picked up the envelope and started to get dressed. Then I stopped and ripped open the envelope, sat back, and re-read the letter. Then I read it a third time. I decided that I was committed to what I had written, and I sealed it again. I threw on some sweats and rain gear and decided to jog the ten blocks up the beach. Some days, the beach was more active in stormy weather than on sunny days; but this morning, I was the only human in sight.

It was overcast and misting rain. The first cold spell of fall had arrived. The Atlantic was an angry black, and the sea foam was blowing across that beach. I took my time, and within forty-five minutes, I was walking up to Andrea's beach house. I knocked on the door and rang the bell for a short time. There were no lights visible and no activity inside, so I placed the envelope in the mailbox, hoping that the rain wouldn't damage it or that it wouldn't get thrown out with the junk mail. I didn't want to stir up too much attention, as the neighborhood was closely watched and guarded.

I began the walk back up the beach. My sweats were soaked from the surf, and after a while, I stopped trying to avoid the waves and surf run-outs. It was cold, but it felt great. As I looked up the beach and saw that familiar shoreline curvature disappear towards Jones Beach, my mind traveled back twenty-five years to my Scouting days, when I had walked that same beach and played in the surf during the summer of '57. It had been a strange loop of life that had returned me to that place. In my world, everything happens for a reason, and this was no different.

I had taken my camera with me, and I captured a few nice seagulls against that black-clouded horizon. The surf was really beginning to kick up. I had a feeling that a Nor'easter was about to hit. I hadn't heard of any storm reports, but there was definitely one just off Long island and heading my way. The weather reports were accurate back then, but the information was not as readily available. Winds were ten knots when I walked down to Andrea's, but they were at least fifteen knots when I walked back. Now they were picking up even more. We were definitely in for a blow. I neared the apartment, and sand was stinging my face as I reached the door.

I helped Mrs. Julliard store the beach chairs, hugged her goodbye, and went into the apartment. I supposed that was it. By then, it was 6 p.m., and I was packed with the car loaded and ready to go. I decided to take a shower and sleep until 2 or 3 a.m. on Saturday. Then I would hit the expressway across the Verrazano Narrows Bridge and head home with no traffic to speak of. Within sixteen to eighteen hours of driving, I would be there.

As I finished the shower, we lost power. That was very unusual on the island, but we lost it nonetheless. I climbed into bed, still damp, and went to sleep with the wind howling outside. Because of the storm, I wouldn't be traveling as planned.

Great. No power, little food, and a Nor'easter blowing for another day or two. I had not called Marie because I had planned to surprise her. I had not even told her about the job. So there I sat for another twenty-four hours until the storm subsided, and then I learned that the roads to the south over in Jersey were impassable because of downed power lines. I did have a transistor radio, and that was about it.

On Saturday morning, after the storm, I walked to 116st and found a bodega open, where I bought some groceries and ice. I borrowed a small cart from them—with the promise that I would return it as soon as possible. I bought Mrs. Julliard a few things also and walked back, pushing the cart full of groceries. The power company said that it would be ten to twelve hours before I could drive out. I returned and unloaded the groceries. Mrs. Julliard thanked me profusely, then told me that she didn't like that brand of coffee.

"That was the very reason that I bought that particular brand for you," I joked. She chuckled.

I decided to wait another day to start out. Again, everything happened for a reason.

The storm was over for the most part, but it was high tide and the waves were still rolling in toward the seawall close to the house. At least it wasn't snow. It was getting late, and the roads were still blocked with debris. Beach 131st was no different; even though the freeways had been cleared, I still couldn't get out, so I just stripped down again and went back to bed. At 8 p.m., the wind was still howling, but I was quickly sound asleep.

By 11 p.m., the wind picked up even more. There was a tapping at my door, and it frightened me at first. Mrs. Julliard always knocked on the wall as she was coming down the stairs, but never at the door. I could hear her still rambling around upstairs in her own kitchen. Everybody else I knew was out of town for the week.

I wrapped a towel around me and was looking for something to wield as protection when I heard Andrea's voice. "Tony, it's Andrea. Please let me in."

"Andrea?" I asked, surprised. She was supposed to be away for another week.

I immediately let her in, and she fell all over me. With tears in her eyes, she threw her arms around me and started kissing me. I was taken aback and actually fell over the bed backwards with her on top of me.

Then she got herself under control somewhat and apologized. She was crying profusely and asked me to tell her all about where I was going. Before I told her, I asked her how she knew that I was leaving, and she said that her neighbor saw someone place an envelope in her mailbox and described me as that person. Then she asked her neighbor to open it and read the letter.

"Wow. Your neighbor reads the letter and you drive five hours to come back? You left your seminar and resort in Vermont just to come back and say goodbye?" I asked, somewhat surprised.

"I don't want you to leave! I want you to find a way to stay."

I threw on my sweats and sat beside her. "I have a job that starts on Wednesday in Georgia."

The tears kept pouring. "I really didn't ever pick up on the possibility that you had serious feelings for me," she said. "But I do—I do have feelings for you. I didn't really know until I read that you were leaving, and then it hit me that I might never see you again. Have you left your job?"

"Yes, yesterday. It was a great experience and even an adventure, but I had to accept the new position. I must go home."

We sat on the side of the bed, and she continued to tear up.

"Did you read the letter?" I asked her.

"Not yet. What did you tell me in it?" she asked me carefully.

"I told you that I love you, pure and simple. It took me five pages to tell you all the ways that I love you and still, I can't have you. I cannot love you. Too many precious lives would be forever changed and even possibly destroyed. You are my Bathsheba!" I explained, exasperated.

She said facetiously, "Who is that?"

"I'm certain that you know the implications of the story. It applies to us, except that you don't have a husband whom I would have to send into battle to be killed." Then I added, "Do you remember the night when we touched hands for the first time, fingertips to fingertips? Then we gently kissed; do you remember the joy of the moment?"

"Yes, vividly, I remember the shock to my system when we kissed. In all my life, I had never had that feeling that you gave me!"

"Neither had I, not ever. Then suddenly we were separated violently by a definite but indescribable force that threw me away from you, and we were both horrified by it! Remember, that night, I had claimed that I stepped backwards into a hole. Then you said, 'Oh, hell no, you didn't!' Do you remember that, Andrea?"

"I remember it vividly," she said, tearfully.

"Andrea, I walked the distance off later that night. I was propelled away from you fifty feet backwards across the sand."

"How do you know that?" she asked.

"I knew where we were standing, and I finally fell backwards by the lifeguard equipment locker. It was nothing except a simple kiss!" I said, exasperated.

"Yes, but that was definitely a kiss!" she said, smiling.

"Andrea, I'm going to be serious and consider whatever was intended to be. I must respect whatever was meant to be. It's enough to say that it frightened me deeply. It told me that I cannot leave my wife and my family. It told me that I must return home."

Andrea had been leaning against me on the side of the bed all that time. I leaned back against the headboard and pulled the cover up over us both as she slept on my shoulder with her arm around me. I held her with both arms like forever, then we fell asleep.

Outside, the storm continued to rage.

CHAPTER SEVEN:

One Last Night On Liberty Street

IT WAS DAYBREAK ON SATURDAY MORNING. DEPARTURE DAY!

I gently kissed Andrea awake. I could tell that her eyes were slightly swollen from the tears, and there were a few leftover tears dried on her cheeks. I wiped them away with a damp cloth as she woke up. She seemed accepting of the fact that I was leaving sometime that day. But she definitely wasn't accepting of the fact that we might never see each other again.

That storms were gone for now, and the October morning was incredible, but there were many much larger storms looming on the horizon. The Atlantic was glassy smooth and so reflective that the sky was almost indistinguishable from the water at the horizon line.

Andrea went into the bathroom, and I heard her taking a shower. She came out in my bathrobe, drying and wrapping her long brown hair with a towel. I couldn't help but just sit and admire. It would never do to let her know that I was fending off strong second thoughts about leaving. It was still early daylight as she dressed, and she walked over to pick up her purse on the table. Then she stopped.

"What is this?" she asked.

"What?" I answered. "The art?"

"Yes, the art!"

"What about it?"

"You did that?" she breathed in a tone of pure awe.

"I suppose I did. I must have been in an altered state, don't you suppose?" I said, smiling slightly.

"You didn't tell me that you were an artist!"

"I think I recall having mentioned it to you on one occasion. It was a while back and only in casual conversation. Other than that, I saw no reason to mention it. It is really no big deal. I never mention the fact." I shrugged slightly.

"Tony, that is a great watercolor," she said, still looking at it.

"Thank you. There was a time in my past when I thought that I would pursue a career in art. I was taught by a master, who was internationally known and one of the best in the world. Anyway, thanks! I want you to have it. I painted it for you. It's a Breezy Point winter scene. It's something for you to remember me by. You can hang it in your closet." I gestured to it.

"It's mine? No closet for this!" she declared, lifting it up to look at it.

"Sure. It was meant to be a surprise. I was going to mail it or buy a mailing tube for it and hand-deliver it today, but anyway, it's yours."

She was biting her lip and holding back the tears again. "Must you leave today? Can you wait one more day?" she asked me, hopefully.

"Well, I need to get started for home, and soon. Any particular reason why?" I asked.

"My brother is having a casual late dinner party this evening on the rooftop of his apartment in Manhattan—you know, the one I told you that I shared with him and Sam in Lower Manhattan? It's on Liberty Street. You're invited, and I didn't have any idea that you were about to leave. Besides, if I had not come home, what then?" she said, smiling.

"Andrea, I had to get back to Georgia for my new job. You were supposed to be away until midweek. Please forgive me. I wasn't thinking, in all fairness. I will stay one more night and go to the party, if you like. I suppose that I could leave from there afterward. I would enjoy seeing both of them again, and also the apartment," I said, talking myself into it.

"Even better, you could use the spare loft tonight and leave from there tomorrow," she suggested.

"Well that's an idea! Sure, why not. It would be into Lower Manhattan, then over to Jersey on a Sunday morning with no traffic, and it would make a good escape route. Do they have off-street parking?"

"Yes, we have four guarded spaces that we pay a yearly fortune for," she said. "And we do have a spare."

"I suppose that I could drive in late today if I can use the parking," I agreed.

"Great, I'll get your tag number and they will allow you entrance. Can you be there by six?" she asked, seemingly pleased.

"Sure, I'll try. I may need more time."

"You never mentioned to me that you were going home!" she said, cornering me with that.

"I was going to let you know. I've been waiting for a call ever since they informed me of the possibility of a position. Well, I found out about the position on Wednesday and accepted it. Besides, you were away. I had no way to let you know, except by letter or your office phone or your maid. Anyway, I'm glad that I wrote the letter for you, and I'm also glad for nosy neighbors, I suppose!" I chuckled.

Andrea wrote the Manhattan address on two separate business cards—one for my shaving kit and the other for my wallet. She kissed me and walked out. Then she turned and came back, picked up the watercolor, kissed me again, started tearing up, and finally walked out crying.

"Andrea, remember the tag number," I reminded her. "And please don't cry. See you at six!"

"Got it!" she said, sniffing.

Leaving Andrea was going to be heart-wrenching, for us both.

Later that morning, I let Mrs. Julliard know that I would be leaving later in the day rather than that morning. She told me that the cleaning lady wasn't scheduled until Monday anyway. I had about five hours left to enjoy the beach before I would leave for Manhattan. I would walk the beach for what I thought, at the moment, would be one last time.

I asked Mrs. Julliard if we could have lunch together on the covered deck before I left, and she thought that was a great idea. This time, my last beach walk would be to the jetties. They were at the divide between the Riis Park beach and the municipal beach at Neponset to Belle Harbor. It was one month before my thirty-ninth birthday.

I was having a difficult time with that fact. As I walked, again I could remember the Valley Forge trip for the National Jamboree, with the Boy Scouts staying at the old barracks at Old Fort Tilden. We had a dozen or more guys who walked down the beach and swam in the cold Atlantic for the first time ever. That place was only a hundred yards or so up the beach. I remember that I had fallen and badly skinned my knee. The Scout masters, Lee Foy and Bo Moss, had been fun leaders at that time, but they were short on the Boy Scout Handbook Regulations. We had absolutely zero first aid kits and had absolutely nothing to dress the wound. Talk about being prepared!

I had thought at the time, *Be prepared for what? To die?*

Anyway, Mr. Bo told me to hit those waves and wash that wound in the saltwater. It stung badly at first, but later it felt much better.

Like always, I recalled everything—even conversations with my first-grade teacher. I continued to walk up the beach along the surf's edge as midmorning approached. The sea remained glassy calm as I reached the jetties. I climbed onto the shore end of the rocks and sat there, looking back north toward Jones Beach. I remembered the commissioned oil painting that I had painted for the lady ten years earlier. As I sat there, I felt that I was looking at that painting again. I always wondered where the painting was. I sold it to a lady in Birmingham and questioned myself as to whether it was still on a wall somewhere or in a yard sale.

I am almost thirty-nine. What would the next thirty-nine years bring? It was not a subject on which I dwelled excessively, but I had a tendency to self-audit on occasion. When I did look in the mirror, I always felt that I could accomplish much more with my talents. Even though I had been well-educated and had accomplished much, even my friend Mike O'Donnell had asked me why I didn't reach for higher goals and accomplishments. "Underutilized" was his description of me, when he sized me up.

I laughed at the thought. After a very short hour of beating myself up, I climbed down off of the jetties and started that last walk on my old summer playground. Almost an hour later, and as I approached the apartment, I noticed a group of people on the deck. To my pleasant surprise, Mrs. Julliard had assembled a small group of my acquaintances and friends for a little going home meal. What a pleasant surprise!

Mrs. Juilliard was standing there with Flora and her friend, the transit cop, and also Dr. Christopher. They were all there to tell me goodbye and to wish me Godspeed and a great life. They all realized that I would never be back. We ate and visited for an hour or so, and I showed my appreciation and then said goodbye. I shook hands with Dr. Christopher, then looked over at Mrs. Juilliard and reminded her that God always places special people in our lives at the right time and for a purpose. I hoped that she understood that Dr. Christopher had been there to save her life for a reason.

I hugged necks, waved farewell, then drove toward Breezy Point past Riis Park one last time. I turned passed the Verrazano-Narrows Bridge, through the Carey Tunnel, and in toward lower Manhattan. An hour later, I was at Eric's parking garage. I hoped that Andrea had made the arrangements for me to park.

Eric's apartment was at 2236 Liberty Street, Apartment 2223 on the 22nd floor. It was located on the south side. The street ran across lower Manhattan a short block from the South Tower, so it was simple to locate. His parking garage entered on Trinity about a block away, so I left early to find the garage. As it turned out, the garage was just up the street from the apartment. Before I parked, I decided to kill a little time with my camera down around Battery Park. I wandered the neighborhood, sightseeing for a while so as not to be too early before going up. I tried to capture old storefronts and any local people who didn't look like tourists.

Battery Park was beautiful, with the hardwoods beginning to change to fall colors and the lowering sun gleaming off of Lady Liberty. Some New Yorkers never give their special uniqueness within this the world a second thought. They are truly blessed. I started my walk back towards Eric's apartment building with my backpack and camera in hand, snapping up rolls of Kodachrome. I reached the building, then entered and met with the doorman.

"Mr. Marchant?" he asked me.

"How did you know, sir? You could tell by my cheap jeans, right?" I joked.

"No sir, but I can tell a Southerner when I see one!" he quipped back.

"Is it that obvious? Around here, I suppose that may be a bad thing. Am I correct?" I asked with a chuckle.

"No, sir, not at all. I happen to be from next door over in Alabama."

"Well, I'm more than pleased to meet a fellow Southerner! Your name, sir?"

"It's Samuel, sir. Mr. Eric explained that you would be attending, sir."

"Well, Samuel, I'm happy to meet you also! Then it's going to be a great night?" I asked.

"You can count on that, sir!" he said, winking.

It was a funny exchange. I couldn't stop smiling.

"Mr. Eric really knows how to party," he said with a sly smile.

"Thanks for the heads-up, Samuel," I said, cheerfully.

He buzzed me up onto the elevator and onto Eric's floor lobby. I had never met either Eric or Andrea's sister, Sam. However, they both met me at the door. I was the Georgia Boy. I supposed that I was to be the curiosity *du jour*!

I was then welcomed into a fabulous open concept of a contemporary three-story apartment with white spiral jailhouse stairs leading to a balcony loft. There were three vertical stories of glass that faced northwest across the corner of the apartment, which framed the full view of the South Tower of the World Trade Center. It had incredible architecture and a stunning entrance view as I entered. Eric offered to store my gear, and Sam hugged my neck—twice! Then she kissed me on the cheek! It was a nice intro, for sure! They were a very attractive couple of young New Yorkers. I remembered seeing their parents in a photo back at the beach house.

Andrea had great-looking parents, and it was revealed in their children.

"Anthony! Tony! Come on up!" Andrea called.

I laughed along with Sam and Eric. I quickly introduced myself, then swiftly climbed the stairs at Andrea's beckoning. She was waiting on me. From the top interior balcony, she showed me the apartment, then showed me *our room*—as she described it. It was truly just a third-floor balcony with an open mezzanine, with its own bed, an open bath concept, and a hot tub located next to the balcony rail. It was open to the three floors down to the main floor below. The three-story trapezoid-shaped window was designed to frame the South Tower, and the architect had done a fabulous job.

When I reached the balcony, Andrea threw her arms around my neck and hugged me for a long time. She then placed her forehead against mine, looking down and saying nothing for a long time. Finally, she hugged me again, kissed me long on the lips, and thanked me for coming. She didn't say much, as I could tell that she was deeply upset.

"Here are some party clothes for tonight," she said. "Would you mind wearing them?"

"Party clothes?" I asked, curiously.

"Yes, Eric has a dress-up party a couple times a year, and a crowd is coming at nine," she explained.

"Okay, not that I'm anti-social or anything, but I'm not a big party person," I said, nervously.

"You will do fine. Will you, please?" she begged me.

"Are these the clothes?" I asked, looking at them. "I suppose I will, as long as they are not something weird. Something like women's clothes and clown outfits would be out. I may feel a bit like I may be the resident clown before the evening is over," I said, but I wasn't really joking.

"No, you won't be a clown to anyone. These are 1930s-era with slacks, a big tie, and a sport coat—complete with tan and white wingtip shoes with spats."

I got to wear spats. I smirked. "Geez! What's happening tonight? Are we going out dressed like this?" I asked.

"No, we are staying in. That's because Eric has hired a small-group Big Band for our rooftop garden party entertainment. It will start out there and probably spill over in here as more people pile in or it gets late or early or whatever. He wants everybody dressed for the occasion. Would you mind?"

"Not to worry, I'm in," I reassured her.

"All of our friends and guests will be dressed in similar attire. It will be fun," she said.

"Is that a rooftop garden?" I asked, glancing that way.

"Yes, there is a garden out there on the main level beyond the glass wall with a covered area where he sets up the bands. It's a neat area for dancing. There are round tables and chairs, and there is an outdoor service and bar."

"Well that's nice. Just like home," I said.

"I knew that you would appreciate the architecture. Let me borrow your hand," she said as she pulled me up the stairs to show me the vista.

"Amazing!" I said, looking around. "I am impressed. We are above the adjacent buildings, and the window perfectly frames the lighted South Tower."

"Yes, that is the way Eric envisioned it when he bought the top three floors. He had three stories of the corner chopped off at an angle to set that window facing the Towers. If you lay in the bed, from this angle, you can see the upper eighty floors reflecting both the sunrise and the sunset. Totally amazing," she said with a wistful smile.

"Andrea!" came a voice from downstairs. "The guests are arriving!"

"Got to run. Come down anytime," she said, heading down the steps.

I took a long shower and dressed in the clothes that she provided. One look in the mirror and I realized that I didn't look half-bad. I realized where I may have truly belonged: in the 1930s, of course! As I started downstairs, I heard a saxophone running some scales and warming up. The band had arrived.

Goodness! How many people could be crammed into this place? The word and conversation of the day among this group was penny stocks! Everybody had their pick, and everybody had the daily newspaper folded in their pockets with the penny stocks listed. As usual, the only people making any money was the broker catching them going and coming, and also the little penny stock news publishers.

Eric's front entrance was beginning to look like a subway unloading. More caterers were arriving, and the drummer was lugging case after case of drums and cymbals for his trap set. Andrea was tending bar until the barkeep arrived, so I walked over as she was holding court with several friends. They were all the professor types whom one would assume a clinical psychologist would hang with. She saw me and tilted her head with a wink.

"How many were invited, Andrea?" I asked her.

"Small party tonight, so around a hundred!" she replied.

"Good grief!" I said with a sigh. I smiled just as a trumpet player lined up for a drink, holding his trumpet with a handkerchief. I couldn't help myself when I saw it, and I said that it was a large Bore Martin Committee Trumpet! Man, wow! I couldn't believe it.

The trumpet player heard me and said, "Hey! Yeah, man! That's exactly what it is. You really know your stuff!"

I laughed, and everybody looked at the horn. The others around were murmuring about it being a special instrument.

"Yup," I said. "It's a Harry James. A real deal."

Then someone asked if it was Harry's horn.

"No. It isn't. It is just the type that he played. He and about four other players got together as a committee and designed what was then—and still may be—the perfect trumpet. They named it the Committee Trumpet!" I replied.

The trumpeter asked if I played, and I told him that it had been awhile. Andrea looked at me and turned her head at an angle in surprise and asked, "What else?"

"Well, a long awhile back, I also worked on the Manhattan Project!" I joked.

She rolled her eyes, and I laughed. The trumpeter told me that I could sit in later and play if I liked.

"Maybe I will if you have a spare mouthpiece," I said with a smile.

"Got it," he said. "Come on back later."

As the evening wore on, the band played dozens of oldies from the thirties and forties. The guys were really good players. I found out that most of them were students at Juilliard. There were a few older pro players from the clubs in SoHo. I danced with Andrea as the evening wore on, and Samantha came by and pinched me on the butt.

"The next dance is mine!" she said.

So, for the next dance, Sam came over and pulled me out on the rooftop garden. I danced *Moonglow* with her. Halfway through the dance, she leaned in and kissed me and said, "You know that Andrea is head over heels in love with you."

"What else can be said? I can't say that I don't love her, and I can't stay up here any longer. Down South, they would call that a major conundrum—pure and simple! I must get back. There are too many lives that would be changed forever by my staying here, and all of them would be affected in a negative way. Besides, Andrea knows that, and in spite of it all, she knows how I feel about her. This is a life that I could never continue to live. It's as simple as that. Nobody intends for those things to happen, yet we can get swept away before we realize it," I said, keeping my voice low.

Just then, the trumpet player interrupted and tapped me on the shoulder, then handed me a spare trumpet mouthpiece along with his horn.

"I'm taking a break. Sit in for a while and enjoy," he said with a small wave.

That was perfect timing, as if on cue, to get me out of the conversation. The horn was sweet! Big bore and mellow. What a great sound. I played *A Train*, a bit of *Stardust*, and Miles' version of *Summertime*. What a sweet-sounding horn. I had fun for too short a time until the lip played out and I saw Andrea motioning at me.

"I'm going up for some privacy. It's our last evening," she said, smiling.

It was almost 2 a.m. when I climbed the stairs to the loft. She closed the door and immediately kissed me.

"You do play great trumpet," she said.

"Thanks! I've had practice!" I said with a grin.

"I want to know, when are you going to play *me*!" she said pointedly.

I smiled as I told her, "Andrea, our lives are simply too much out of tune."

She bit my lip and she said, "I like blood!"

"How, well I know!" I gasped. Ouch! The blood poured out! *I can never play trumpet again,* I thought as she got a wet cloth. She didn't apologize. Did I need a stitch?

I smirked. "Our first argument and you try to bleed me to death!"

As the noise and music died down, we lay back on top of the covers and looked out at the massive lighted Tower as it pierced into the low clouds and the fog over Manhattan. The guests were departing, and Eric had turned on his sound system. I placed my hands behind my head and lay back on the pillows, looking out the window as Andrea lay beside me and held me for the remainder of the early morning hours.

We said nothing, and we didn't sleep—at least, not at first. No talk of love, affection, or the future. No talk of our good times past. There was nothing left that we could add. We just held each other. I simply must go home! I knew that it might be the last time that I ever saw her, and she knew the same, so we dispensed with the emotions as best we could and simply watched the pink of the morning light cast against the tower.

In a while, there was a knock at the door. It was Sam.

"Hi guys, I just wanted to let you know that it's noon—if it matters."

"Thanks, Sam!" I whispered.

Andrea lay there in a deep sleep while I tiptoed around and slipped into the bathroom for a quick shower. It was late, and I had to get started. I quietly dressed and grabbed my gear, then leaned over Andrea and kissed her awake.

"Goodbye. I've got to go," I said to her. She said nothing, but quietly teared up again as I pulled away and walked out. Eric and Sam were out in the roof garden, and I stuck my head out and said goodbye and thanked them for their hospitality.

"Be in touch, please?" Sam said. I nodded as I hugged her and shook Eric's hand, and then I made my way up the street to the garage and let the attendant pull the P-1800. As I started to get in, I saw Sam and Eric walking hurriedly toward me.

"Tony! Can we have one more word?" Sam said.

"Sure. What is it?" I asked, pausing for a moment.

Sam asked if I would reconsider leaving. She knew of Andrea's feelings for me, and she was simply championing for her little sister. I told them both that, at any other time of my life, I might have considered staying; but there was something much greater—even than my responsibility to my wife and family—that was drawing me to return home. I had an internal force guiding me—one that I could never describe or explain. I only knew for certain that my remaining future was not to be in New York City.

Eric and Sam were both aware of those guiding feelings that I get, and I seem to be required to respond to them—otherwise everything with me goes haywire, and I become anxious and unsettled. Sam knew how I felt about Andrea, but she also understood that my life was not meant to be lived in New York, away from my wife and family. I chose not to leave the wife and family. I hugged and kissed Sam goodbye again and shook Eric's hand.

As I left, I told Sam that she had to understand that I felt God had future plans for me that I had never even dreamed of, and I felt that they were important—not only to me and the family, but to others as well. I had to find out what they were. Just then, the attendant started the Volvo and drove it down the ramp, and he left it running. As he got out, he also asked to buy it if I were to ever consider selling it. I smiled and tipped him, and then I revved the little red bullet, waved goodbye, and started towards home. I was as sad as they were, but I could never let on that something was wrong. I had to go!

It was Sunday in New York, and the streets were empty as I turned south. It was fun navigating and echoing the twin exhaust through the metro canyons as I left. Never in my wildest dreams had I ever envisioned living in this place—even for a brief time. But now, it was over. It was a new start: a fresh start, a reboot, or whatever. It was time to get back to the reality of caring for my family down South.

It would be a long sixteen to eighteen hours home, but then all of this would be placed in the memory closet and locked away. I turned on the radio and drove away to *Eye of the Tiger.*

The trip south was scenic, but otherwise uneventful. I was about to enter the country of my dad's childhood. I slipped the Volvo over to the Shenandoah, then down the Blue Ridge to Mabry's Mill before turning back to the Interstate. The little P-1800 was a dream to drive on the open road, but the party was over. My thirty-ninth birthday was around the corner, and all I could think of was that—except for my family—I had absolutely *nothing* to show for it. But a strange change and a different direction in my life was on the horizon. I just didn't know of it yet.

For now, I forced myself to not dwell on that as I drove home to see my family. It was late after lunch when I crossed into the Tennessee Valley. Every time I ventured through there, my thoughts would drift to my dad and his childhood. They were never pleasant thoughts, except for the fact that he pulled himself through his childhood.

This was the valley where his divorced mom kidnapped him in 1912 as a six-year-old from his dad, and then climbed aboard a southbound train in northern Tennessee that was headed toward Alabama. Near Interstate 81, I could see the same steel rails of the 1912 train route from the highway as I drove toward Knoxville. The local authorities were told that he was missing from a train station where he had been seen with his visiting mom on her return trip to Alabama. A sheriff's posse on horseback stopped the train below Knoxville, pulled him off, and sent him back on the next northbound train to his dad in

Tazewell. That was his great adventure, I suppose, and I considered the times in New York City to be mine. I thought later that if I had only known what was ahead in the coming years, I might have turned the car around then and there and returned to New York.

In another two hours, I was in Chattanooga, where all my cousins had settled. My uncle always wanted to live near the Chickamauga battlefield, where some distant relatives had fought in the Civil War with the South. It was told that they deserted in the heat of battle and were captured. They later swore allegiance to the U.S. government, signed a document, and were sent home. Many were later hunted down by other Rebels and shot for treason to the South. That was not a pleasant thought that we discussed around my uncle's dinner table every single time we visited Tennessee. That's all he ever talked about. We had relatives on both sides in the Civil War.

My dad's brother was a bit weird. He kept a stack of books on various religions on his nightstand. My Aunt Mary used to say that Jed was going to make sure he gets into Heaven, and that he believed in every one of those books.

I was a Christian ever since I was a child. As a young adult—and later, as Uncle Jed was getting older—I became a bit concerned with his salvation. I asked him to go for a ride with me through the battlefield during one visit. I asked him point-blank whether or not he believed that Christ was the Son of God.

"Oh, not to worry, Anthony, I do!" he'd replied. "I've been baptized six times."

"Well, that's good to know, Uncle Jed. It seems as though you are good to go," I said.

Finally, the road turned around Moccasin Bend, and I was nearly back in Georgia. I had not told anyone that I was coming home. It was to be a total surprise, even to Marie. I was getting both excited and anxious as I neared Atlanta. The Interstate around the metro was a nightmare with construction everywhere.

A few years ago, I had moved the family near Chamblee and out into the rural countryside. As I neared our street, I down shifted the P-1800, backing off on the twin pipes. My son ran out of our garage to see who it was. I saw him yell back into the house as first Jen, and then Marie, hurried out to the driveway.

Amid all the excitement, I paused and said, "Thank you, God! I'm home."

I was so glad to be home and away from anything *New York*. It was Monday evening and a great start to a new week.

Late that night, the children went to bed early. It was a school night, after all. Marie and I slipped down to the dock on the lake and lay there together, looking up at the clear Southern sky. I was finally back home. We were both very happy in that moment. It would have been so easy to stay in New York, but I was happy to be home with my family.

I would take a week or two off, and then I would leave for my new job. At least the family would be together on weekends. The Savannah Project was not that far across the State, and they could visit me at my apartment on the river or I could return home. I was supposed to be on the job on Wednesday, but I called, and they said that I could delay. My actual project was still two weeks out. The children were in school, so I attended a couple of football games to see the kids cheer and play.

It was nice to be back. I tried to not think about everything that I had missed at home or left behind in New York.

It was to be a new chapter in my life!

CHAPTER EIGHT:

An Epiphany And Seven Words To Live By

It was 1984 and I was at home. The time passed quickly, but the memories never faded, and I continually felt as if I were always waiting for the other shoe to drop.

A year flew by, and my life was beginning to become much more manageable. Our family was doing well—except for Mom. She remained in the extended care facility. My dad visited every day and spoke with her about the day's activities, even though she could not communicate or even respond. He was a great Pop, and he carried on. He deepened my love for him as he remained loyal to Mom in spite of the devastating circumstances. There was no cure.

The children were busy growing up, and Marie was working at her own retail store. We had opened it to earn extra income and we were having success, but the budget chains were threatening with stiff competition. There was always some kind of pressure to compete. Fortunately, we were able to sell our home, and afterward, we decided to build another.

Our new home was the first home to be constructed in our area in over seven years. As our parents remembered the Great Depression, my generation had its own hurdles to contend with. Jimmy Carter's nineteen-percent interest rates for housing loans played a big part in drying up the market, but the retirees who had savings stashed away loved it.

I was still employed out of town and living away from home during the week. I would occasionally call New York, and if Andrea was there when I called, we would talk. She never tried to call me, and rarely would she return my calls, and I didn't blame her. I would call on my new Nextel wireless phone that I used on the job and never on the landline. Cell phones were the up-and-coming thing, but only if you were near a tower.

I had always promised Andrea and Phil that the first time that I had one of *those unusual moments*, I would call them and discuss the event. However, in all the time since I had left New York, nothing unusual—or of any consequence—had ever happened since that strange night on the beach at Rockaway. It seemed like such a distant memory, but every time did I recall it, it still appeared vividly in my memory and gave me cold chills. Andrea had been affected in much the same way. It was a strange thing to be pushed or thrown like that; it was real and otherworldly.

Andrea had never remarried, and I had thought—and even hoped— that she and Phil might get together; but I was mistaken. She continued with her work and published articles regarding her ongoing research on childhood memories and related subjects. She never told me, but I'm almost certain that my contributions were included in a paragraph or two.

When we sold that home in 1979, we intended to build a new home immediately and relocate. For a short time, we intended to lease a house while we rebuilt. As the real estate market would have it, we were then selling everything we built as fast as we could construct it. Our six-month temporary rental that we lived in turned into an eight-year stay. There were mixed blessings but no real happy campers at our house. We enjoyed the income, but the family wanted to move out of the rental. Marie and I both began to occasionally annoy each other in our tight quarters, and the children were living and growing up in a house where they didn't enjoy having guests over, and that was mostly attributed to its condition.

It was now 1987, and my eighty-year-old dad had a heart attack. My sister had found him with photos of another woman in his wallet and had an uncontrollable fit there in front of God and everybody. He had a slight traffic accident and asked the investigating officer in LaGrange to call her so that she could help with the paperwork and the accident report at the accident site. It turned out that he was at fault.

When my sister arrived, she retrieved his driver's license for the police and some secret photos of this lady—or hussy, as my sister called her—fell out of his wallet. Immediately realizing what they were, my sister screamed in disappointment and ran all over the K-Mart parking lot, screaming and crying. The policeman was standing there with his eyes popping out. He didn't know whether to tackle her or shoot her and put her out of her misery. Her entire world and her respect for my Dad had been destroyed right there on the spot.

I never blamed my Dad; the pressure of eight years of loneliness was tremendous, as Mother had always been at his side. Now, for those eight years, she was like a zombie—unable to communicate in the nursing home—and he was as lonely as he could possibly be. I didn't mind his secret arrangement. I understood, except for the fact that his so-called lady friend was surely after his money more than his company.

Later that night, after the wreck and all was said and done, Dad again went home alone and, within a couple of days, he laid down and had a debilitating heart attack from the stress.

Be sure that your sins will find you out!

Now we had three invalids: my mom, my dad, and my sister, who was forever screwed up over it all. Christians should appraise the situation, quickly forgive, and move on! That's life. I am amazed at those who never considered that option. With that premise, it's tough to mend broken relationships.

It was a changing time for our family. Marie wanted to repair the rental house to make it presentable, but I refused. I wanted to build a new home and get the heck out of the dump. We had begun to argue frequently. Over time, conversations would arise concerning a new house, kids in high school, college, and debilitated parents in nursing homes. Occasionally—actually, more often than not—I would allow my thoughts to drift back to that wonderful beach at Rockaway.

It always remained the same in sun, under moon, and in all kinds of weather. I missed the solace that I found in the seashore. I began to miss even more being with Andrea, whom I had admired as my beautiful Israeli. Marie never knew, but those violations of my vows to her were wearing on our relationship. It was not a pleasant situation for anyone related to it. Life was becoming tedious. Was it a midlife crisis, perhaps? Surely, Marie and I had our share of struggles. I'd worked out of town and tried to manage the family affairs as best I could around the weekends. I was now forty-three and climbing in age.

Marie and I finally agreed to build our new home. It was now late 1986.

Marie was anxious to get out of the rental. Both Jen and Mark had friends whom they wouldn't dare invite over. We had a lot of living to do ahead of us and many directions that we could go. *And miles to go before we sleep, and miles to go before we sleep.* I suppose that our situation was the reason why that poem was my favorite. I had a lot on my mind, but I never considered whether I was overly pressured or under stress. I simply went forward to a goal that was set by a Power that was higher than I could ever have imagined.

Finally, after all the transitional stress, something miraculous occurred that I would be recalling in minute detail for the remainder of my life. I couldn't discuss it with anyone—not with Marie, not my children, or even my pastor.

It was something so astounding that it could never to be discussed as to its possible intended meaning. Any attempt to define it would have been purely conjecture and disbelieved among any who heard of it. I certainly would be calling Andrea and Phil in the near future; I would have to let them know.

I was gifted with both an incredible joy and what would become a burden of suffering in one fell swoop, but it would be a burden that I would gladly bear. At the onset, I could never readily understand the *why me* of it. I was arguably at a low point of my existence, and it would be many years before I would have the slightest clue as to why I was allowed to see what I saw.

THE ULTIMATE INTERVENTION!

1986. It was morning, and our house was empty except for me. It was an hour or two after sunup, but it wasn't all that early. It was just like any other morning— nothing special. Marie had gone to work, and we'd had a minor disagreement but then resolved it almost immediately before she left. I lay in bed for another twenty or thirty minutes or so. I was neither angry nor joyful at the time; it was only another weekday morning.

The room was darkened as I threw the covers back and placed my feet on the floor. As I sat up, I looked around at the sun peeping through the edges of Marie's dark curtains. I do remember yawning and stretching a bit, and thinking about preparing myself to start the day.

Suddenly and without warning, I was no longer in that room. I repeat: I was not there!

I was taken away—perhaps not physically, but at least mentally—for an unknown period of time. When I say *away*, I mean very far away. I was away from Georgia, the United States, and even the Earth itself. Then and there, I was allowed by Jesus Christ to see Heaven close up and for a brief but very informative time!

Yes, I said Heaven. I would never make such a claim without it having happened and I certainly would not put it into writing. I would never make light of my time there, but I will tell you this: it is everything God said that it would be. His promise to us as believers is assured, I can vouch for that! To all who simply believe in Jesus, His incredible reward is awaiting you in Heaven for eternity. Eternal joy and peace! And He allowed me to see it firsthand.

During that time, I was allowed to see and observe, and I was given a short but detailed message. I was very briefly and simply instructed.

As I write this, or even think of it, it brings tears to my eyes. I can still see every astonishing thing that I was shown. Every finite detail is etched in my mind. As I age, it never goes away—no matter the place or time of day—and it will be with me until I leave this Earth, *again*. I cannot un-see the magnificence that I observed, nor would I ever want to.

I spent the next few days, even weeks, totally enamored and in a bit of a daze. For years, I never told Marie—or anyone else, for that matter. It was an astonishing place to see, but everyone would have said that my testimony was just craziness. Marie noticed a change in one Mr. Anthony Marchant. It was too much to mentally grasp; but for me, the huge question was *why*. Repeatedly, every day, I asked: *Why? Why me, Lord?*

If I had told Andrea and Phil, they in turn would have immediately suggested a visit to the psychologist—and then to a medical doctor—to check for Parkinson's or some other physical or mental issues. How on this Earth would anything like that just interrupt you as you start your day? A person could never foretell such an event, or even prove that it had ever happened. The gravity of what I observed was one thing, and its meaning and the eventual reason for it would not be realized until years later, and then it would be related to something else entirely.

At that moment, as far as I was concerned, the most significant question of them all was why Anthony Marchant, a builder and an electrical construction superintendent, would be allowed to see with his own eyes all that he saw and heard with his own ears. Why would he receive the message that he was given? What was the true purpose of having been allowed to see and hear it?

All my life, I have known God through Jesus Christ, His Son. I never imagined Him in any form other than in the Biblical persona of Jesus—and then the Holy Spirit, as described in the Bible. He was a Jewish man, and he was young, strong, loving, forgiving, and also *all-knowing* in His intellect and teachings. And according to Scripture, he was made strikingly similar in the image of his Father; and after all was said and done, the Scriptures said that He was perfect. And He is!

Then, later that week, I worked up the courage to call Andrea. After a long discussion to catch up on our lives, I explained what I had seen for more than an hour. She listened without a single comment or interruption. I explained in detail what I heard and what I was shown. Then I told her what was said during the epiphany. Again, she listened intently and quietly. Eventually, after a long silence, she spoke.

"I'm astounded, to say the least," she remarked.

Then, again, there was total silence for a while.

Finally, she said in her very quiet and loving voice, she went on. "Anthony, I know that you don't make things up. Also, I will never forget the strangeness of our first night together on the beach. Again, as you tell me this, I remember all the crazy coincidences that you have observed and have been subjected to in your life. In my opinion, I suggest that you may have garnered favor with God for whatever would be His purpose with you. Certainly, to be allowed to see Heaven and all that you saw would be a blessing so unique that it must be for a purpose known only unto Him. He is telling you something, or allowing you to observe something in a very Biblical sort of way, and—I might add—in a most uniquely privileged sort of way. Also, Anthony, I must tell you that it weakens my knees as I even tell you that."

I knew in my heart that, if anybody would believe me, it would be Andrea. Her calming assurance and Jewish nature were what I had hoped to hear.

"Anthony, what purpose is there for you in this life? I could never say. No theologian, Rabbi, or priest could interpret the meaning of what you have just told me; but there is a purpose in it, and I believe it must be a very special one. I will say this: I feel that you will know the purpose when the time comes, and I believe that it will possibly come soon. Before I discuss anything else about this with you, I need to discuss it with Phil." She paused for a moment. "Anthony, may I tell Phil? I won't tell anyone else."

"Andrea, answer this first: if you had never met me and I told you this as a perfect stranger, what would you now be thinking?"

"After what you just told me, I would be suggesting that you seek counseling from a professional—that is, if I had not known you. But I *do* know you, Anthony. I really know you—perhaps more than you know yourself."

"That's what I thought also. Let me say that, had it not been for living a life accompanied by strange or unusual occurrences, I would totally agree that I should have my head examined. What I was allowed to view recently simply adds to it." I sighed. "Andrea, what I saw that morning would be considered by some to be similar to epiphanies described in the Bible. I observed it, and I didn't imagine it in any way. It was shown to me. I saw an epiphany, and I was given a message intended for me. I can never un-see it nor unhear it, and I will never forget what was said to me. Never!"

"Anthony, don't doubt for a moment that I believe you. For whatever purpose you saw the images, or epiphany, or whatever it was, it must be very important. Also, it may be that it is only for you or even for the future! Have you thought about that? Do you understand? Like a gift to help you along and give you inspiration and guidance in the future—or, perhaps, a message or guidance or even a reference for future events. Think of applying it in those terms," she suggested.

"I didn't understand it as that type of message. And you may be right; it may have been solely for me," I said, considering her words.

"Anthony, I just don't know what else to say about your epiphanies. I am at a loss for words, but certainly not for expression. All I could ever say was, *wow!* Also, I certainly don't know where God would want what you saw to fit in this modern world—as compared to those epiphanies that occurred in the Bible. Tony, I do know that I will never forget that night on the beach, ever! I will never forget the event, and I think about it every day. For me, that incident was otherworldly and cause for deep contemplation—even alarm! It still bothers me to even think about it." She sounded thoughtful.

"Andrea, thanks, as always. Please hug yourself for me. I have got to go now. And by all means, you have my permission to discuss it with Phil. I promised him that I would share any event or occurrence. And this was certainly an event to be noted, at least in my life."

I ended our conversation there. I never fully described to Andrea or Phil all that God had actually allowed me to see. I simply told her about fully seeing Jesus before me, and that He gave me a seven-word message intended only for me. I felt that I needed to hear what Phil had to say about it, so I told Andrea that we would talk again soon. Little did I know that it would be months before we were able to call each other again.

Over the next few months, I never mentioned anything about it to Marie. We were busy working to save for our new home, and I felt a constant dread hanging about me. The next few months passed, and we were constantly busy with family and our project. I had never bothered to call Phil, and when I did speak with Andrea, there was never any further mention of *The Epiphany*. I suppose that they were simply avoiding the subject. I didn't mind; after all, what could be said?

My dad was steadily losing ground with his health. His last days were filled with visits from family and friends, and as the year's end approached, his closest friend from Massachusetts—who had expressed that he would be coming to pay a visit—called and told him that he could not come because he was now suffering from acute mesothelioma. Within a week of the call, we were informed that his friend had passed away. Also, Dad had a first cousin, a niece, a brother-in-law, and also another close friend who all passed away in short order. It was Christmastime, but in spite of all the family deaths, I don't remember it being overly sad. They had all been in their late seventies and early eighties, and now they were all having fun in Heaven together. They were all Christians, after all. Even so, it was stunning to see the herd thinned so much and in such short order. I loved them—each and every one. They all had gone to Heaven, and they are all together in that unimaginable place that I was briefly allowed to see.

My dear sister and brother-in-law thought it best to immediately visit the healthcare facility to tell Mom about Dad's passing. Much to my chagrin, they didn't discuss it with me before going. They walked in and told Mom that Dad was in Heaven. They meant well, and they never believed my story about Mom constantly dreaming of being trapped in a casket but not able to converse. Not long after that unnecessary visit, Mom left this Earth also. I believe that she had understood every word that they told her. That should be a lesson to those with relatives suffering from Alzheimer's. Odds are, they can understand what they hear but are unable to respond. I never mentioned my dissatisfaction with them for doing that. Why aggravate the situation and let it lead to more family bitterness and regret?

It was 1990, and I had actually gotten into a great building career. Within a relatively short period of time, I had constructed several million dollars' worth of real estate. I became a developer and a designer/builder overnight. I had a great deal of help from the real estate agents and agencies. I built for very nice clients, and also for a few certifiable loony tunes. I could write a book about that part of my life—maybe, at some time in the future, I will; and if I do, it will certainly be under a pen name.

As the months passed and I kept searching for a place to build our personal home, I finally found great lots to build on. But they presented major challenges. I asked Marie to take a weekend to visit the property with me. She had no idea where we would end up. We were driving toward the northeast Georgia Mountains, close to her birthplace, and she began to smile as we approached a mountain road that she said had bordered her grandfather's farm in the late 1800s. Several other homes had been constructed over the years, and the only remaining lots were high on almost solid granite and overlooking a valley, which was eight hundred feet below. The view was incredible!

We ended up on a lot that faced the southeast. The rising sun would illuminate our kitchen and breakfast area. Then the shade in the afternoon would be on our deck, which would be constructed out over the cliffs. The view was one hundred miles into eastern Georgia and South Carolina. Marie was ecstatic.

"Do you like these lots?" I asked her. She smiled and just nodded her head, then hugged and kissed me. Needless to say, we bought them that weekend.

The gentleman who sold the lots to us had informed us that the highest lot had a large hole through the cliff where, millions of years earlier, a giant tree had fallen into the sand of the ancient ocean bed. As the sandstone had formed, the tree dissolved and made the hole. The hole was scorched to a bright red patina from signal fires and native ceremonial fires that burned in thousands of years past. I simply planned to clear the underbrush and to landscape around it. Marie was excited, choosing plans and working with the decorators as we planned that construction.

Three more years passed, and it was 1993. The construction went well, and nine months later—around Thanksgiving—we moved in. The novelty of living there never wore off. During all seasons, the sunrises, the storms, and the shady valley sunsets were visible from almost every room in the house. We loved the house and never wanted to leave it—not even to vacation. We were constantly on vacation the whole time we were there.

However, my friend Jim called early in November and told me that he had tickets for the guys to fly to Denver during the first week in December to catch an early-season ski trip. I asked Marie if she minded my going, and she said she didn't mind at all. It would give her some time to kick back and enjoy the fireplace, soft music, and the views. Our daughter was home for the holidays and stayed with Marie during the week that I was gone.

Jim, Ricky, Michael, Bill, and I always planned a guys' trip to Colorado every year. This year, Jim wanted to go early, so we picked A-Basin because it was the highest-elevation ski area in the world and would have the most snow. That week, the early season powder was incredible. We skied the entire Summit County and Copper Mountain, and before we knew it, the trip was over. What great fun and memories! I had called Marie daily to check on her and the children, and also to check on the house. I always asked about the house because it was new and might have had an issue or two. She said that everything seemed to be well, except that the lights had flickered a couple of times.

Flickering lights? That was a cause for alarm, to think that we might have an issue with the electrical. I looked at Jim because he had wired it. He called his partner at home and sent him right out. Marie called and said that the guys checked everything and found nothing. I thought nothing else about it, and we enjoyed the remainder of our trip. What a memorable and enjoyable ski trip that was.

After I arrived at home, Marie described the enjoyment of living there as if it were a resort. I told her that I would wager that the Natives had enjoyed it with ceremony on all of those moonlit nights thousands of years ago.

She said, "Do you suppose?"

"I have a feeling they did that very thing in that hole in the cliff. They lived here for thousands of years, so there is no telling. Tribe leadership ruled the day, and they had their rituals. There are centuries of evidence burned into the walls of the cave."

"Do suppose that their spirits are still around here?" she wondered curiously.

"I have no idea, but I did do my thing before we bought the lot and started building on it."

"What did you do?" She seemed rather inquisitive.

"All these years since I built our very first home when we were twenty-six years old, I would go out on the lot or property and kneel down and pray," I said, glancing toward her.

She smiled. "I didn't know that! What do you pray?"

I chuckled. "Well, now you are getting nosy."

Then I explained that I simply pray that the job will go well and that no one will be harmed in any way during the construction. "And I also pray that the new owners will be blessed by having lived there. Then I close my prayer until after the house is finished, and then I have a similar prayer, thanking God for the work."

"I didn't know that!"

"Well, now ya know," I concluded.

Marie hugged me tightly, and I settled in after the trip. We had furniture on order, but the master bedroom furniture had not yet arrived. We were sleeping in the upstairs guest bedroom just across the hall from my corner office. The office was built over the cliff and had a walk-in filing and storage room. The opening of the closet faced away from view toward the back of the office, and the door to the closet usually was left open.

In the middle of the pitch-blackness of the night, I was awakened by a sizzling sort of welding-type sound. That is the most accurate way that I could describe the event. In the office, I could see an extremely brilliant white light that was oscillating enough to cast wavering black shadows on the back wall of the office. The light was reflecting off the inside of the office windows.

"What under the heavens was that?" I asked Marie, but she said that she was facing away and only saw the ambient bright light. It was a brilliant illumination, much like a welder's Heliarc welder, and it lasted only a few seconds. After ten to fifteen seconds, it was over.

Marie screamed, "What on Earth was that?"

"I suppose it was a couple of local dudes ordered out by the Holy Spirit. God had led us to have the property. We asked blessing over it, and it is ours. I knew that fact for certain!" I said. I was half-joking, half-serious.

Marie was almost screaming. "Anthony, please stop your joking! Whatever that was, it was frightening!"

She and I repeated the same question over and over again. It became our mantra for the night: *what on Earth was that?*

"If this house is haunted, I'm packing up!" Marie said. Naturally she stayed awake for the remainder of the evening.

After spending a couple of hours wondering if it would happen again, I drifted off to sleep.

The next morning, over breakfast, Marie asked a question out of the blue. "Anthony, how did you know to choose these lots and how did you find them?"

I glanced at her. "Why are you asking that now?"

"I want to know how you found them!" she demanded.

"Why?" I countered.

"Answer me!" She was getting irritated now.

"It doesn't matter, we aren't moving!" I said with finality.

"Answer me!" she still demanded.

"Alright! When I was five years old, my parents brought their friends to this lot. They had a five-year-old daughter named Janie whom I had fallen in love with. They made photographs of me and my sweetheart, little Janie. One evening, I found the old black-and-white photo while we were packing to move. Here it is—I found it! The little girl and I are holding hands and standing on a cliff somewhere. I had always thought it was on another mountain." I sighed. "As it turns out, that photo was taken on this cliff, standing right underneath our great room floor. I didn't realize it until I was telling Jim about it on the ski trip, and then it finally dawned on me where we were. I got the impression that it meant that we were meant to build our house here."

"Then what do you suppose that light was?"

"I don't know, but I'll look again tomorrow," I tried to soothe her.

The next day, I went into the office and peered into the file room. Nobody else was in there for sure. I looked all over, around, and in the corner and I saw nothing at first, then suddenly, I saw it. It gave me cold chills. When I first realized what I saw, I was held in disbelief for a long twenty to thirty seconds.

Then I called Marie. "Honey, come look at this."

"What did you find?" she asked, breathless.

"Look!" I exclaimed.

"At what?" She peered around.

"Over on the wall behind those white filing boxes—see there." I pointed.

From the horrid reaction on her face, I realized that she had finally seen the markings. I shouldn't have shown her. Now she was frightened, and it would take at least a week to settle her down—if ever. She asked again about what it may have been, and I told her that the mark was a burn mark, like a lightning strike. It had blackened or smoked the new paint like a flame and had left a linear vertical mark in the drywall. The walls were smoked a bit, but not to the extent that the drywall had scorched. There was simply black smoke residue, distributed into making an unusual pattern.

Marie said, "I didn't hear any thunder!"

I told her that I didn't either. There was no weather last night—not even a cloud anywhere.

"Anthony, what on Earth was it?" she asked, frightened. "I don't want it in our new house. Get it out!"

"It may have been lightning, but there was no weather system around. It may have been a lost Native spirit wandering through on its way to leave this place. There wasn't much of a chance of lightning in December. Anyway, it has left the building, I suppose. Don't worry."

"Aw Tony, I don't want to hear that!" she anxiously said.

"It's gone, trust me," I soothed.

"What a way to start life in a new home!" she said, exasperated.

"Marie, do you recall what I told you while standing out on this rock—long before we started construction?"

She sighed. "I don't know. I suppose you should remind me."

"I told you that I had prayer before I started the first survey. I stand firmly on what I prayed about, so that's that," I said, firmly. "Forget about it, and let's go try out the new grill. It's going to be cold out there. It's thirty-eight degrees right now and going lower." I smiled at her. "We cook out in Colorado every time we go skiing. We don't give it a second thought. What's the difference? We soak in the hot tub out there in ten-degree and below-zero weather, but it seems to be even colder here up on this cliff."

Marie left to run errands and pick up a few ribs to grill later that evening. While she was gone, I quickly picked up a screwdriver and removed all the electrical plates and panel covers in the area of that room. I found nothing amiss whatsoever, and to me, that was very disappointing. No electrical issues, no electrical storm, and no construction debris anywhere near that office closet. I was playing the brave guy, but what I saw and heard was extremely unusual and unsettling. Later that evening, we had our first official cookout, and it was in the dead of winter. The light anomaly never happened again, but every time I went out on the cliffside deck at night, I kept an eye on that big hole in the cliff.

The next day, I got a very surprising phone call. I was on my way back to work in Georgia when my car phone rang. It was Andrea! I pulled over in a rest area and shut the engine off.

"Hi!" I greeted her excitedly.

It was really nice to hear her voice. It had been several months. I could not have imagined going that long without talking with her. I was totally surprised and so happy that she had called. I had decided months ago that I wouldn't call her. If we were to talk, then she needed to call me. I had nothing much to add to the current conversation, except for the strange thing that had just occurred in my new house.

I decided not to mention it. Then I thought: *what a coincidence! Or was it?*

I asked her if anything had prompted her to call me, and she said that she just wanted to talk and hear my Southern accent. She also had some surprising news. After talking for a while, she told me that she had leased my old apartment at Beach 131st. I asked her why she moved from 140st, because she owned that beautiful home on the beach.

She told me that she had a nice lease for her house from a couple who wanted to live on the ocean for a couple of years, and she decided to let them have it—on the condition that my old apartment was available. She told me that Mrs. Julliard had passed away a few years ago and the dentist had bought the house. So everybody knew everybody, and that it made it easy to adapt. She asked me how I was doing, and I told her that we had constructed a new home on a cliff.

"Oh nice, send photos!" she said. then she asked if I ever thought about visiting New York.

"Yes," I replied. I told her that, this next Christmas, we were coming as a family for one last vacation trip with my son, who was about to be married the following March. The trip was a year away, but we were planning on coming. I asked how Sam and Eric were, and she said that they were still living in the family apartment in Manhattan on Liberty Street and would probably die there. Neither had remarried after their divorces.

"Andrea, I never knew that either of them ever got married in the first place," I admitted.

She laughed. "Well, that's my fault for not keeping you informed. They both have children, so it is a bit sad. The weekends are great because we all crowd into those three floors and wreck the place while playing with the children."

"What about you, Andrea? Anybody?" I asked, quietly.

"No, I would have called you if I had. I was rather *hoping*, but I gave up on that situation a long time ago when this crazy guy I knew moved back to Georgia. So, I buried myself in my research. You remember, Anthony? My research?"

"Am I the weirdest guy you've ever studied?" I asked her.

"So far!" She chuckled.

We both laughed. "How about Dr. Phil?" I asked.

"He moved Upstate and received tenure at a college. I don't hear from him often, but when I do, he always asks about you. Anthony, when you come at Christmas, how long will you visit?"

"I know this will disappoint you: we are definitely going to come, but for now, we will have to put that trip on hold for a later date," I said.

CHAPTER NINE:

The Olympics, A Vision, And A Bomb

By 1996, my routine was returning to normal for the first time in a long while.

Jen was away at college and Mark had announced his marriage date for the spring of '97. So we had time to straighten things out around the house and plan for the wedding. Marie was excited about the trip to New York. She had never been to Manhattan; even though we had changed planes at JFK several times, she had never been into the city. Now she had the added planning for the trip to Houston for Mark's wedding.

I was excited also, and I would certainly have liked to have time for a visit with my friends, but I knew better than to even bring up that subject. I had to limit the visit to only four nights. The Waldorf was expensive, and I really didn't want to stay anywhere else. Marie didn't know the history of that old hotel and she would not have appreciated the experience of staying there. We planned our visit around the available nights at the Waldorf.

I was leaving in a couple of days for another two-week stint at the Savannah project and had several errands to run for Marie before I left. Marie was a bit perturbed about something, and I asked her what was bothering her.

"Nothing really, except that you are leaving again. I don't like the idea of you going anywhere anymore to be away from home. The children are gone, for the most part, and you have to work away from home. I love the new house, and I'll stay busy decorating it, but I'm hoping that you can find something closer so you won't have to travel, and we can enjoy our home even more."

I didn't like it any more than she did. I asked her if she would come to Savannah with me for the two weeks, just to get away. She could take a tour of the area and enjoy the beaches and scenery, but she rejected the notion.

"I need to stay and help Mark plan his wedding arrangements for the family that will be traveling to Texas." Marie wanted to get everything completed before the fall. She was unusually perturbed about something. As I talked with her, I got that feeling a guy gets when his wife is unhappy.

I asked her again, "Are you alright? You aren't telling me everything. What's up?"

She seemed hesitant to speak, and finally she asked me about a call from New York.

"What call from New York?"

"On your cell phone while you were in the shower last night."

"Did you answer?"

"Yes, I answered."

"And?"

"Nothing, they hung up."

"How did you know it was from New York?"

"I assumed that it was."

"If it was, it was probably from Dr. Phil or Andrea," I said. "I don't see why they would have hung up. The last time Andrea called, I told her that Mark was getting married and that we were planning a trip to New York as a sendoff. If it was her, she probably wanted to find out about the dates of our trip."

"Why would she want to know that?"

"Because she wanted the opportunity to meet the family, so she would have asked for our trip plans. She and Dr. Phil are really nice people, and I still can't imagine either of them hanging up on you."

Marie was in no mood to talk about my New York friends, and she stormed out of the room.

So we had our first argument in the new home. It didn't last long, and it wasn't a bad argument; but that night she chose to sleep alone, and I didn't argue the point. I grilled a burger—only one for myself—and I ate it while standing up near the railing as I watched the moon rise at the end of the valley. It was a great cookout—party of one! It was the best burger that had ever been grilled by anyone, ever!

Marie never came out of her room except to grab a late-night snack, and she also ate that standing up. Then she went to bed. I decided not to disturb her. Around midnight, I went upstairs and decided to sleep in the same bedroom that Marie and I had slept in on our first night in the home.

It was dark around the house as the moon had set. I turned out the lights and went to bed. I wasn't angry, not by any definition of the word. Marie was besieged with wedding planning and scheduling trips, and her only son was never coming back home as a single young boy. I understood all of that and I didn't try to console her; I just went to bed.

Not long after midnight, I awoke to a strange sound in the room. I thought to myself: *Oh crap, now what?*

It was as if something, like cloth material or even heavy canvas, was being slowly ripped apart. I rose up on my elbows and was almost frightened out of my wits. It sounded as if the room was ripping away from the house, and that was my first conclusion. But that wasn't what it was. What kind of nightmare or dream was this?

There, immediately before me, somehow, I was given a view to a scene out on the rock where we were landscaping around the famous hole in the rock. There was light being cast into the pitch-black night. The light was coming from my direction and was being cast on two men who were standing together on the cliff rocks. *Frightening* doesn't begin to describe the intensity of the vision. I knew immediately that was looking at the Enemy and his minion, the Antichrist.

In the moment, I checked myself and my surroundings. It just couldn't be! I was looking at the wall at the end of my bed, but the wall was no longer there. I looked again in disbelief.

Then I remembered my earlier vision from a few years past. That was no dream, and this wasn't a dream either. This was another vision! What on Earth, and for what purpose unto God, was I being shown this? I was surprised at the occurrence, but I was definitely NOT frightened because I immediately knew personally in Whom I had believed! This was another vision unto God's purpose, and I immediately realized that I was to simply observe.

Meanwhile, the two men said not a single word. All of these thoughts were slamming my mind and, at first, I thought that the men were actually standing outside my home. I started to reach for both the cell phone—to call police—and my gun, and then it dawned on me that I was well inside the center of my house with no possible way of seeing outside in the direction of the rear cliff.

No way!

That's when it became even more apparent that what I was definitely seeing was another vision, much like the first one from thirteen years earlier; yet this vision was being cast in an entirely different place. God had graciously shown me Heaven years earlier, for a purpose known—at that moment—only to Himself. Now He had allowed me to see the gates of Hell, along with the actual face of the coming Antichrist.

I repeat, God allowed me to see his actual face: the face of the Antichrist! He was a famous man whom I had never seen, but I would come to know him after a shocking future revelation.

I had always been curious as to what Biblical visions were like and how they manifested themselves to God's intended viewer. I understood that the visions illustrated throughout the Bible were fully described. The simple fact of the matter is, until you have been presented with one, you cannot even begin to fully understand the magnificence of Heaven or the terrible horror of the Lake of Fire!

I cannot adequately describe what I saw. The English language hasn't enough descriptive adjectives. Now, at this stage of my life, I had seen two visions. A blessing and a privilege? Yes! I considered it a most high honor. I had been given a peek inside Heaven, but only a slight view of Hell.

Again, the greater question would be: *Why me? And for what purpose? Why me, Lord? For Heaven's sake, why am I being allowed or chosen to be the one to view these individuals?*

I am normally a calm and collected individual, but I was about to lose it for certain as I had seen enough. Then I exclaimed, "GET THEE BEHIND ME, SATAN!"

As promised in the Bible, and just as suddenly as it had occurred, the wall closed up like a rolled scroll. The blank wall was again staring at me in the dark room. Satan followed God's orders. He got behind me! As explained in the Scriptures, he had no choice upon hearing that command from a Christian.

What on this Earth was that all about? Why me, and for what purpose?

As I had mentioned before, I have been a Christian since that age of nine. Everything unto God's purpose is what I was always instructed, and everything is to be unto God's own reasoning. I accepted that which I had seen under those beliefs.

After a long while, I slowly lowered myself off of my elbows. I brought myself to the point of accepting what I had seen and filed it away under the "There is a reason for it" category.

That wall may have closed, but I recalled every minute detail of what I was shown—and I still do to this day. God knows that I will recall everything when the time is necessary. God is well aware that I will connect the dots when the time is given for me to do just that.

When I had gathered my wits about me, I was concerned that what I had just witnessed had not come from the Lord, but rather from the power of the Enemy. After thinking and praying about it, I realized that God was possibly allowing me to view into the future. He has given me many gifts, and apparently one of those gifts could possibly be that of prophecy.

What other reason could there be? Years earlier, He had shown me Heaven and had admonished me and my sinful actions so that I might remain acceptable unto His call. In my own assessment of the condition of my own mind, I simply had not remained acceptable to His call. Even after He had allowed me to see what I saw, I had still lived a reckless and irresponsible life. I hadn't lived for Him, and I regret that I had lived those years mostly for myself. However, He taught me, gave to me, and placed His arms around me—even though I was never worthy.

I didn't realize, until years later, that He was allowing me to see what I imagined that possibly no other no man had ever witnessed. He was allowing me to see the principals who would be the leaders in the End Times. Again, I asked: *Why me? I saw what I saw, but why me? Why did I have the privilege of seeing Heaven? Was I like Moses in any way? Had I disobeyed the Word so much as to have to be personally admonished while on Earth?*

That is exactly what Jesus did!

"TONY! Remain within the cleft of the rock!"

A seven-word commandment from my Savior's own mouth, and it was never lost on me that the voice that I heard was the same voice that had commanded Moses to strike the rock. If you are a Christian, you too will hear it one day; it is definitely like nothing else that you will ever hear.

As with the previous incident thirteen years prior, I came to an acceptance of what I had seen. Again, every minute detail was burned into my memory. Every waking day from that moment forward, until even as I write this, has been filled with these two strange visions—both allowed to me by God. It wouldn't be for another ten years until I could begin to lace together the remembrances of what I had seen during those two early mornings that were thirteen years apart. There had to be a purpose for me to have knowledge that was simply not privy to many—if any—other souls on this Earth.

I got up early and packed my bag for Savannah. Marie met me in the bedroom as I was about to go for a shower.

She said, "I apologize. I love you and miss you, and I do not like your not being here. I'm tired of seeing you walk out that door to God knows where, just to earn the family a living."

At that point, I had been traveling for my work off and on for almost twenty years. The pay was good, but it was beyond burdensome. I told her that those were my sentiments exactly, and I promised her that I would do my best to make a career change.

While I took a shower, Marie cooked a great breakfast, and we later enjoyed it together on our deck. I kissed her goodbye and told her that I loved her, and I asked her to finish the planning for the trip. Then I left for Savannah. I never even hinted at what had occurred in the upstairs bedroom the night before. If I had told her about that episode, added with the bright light in my office that she had already witnessed, I might as well have set fire to the house and bulldozed it off the cliff. She would have moved out and never come back. I just kept my mouth shut.

"See you in two weeks!"

I drove all day back to Savannah and settled into my apartment. I was glad to get back to work, even though I still had to live away from home. I was anxious to call Andrea and share with her the latest strange event in my life. I attempted to reach her, but I ended up leaving a message for her to call my cell.

The next evening, Andrea returned my call.

"Hi Anthony! I'm glad that you called."

"Hi Andrea, I just wanted to hear your voice again. I wasn't able to converse the last time we spoke. Are you well?"

"I'm good, Anthony. It is always wonderful to hear that Southern accent. I miss it."

"I thought that you might be most interested in hearing the latest event in my spiritual life. It may be interesting fodder for your research, or book, or whatever place you may find to put it."

"Really? Now what?"

"In the middle of the night, there were two men standing on the huge rock outside our new home, and they were looking toward my house and, I suppose, at me personally."

"WHAT? Did you call the police?"

I laughed. "Even if they had been called, they wouldn't have seen them. I have a sneaking suspicion that only I could have seen them."

"Anthony, what are you talking about? What were they there for?"

"I have no earthly idea, but I have been allowed to see two visions now within thirteen years. We have discussed this before."

"Are you telling me that you have had another episode, Anthony?"

"You call it an episode, but I call it what it was: a vision."

"Oh, I do understand. I believe it is for a purpose. I honestly believe that. Remember, Anthony, it isn't just that they are epiphanies; some would say they would have to be interpreted. If you are seeing these things, you are seeing them for a reason. Anthony, would you be willing to speak to a precious Rabbi that I know and tell him about your revelations? When he speaks at the synagogue, he speaks almost exclusively on the prophets. He is very intelligent and so very nice."

"Andrea, I'll have to think about that. It certainly isn't something I will discuss with a stranger over a phone."

"What about during your trip this December to New York?"

"I think that certainly may be impossible as well. We will be really pushed for time."

"Anthony, I'll think of something. Go ahead and plan your trip, then give me your schedule. We may be able to work something out so that you can talk with my Rabbi in person. I know that he will want to meet you. I will be in touch."

"Thanks! Bye, Andrea. Please take care and be safe!"

"Goodbye, Tony. Call me soon!"

It was June, and Marie wanted to take a trip to Destin before Jen returned to college, but Jen insisted that she had plans to go to the Olympic Park in Atlanta with her friends. The Destin trip was still a month away, and I agreed to allow Marie to visit the Olympic Park as long as someone else drove, since the traffic in Atlanta was horrendous and was becoming a thing of legend.

Marie finally worked out a deal with the girls that they would gather at our new home in North Georgia and stay for two or three nights. We would entertain them, and on the last night, they could travel to the Olympic Park and spend the last evening in a nearby hotel. It was over a month away, and I actually had a sleepless night or two from concern for their safety. I asked Marie not to plan our trip to Destin until August, which would allow the girls' weekend plans to pass. Jen was in music grad school in Fort Worth at Southwestern. She was scheduled to graduate within a year, and we were all anticipating a big trip to Fort Worth for that celebration.

It seemed like we were on the road a lot in those days and rarely ever home, but Marie didn't seem to mind. She just wanted me to be home and not to travel. The children were just about grown and gone. We would later relish those college weekend gatherings as we got older and the house grew quieter.

When July finally arrived, Marie planned a cookout for her family members who were driving over from Alabama. They hadn't seen the house and wanted to visit, so we lived on that deck for three days. Her brother and sisters wanted to know about the hole in the rock. Of course, they asked the same questions that everyone else had asked, and those were: *Was the hole in the rock haunted?* I finally got tired of the questions and the discussion, and I told them all that yes, it apparently was haunted.

Much later, after a thousand Indian stories and a thousand Headless Horseman tales, the weekend came to an end, but I loved them all and enjoyed every minute of our visit. Marie told Jen to plan on going to the Olympic Park by checking into the hotel, then to ride the MARTA to the park and back. They selected three dates to choose from because the hotels were getting booked: July the 25th, the 26th, or the 27th. Her mother suggested that they go on the 25th, and if they really enjoyed it, then they could stay an extra day. Jen said the girls could only afford one day, so she decided on the 26th of July. For some crazy reason, I didn't feel well about either the journey to the park or the visit. I didn't say anything, but on the morning of the 25th when they were about to leave, and I told Jen where all could hear me, "Jen, please be careful; there is going to be a bomb."

Why I said it, I will never know. But I said it, and all who were in my presence heard what I said.

Jen said, "Oh, Dad! There isn't going to be any bomb! Don't say such things."

"I hope not. Just a feeling. Please be aware and careful."

Thank God they made it home safely on the morning of the 27th because, that very night, Eric Robert Rudolph set a bomb that exploded and killed a person, and the rest is history.

Marie screamed when she heard of it, and Jen didn't recall much about my saying that there would be a bomb. However, there was a bomb, and I called it before the event occurred.

"How do you do that?" Marie asked.

"I just get a gut feeling, and then I go with it. Sort of like when I met you. I got a gut feeling, and we have been married thirty years. I really can't describe what it is like."

Jen later told me that one of her friends thought I was weird, and I took that as a supreme compliment. I told her that whatever gift I had was indeed weird, but the gift was given to me by God and not by the other guy.

She laughed and said, "Well, whatever it is, I'm glad that you have it."

"Me too, kiddo!"

Mark was on his way back to work in Dallas, and Jen was headed back to Fort Worth to finish out her summer studies. It would be a busy fall with all that was planned. That left me to go back to work and Marie to plan our excursion to the Big Apple. I never thought much about the bombing that I had predicted. That sort of thing was a common occurrence in my life and somewhat prevalent in my dad's family. My son would never watch a football game with me because I would call all the fumbles and intercepted passes before they occurred. Don't even ask me how I knew to make the calls; I simply don't know.

Still, as accurate as I was about the calling the bombing, it always rattled me when I was correct. That autumn, Marie and I put our final plans together for the New York trip. We confirmed with the kids and set the dates for a December 19th arrival and the 23rd for our departure to return home. I made the hotel and air reservations, and we were all set. In the hopes of convincing Marie to go out for an evening dinner with my friends, I asked her to at least consider the thought. She was in a better mood, and she said that she would.

I waited a few weeks, then called Andrea one evening and told her our schedule. She was delighted that Marie would even consider it. I told her not to make dinner reservations because I wouldn't believe it until I saw it. I hoped that, during our trip, I would have the time and the place for an extended sit-down meeting with Phil and or Andrea's Rabbi. I had so many questions that had never been answered. I had not found anyone who could determine what was going on in my life. Some might say that I was gifted. Others might say that I had a mental issue. The problem was that my foreshadowings kept happening on an increasing basis, and to date, they all have been proven to be true.

The first order of business was that these visions, and what they contained, were constantly on my mind. They were seared into my memory like the light from an old flashbulb. They were never settled through reasoning or any type of logic. I needed to speak with someone who was known for deriving logical conclusions about illogical occurrences. In my second vision, the two subjects who were standing near the rock are people who are alive today. Who they were, and what part they would play, would be revealed to me in the order that the Lord would determine. I had much that I wanted to discuss with some notable theologian.

Even though my local church pastors had doctorates in theology, I had always felt that they were still not versed well enough in the Scriptures to satisfactorily explain the knowledge that I had received through either of the visions. It is *End Times knowledge* that I possess. What use is it?

Perhaps to stand on a street corner and yell out, "THE END IS NEAR! THE END IS NEAR!" along with the same advice as always: be certain that you are a Christian or your eternity is going to be as horrid as you can imagine. How do I give warning? Who would believe? No one believed Noah, and yet the rains came.

START SPREADING THE NEWS! WE ARE LEAVING TODAY!
(To New York City, not the Rapture.)

It was Wednesday the 18th—a week before Christmas. Jen was home from Texas, and she rode to the airport with us. Mark flew in from Dallas and met us in Atlanta. It was the same flight that I had always taken when I worked in New York, only earlier in the day. It was fun for a change, being on the plane with my family and going somewhere to enjoy the Christmas holidays together.

I thought of all those commutes from Atlanta while I was in New York, and I couldn't help but think of Andrea going to sleep on my shoulder on that moonlit night flight when we first met. My marriage could have gone either way in those days, but being surrounded by my family as we approached JFK, I was very happy that I hadn't left them. It would have been devastating to everyone and immeasurably selfish on my part. As we approached JFK, we flew over the tip of Rockaway, and the guided tour began as I explained the place where I had lived. It was late afternoon and the lights were just beginning to come up in the city. The fun was about to begin.

We grabbed a limo, and the first thing Mark and Jen said was that they wanted to go to Rockaway and see my apartment. I laughed and explained that it was a long way out there, and we just wouldn't have time on this trip. I didn't want to tell them that Rockaway held a special place in my life. I didn't necessarily want to share it with them—not until perhaps I could possibly write a book about it someday. That was simply the truth. At twenty-six years old, I had been told to write a book, and I was currently living its subject matter.

We had flown all over the country on various occasions, but they were mostly ski vacations. This was their first trip to New York. After a twenty-mile ride, I asked the limo driver to take us across 59th Street Bridge rather than through the tunnels. The family was excited and commenting on every landmark, and the Russian driver was having as much fun as we were while he pointed out all the sights in Russian. After making a huge U-turn on Park Avenue, we arrived at the Waldorf entrance.

The novelty of the hotel would be almost as enjoyable as seeing the city itself. As we unloaded the luggage, I looked around to see if I could see Trump Tower from there, but I couldn't. I wanted to show the family, but we could see that later.

I couldn't help but think about Andrea and her family there in the city. Their apartment was only a few blocks from Trump Tower, so we might be able to see it as we toured the Battery Park area. It had been so long that I had come to miss them. It was something that I just needed to let go, and I certainly wouldn't let it interfere with the trip.

Wow! What a hotel! The Waldorf Tower's 43rd floor was where we were booked. The 43rd floor was Mary Tyler Moore's permanent residence floor at the time, but we certainly didn't see her. It was late, so we grabbed a bite at the Grille and returned to our suite. You can appreciate that you aren't at Motel 6 when the double French doors to your suite have golden handles.

We were nearly settled in, and I really needed to let Andrea know that we were there. So I slipped down to the lobby and attempted to call her on a pay phone, but I got no answer. Then I called her old number at her house at Rockaway, and no one answered there either. There was no way to leave a message and her offices were closed for the holidays at the college. I had given her our itinerary, so perhaps she would contact us.

Marie was settled on the idea that I would meet with Andrea, so I didn't have to deal with that aspect of the matter. When I went back down the elevator to the tower's lobby, a steward approached me and excused himself, then asked if I was Mr. Marchant.

I said, "Yes, I am Mr. Marchant."

"I believe this note is for you, sir. Would you please check to confirm?"

I confirmed that it was from Andrea. I laughed to myself; I should have known full well that she would be on top of the situation.

The note read:

Hi Tony,

Tomorrow evening at 11 PM, if you can slip away, Phil and I will be in suite 4323 Waldorf Towers. We will be there late to meet with you so as not to interfere with your family and your vacation.

P.S. I can hardly wait to see you, and I will have my favorite Rabbi along with me.

I asked the steward to confirm the contents of the note to suite 4323. He smiled and said, "Right away, sir."

I had been thinking that we were going to run a tight schedule anyway, so I had opted to abandon the attempt at a meeting. We were going to see the sights, but now, the meeting was set for late at night and wouldn't interfere with our schedule. I was both very happy and very nervous. I had a great deal of strange information to talk about, and I didn't know if I had the courage to divulge it entirely. I would definitely have to pray about it. The next day was scheduled to be very busy anyway, and with the added late-night meeting, I questioned whether I would have the stamina to give a clear and concise presentation.

I returned to our suite, and Mark had a fire going in the French fireplace. Marie had her jammies on and was wrapped in a Waldorf bathrobe. She told me to have a seat because she was done for the day. She had ordered House specialty sandwiches and was glued to the fireplace.

Jen and Mark later ventured down for a tour of the lobby, where Cole Porter's white grand piano was setting above the entry. Mr. Porter had a penthouse suite in the hotel, and he had made his permanent residence there. Frank Sinatra had leased the suite for a year for one million dollars. What a place! It was that kind of place, and I was happy that my family and I were able to spend Christmas there.

The maid came in promptly at nine-thirty and turned down all the beds, placed a silk mat at each bedside for our bare feet, placed mints in the trays, and replenished the bar fridge. We were all set for the following day. After we turned out the lights and got into bed, I told Marie about the steward presenting me with the note from Andrea. She immediately sat straight up in bed, looked out the window down toward the Chrysler Building, and then lay back down again, turned away from me.

"Are you okay?" I asked.

"No, I'm not okay!"

"I am going to meet with them at eleven tomorrow night for a little while. You are welcome to join us."

"It's not the meeting, Tony; it's Andrea. How naïve are you? I can't stand the thought of meeting her."

"It was a million years ago, and nothing happened! Nothing! They are nice people. They became my friends while I was trying to support you and the kids. They broadened my life and opened my thought processes to new and different attitudes than those that I had been accustomed to in the South. I also gave them a few things to think about in my discussions with them. Besides, they were head over heels in love with the group *Alabama*. They can't be all bad!"

I talked to her for over an hour until I finally realized that she was asleep, because I heard her snore.

I thought*: It is hard to believe that I am going to finally divulge all that God has shown me over the past thirteen years.* I was hoping that I wouldn't leave anything out. The meeting was less than twenty-four hours away, and I was counting those hours down.

CHAPTER TEN:

A Towering Reunion

The following morning, we gathered for the breakfast buffet before leaving the hotel. It was an early start for a long day with a walking tour. The weather was slightly overcast and cold, so we ended up riding the subway to the World Trade Center's Twin Towers. I had wanted to take a taxi, but the family had never ridden a subway before, so I was overruled.

Once we arrived, I walked outside and looked up. I couldn't see the top of either tower for the low-hanging fog. We took a chance that we still might be able to view the city and went on to the top of the South Tower to the restaurant and observation deck.

Through the years, I had been to the top on several occasions. I never much liked going up there for some reason. I couldn't explain the feeling I always had when I walked out onto the observation deck. It was probably simply the sheer height of the structure. However, upon reaching the top, the first thing I did was to look down on Liberty Street where Eric's fabulous apartment had been located. I knew that it should be easy to spot because of its unusual shape and the three white-brick stories of an all-glass atrium window on top of a brownstone. I hadn't spoken to Eric since I had returned to Georgia, and I had never asked Andrea if he still owned the place. It had been thirteen years since the morning I had driven away in the Volvo. While standing up there, I visually traced the streets through the fog as best I could, following the route where I had departed Manhattan. I remembered that morning as having been joyful, as I was headed home.

The view was still a bit foggy, but New York City leaves on its lights on during foggy days, and the streets were reflecting the lights through the fog. That view made the visit worth the trip to the top.

We ended our day uptown with a late lunch at Trump Tower, and Marie and I walked back to the Waldorf while Jen and Mark left for an afternoon tour of the Met and the Modern. It was still spitting rain and turning much colder. I suggested to Marie that it felt like snow was a possibility.

I simply wanted to spend the late afternoon lounging around in the Waldorf lobby, listening to the pianist and watching people. It was a fabulous place to rest and people-watch. Every spectrum of wealthy humanity passed by as I listened to the pianist cover Cole Porter favorites. Also, I had reminded myself that the 11 p.m. meeting was coming up, and I didn't want to fall asleep in the lobby.

I was nervous about seeing Andrea for the first time in so many years. I wondered what that moment would be like and whether I could contain myself. Would I even be able to speak?

The information that I would soon relay to her and her friends made it even worse. Just as I had with a few other people, I simply was going to describe what I had seen. However, this gathering would be the first where I would describe both events, as they had been shown to me, with all of the details. I planned to fully describe both epiphanies to them.

I was always concerned with the rebuttal that was sure to come. That no one would believe me was to be expected. I had to keep reminding myself that I didn't have to convince anyone of anything. It was not my place to convince. There were no consequences for not convincing anyone. The same may not have been said if I hadn't conveyed what I had seen.

I was like a newspaper boy standing on the street corner, yelling, "Extra, extra, read all about it!"

The two epiphanies had been given to me. Even one event would be astounding enough, but then seeing another? That was two epiphanies within thirteen years! I had to remind myself that God's clock has no sweep hand.

And after a time, I realized—a few years later—that the epiphanies were ultimately connected. I didn't understand the reason at the time, and I had reconciled myself to the fact that I might never know His reasons. I am thoroughly convinced that He wanted me to convey what I saw, or He would have had no other purpose for showing me these epiphanies.

I suppose the incidents reminded me of the day when I had told my friend that I would be writing a book someday. I strongly felt God's directive that, someday, I would write a book when I had the material or the message. Had that day arrived? I certainly had the subject matter. I had experienced what I had seen firsthand.

But it wasn't time for a book yet. I would learn that the subject matter was not yet complete. Even more connective information was still to come.

Manhattan was a great venue to create that final gathering of our family as a unit and to celebrate a wonderful life with my children. They would soon officially depart for lives of their own. That was my main purpose for being in New York City. I wanted nothing to detract from this last family trip.

It was only at Andrea's request that would I take the time to share what I had discussed with her for so long. We had visited the issue so much over the phone that it would have been a shame to not seize the opportunity to share in person. Also, I wanted to see her again. Thirteen years is a long time. I was both fearful and excited by the thought. The meetings would be only a minor inconvenience for my family, as I would schedule them late at night.

It was also going to be interesting to find out about Andrea's rabbi and which branch of Judaism he subscribed to. It would make a difference to him as to whether what I had to tell him was possibly genuine in his beliefs and opinion. I knew nothing as to what beliefs he ascribed to. It really did not concern me that they may not believe me at all.

Since I was a Christian, I can only say that I was shown what I saw, I didn't imagine it; and someday, everyone on Earth would experience—in some way—what I had been shown, firsthand. Everyone!

That was the good news. Make that GREAT news!

It was getting late, and the children returned from their museum tour in time to join Marie and me for dinner at the hotel. It had begun to sleet, and the precipitation soon changed to snow. Jen and Mark were freezing by the time they returned to the hotel. They were also thrilled to see the city lights and decorations in the snow at Christmastime.

Afterward, I went to the room to shower and clean up. Eleven o'clock was approaching. I was becoming very nervous and even weak at the thought of what I was about to share with a perfect stranger.

I asked Marie one more time if she wanted to join the group, but she suggested that I go alone. She said that it was more for her benefit that she didn't go, and I didn't argue the point. Besides, the little French fireplace was all aglow, and the loveseat was reserved for her—along with a glass or two of merlot. I suggested that she never drank wine before.

She said, "I'm in New York! What's the big deal?"

I laughed and said, "That's what the big city will do to you, so be careful!"

It was 10:45 p.m. I kissed Marie, then left our suite and took the long hallway to the elevator up to the Tower.

The white-gloved Chinese lady who was the elevator operator met me with a smile and a nod. "Floor, please?"

After a short ride up, I was at Andrea's door. The meeting was at hand. I was nervous, and my knees were as weak as if it were my first date or a job interview. I don't know whether I was more nervous about the meeting or about seeing Andrea for the first time in over thirteen years. It wouldn't be long until I would decide that it was the latter.

I rang the bell and, in a few seconds, the double French doors slowly opened and there she stood. Thirteen years shrank into thirteen seconds, and there was Andrea. My knees were weak, and tears were in her eyes. Tears were also in mine. We said nothing as we simply walked into each other's arms.

It was not anything that we planned. It simply happened. I suppose we both knew that it would occur, because neither of us would resist the obvious attraction.

Later, I often wondered if it would still have happened if Marie had opted to join me in the reunion. I wished that she had.

I was lightheaded. I almost passed out.

We said nothing as she closed the door into the small vestibule of the suite. The door was closed into the parlor and the light was off as she threw her arms around me again. And before I could speak or react, she planted a thirteen-year overdue forever-kiss on me that I can still imagine feeling today. That kiss instantly blew open all the old memories and forever re-tattooed my heart.

We both came close to losing all emotional control right there on the spot. All the lures—her scent, her silky soft brown hair, and those alluring eyes—were the things that I had tried to put out of my mind for all those years. In one fell swoop, all the emotions came pouring back once again. This was definitely not a good idea! But I had known that from the outset, and I didn't want to think about those memories. I tried to put our reunion out of my mind, but it was a lame attempt.

This was a crazy mistake for the weak in spirit!

I was already questioning my own true motives for agreeing to this little confab. How would I go back to Marie, who was only a few floors down, and act normal—in any sense of the word? All of the memories were flooding my mind. I held Andrea and kissed her once more and told her that I either must leave or stop it and get on with our meeting.

Why had I really come here? The truth had found me out. I had come to see Andrea, and that was the only truth that I could rely upon in that moment. I needed to regain emotional control or I wouldn't make it through the night, and it was going to be a difficult night.

Andrea smiled, wiped her silent tears, then led me through the long corridor of her suite and into a parlor on the rear corner of the hotel. At first it was empty, and Andrea asked me to have a seat. I looked out the windows as a brief snowsquall was striking the city. The lighted Chrysler building was barely visible from only a block away, and the room was warm and glowing with a fire. Andrea turned down the lights and brought in glasses of wine. In a few minutes, her rabbi walked in. He introduced himself as Michael as I stood to greet him. Michael was a most congenial older man with a large smile, graying dark hair, and a ruddy and robust demeanor. As Andrea continued to introduce me, Dr. Landers walked in, and we had a very nice reunion. Upon hearing about our gathering, he had asked Andrea if he would be allowed to sit in.

I couldn't help but think that she and Phil may have finally started showing interest in one another. I didn't mention it, but I did give them both a questioning side-eye and a raised eyebrow that was aimed specifically at Andrea. When Phil wasn't looking, she frowned and strongly shook her head: NO!

The hour was almost midnight and the conversation had immediately expanded to a half-dozen subjects. Michael said that he was in love with the South, especially the coastal areas of Georgia and the Carolinas; and so we talked and talked, and the snowstorm kicked up to howling outside the buildings. The lights on the nearby Chrysler building were now barely visible, glowing dimly through the storm.

After a while, the conversation turned to the matters at hand, and Michael asked me about my beliefs. I told him that I was a Christian, and that I believed in and loved the Lord in Jesus Christ as my eternal Savior.

Then I asked him about his beliefs. He said that he believed in God, of course; but he had always thought of Jesus as a bad boy, of sorts. He also knew that if Jesus were everything that the Christians said that He was, then perhaps he could be convinced. I confirmed that I truly believed that He was, and then I told him that—as I understood history—you'd had your chance 2,000 years ago and blew it.

Dr. Phil laughed and agreed.

Andrea had sat down close beside me and said nothing as the conversation continued. I sensed that she felt like she might have to referee.

After a while, Michael remarked that Andrea had spoken with him about my events, as he called them. He then asked me if I would care to share what I may have seen and the circumstances that surrounded the events.

I told him, "I suppose the hour could be considered as fitting for what I am about to divulge."

It was midnight and snowing hard in New York City. I also suggested that he and Andrea should simply ask questions and I would explain what I had seen as best as I could. Phil could jump in whenever he wished.

And so, it began.

Michael asked what circumstances were surrounding me during the time I had the first epiphany. I explained that I had sold our home and was attempting to change careers, or at least to reinvent myself.

My parents were elderly, and my mother had been in a nursing home at the time. Also, my dad was healthy and independent. Furthermore, there were no extraordinary stresses in my life—except that Marie and I were building ourselves another home and moving out of the rental. That was our existence in a nutshell. There were no unusual stresses.

We were in the process of planning that home at the time of the first incident. Neither Marie nor I could tolerate living in the rental after having lived in the new homes that I had constructed in the past.

THE FIRST VISION IN DETAIL

As far as the circumstances that led up to the first epiphany, Marie left the bedroom and had dressed early for her job before departing the home. She had been a bit upset about something at work and, apparently, I hadn't paid enough attention to her complaint that morning. She had slammed the door on the way out and further awakened me.

At the time, I was still in bed and about to get up. Marie and I never argued that much, and the arguments were never serious concerns for either of us. We both had the same goals and aspirations to succeed together and to help our families. I was fully awake and thinking about what I was going to wear that day.

Michael then asked if I ever did any drugs or smoked anything, and I said never. I explained that I had never drunk anything, except a glass of tea or a rare glass of wine with a meal, for my entire life. I was drug-free and fully lucid when the epiphany occurred. As I just said, I was thinking about what I was going to wear that day.

Andrea said nothing as I spoke. I knew that, as a clinical psychologist, she would be listening to my story; but at the same time, she would be observing me from a clinical perspective. I also felt that, emotionally, she was wanting to hold my hand through the process.

That didn't alter what I had to say in any way, so I continued the explanation and description of the event. I had volunteered for this meeting because Andrea had requested it, but also because I wanted my unanswered questions to be resolved.

The day in question was a normal fall day in 1983.

It was still early, and the sun was up. Marie had departed and, except for the cat and me, the house was empty. I rolled out from under the covers and sat on the bedside. I was about to put on socks and then, with a joltingly loud voice, "IT" happened.

Michael and Andrea both sat toward the edges of their chairs.

In a loud voice, I heard my name called sharply and only once. He sternly delivered my name as clearly as a bell: "ANTHONY!"

Anthony?!

I didn't have even a split-second to wonder who was calling my name. I looked up, and to my astonishment, I knew immediately that I was no longer on the Earth.

I was looking up at the Lord Jesus Christ, who was standing above me and to my left. He appeared to be twelve or fifteen feet tall as I looked up at Him. Once He got my undivided attention, He lovingly continued and drew me much nearer as he then appeared at a more normal size. Then, with advice given to me as a single command, He said, "REMAIN WITHIN THE CLEFT OF THE ROCK!"

Those seven words from the voice were as two-edged sword.

I was both fearfully numb and in awe of what I was observing. As I looked up at Him and observed Him, I can only say that He is the most beautiful being ever created. He didn't smile at all, but the expression on His face was one of laying down the law to His child. With those seven words firmly delivered, I had just received a loving spanking from my Savior!

He was alternately looking at me and then looking upwards into the pure light of His Heavenly Father. That light from above bathed Jesus, and it emanated the purest brilliance that was being cast over and upon Him as He stood there.

I was stunned!

Briefly, He allowed me to observe Himself in minute detail. God the Father was shining His Light upon His Son as I observed Him standing there in person. Jesus stood at a type of altar or podium, and in His left hand, He held what I later realized was the huge Book of Life.

The Book appeared as large as two huge joined white mattresses—a Book with thick and very large white pages with edges that were gilded in very bright polished silver. Those pages were individually hanging down, with each flowing towards different places on Earth like thousands of flashes of lightning.

Far below, I observed the blue marble-sized Earth where, only moments before, I had been sitting on my bedside. The pages of the Book of Life were ten thousand-fold and were streaming and flashing towards our planet.

As Jesus' left hand held the Book of Life, His open right hand was held up toward the Shining Crystal Sea which was before us and over toward a distant isthmus of land that lay along the opposite shore. There is no way that any poet or artist could verbally or recreate a proper description of the approach to the Shining City on the Hill.

"Please excuse me, Anthony," Rabbi Michael interrupted. "Were you able to see and describe this 'City on the Hill?' And please excuse me for interrupting."

I then told Michael to please feel free to ask all the questions that he could think of and, no, I was not able to see the City as described in the Bible. I was not allowed that view.

I was standing slightly below and a bit behind Christ. He was positioned to the right side of the entrance. I could not see it. I could only see around Him as much as He allowed. The gate and entrance were not visible from my point of view, and I was not allowed to see them. I had a feeling that the full vista is saved for our soul's grand entry. I was standing to Jesus' left and slightly behind Him. He had to turn to his left slightly and look slightly downward to address me.

I was looking over and around the Book of Life that I described, which He held in His left hand. Believe me when I say that I was trying to see all that I could possibly see as I stood there. And that brings up an interesting point. Jesus knows each of us in every detail, including our talents, and He knew that I would leave no detail from my memory throughout my life.

"What else did He allow you to see?"

As I had said, I was able to see over and beyond the Book of Life and out to the incredible beauty of the Crystal Sea. There was an isthmus of land adjoining the sea beyond. Past the isthmus were incredible mountains and meadows with flowing streams that led to the Shining City. The colors were intense and much more profound than these on Earth. I would venture to guess that, in Heaven, we are allowed to see the full spectrum of the colors of His rainbow.

Along that distant isthmus of land were hundreds of thousands of happy souls who were joyfully walking, running, and skipping towards our direction and the direction of Heaven's Gate.

"Did you see the Gate?"

No, again, I was not allowed to see either the City or the Gate.

"Then how do you know that the Gates to the City were there?"

"Because it is described that way in the Bible," I answered. I was not allowed to see the Gate nor the City. Multitudes—perhaps millions— were joyfully hurrying toward it.

I will tell you this: it is not Saint Peter who stands at the Gate. It is Jesus Christ, the Son of God, who calls each and every name of those who have even a little faith—as little as a grain of a mustard seed—in Him, the Son of God!

It is He who allows you in. "I SAW HIM WITH MY OWN EYES!"

And I heard His voice like a "two-edged sword" as he called my name. Then, with that same voice, He uttered those seven instructive words: "ANTHONY, REMAIN WITHIN THE CLEFT OF THE ROCK!" He said nothing else after that.

I began to tear up as I described the epiphany for the first time to strangers. I had previously shared the story with Marie, and she trusted in me to tell the truth.

At that moment, Andrea suggested that we take a break or not even continue.

"No!" I said. "You must hear it all. I am definitely NOT finished. There is MUCH more that you must hear."

Andrea brought me a glass of ice water, and I settled back and looked down at the streets and watched it snow. There was much more that they needed to hear. Thankfully we were booked for two more nights, I thought as I watched the snow beginning to collect in the streets below.

Finally, I suggested that we continue.

Michael asked me for a description of the happy people.

As I had described, there were tens of hundreds of thousands of happy souls skipping and joyfully marching toward us. As far as my eyes could see, there were joyful faces. Their bodies being covered by colorful gowns is the best way to describe their dress, and even their hands appeared to be "ethereal"—as were their gown-covered bodies. I could see through their ethereal hands as they skipped happily toward the City.

There were no "white" gowns dressed among the multitudes—only millions of colorful dresses. There is little doubt about one thing as they walked and skipped along, and that was the incredible joy that emanated from their faces. As I said, there was no white dress among any of the multitudes; there were only various beautiful colors as far as my eyes could see.

I have no idea how long the Lord allowed me to stay at His side and observe that magnificent place, but after a time, I felt myself falling away. As I was being allowed to return, I desperately tried to see His face once again, but He then obscured it—along with the multitudes—as I fell away. I also tried to see their faces once again.

However, I really didn't need to see Him again to know what He looks like. He had already blessed me with the incredible privilege of drawing me nigh! The most beautiful creation ever in God's Universe was standing before me with my personal stern instructions and a warning.

Suddenly, just as it had begun, I was again sitting on the side of my bed with one sock on.

As I returned to familiar surroundings, I remember asking myself, "What in all of God's creation was that about?" I had no trouble whatsoever remembering His voice and what He had told me.

The only question now was: "Why me, Lord, why me?" Again, I was stunned at the event of that October morning. I asked, "Why did you take me, of all people on Earth, up to Heaven and show me what You allowed me to see? Why me, Lord, why me?"

I was back on Earth, and I simply was late for work.

Michael then asked, "Anthony, how was He dressed and how did His persona appear to you?"

Andrea interrupted and suggested another session at a later time if I was too tired to continue. It was 2 a.m.

I said, "No, there is much more, if you can remain awake to hear. I must tell you what I saw later on in the second, most recent, event. But first, to answer Michael's question, He is the most beautiful creation in all of creation. Perfect in every way. He is obviously a Jew and His skin, hands, and face are like none that man has ever seen. His hair is long and dark, and his beard was black and appeared trimmed. As He held the 'Book of Life,' He would occasionally look toward the light and tilt His head back and raise his chin slightly as if to bask in God's Heavenly Glory."

I cannot emphasize enough the pure, sinless nature of what He allowed me to see.

As far as his dress, describing both inner and outer garments, His outer garments were the garments of the day that He walked on Earth. They were a hopsack woven material with what appeared to be cotton or woolen inner garments.

Then there was the indescribable pureness of His final inner garment, which was astounding and can only be described as the essence of purity. It was as if I could take my hand and insert it near any of the white pureness, and my hand would disappear into the "Pure whiteness enclosed around His persona."

The reason for what He allowed me to witness, and the reason that He allowed me to stand before Him, was yet to be determined. What I just described occurred in 1983, when I was forty years old. I knew of no purpose whatsoever at the time, but I knew very well that there had to be one. Thirteen years later, the saga would continue, and eventually the probable purpose would make itself known.

Michael again interrupted and suggested that we return the following evening to continue. He wanted to gather his thoughts and possible questions. He asked that he be allowed to create a list of questions, and I agreed. Andrea asked if I would be agreeable and suggested that they would pay for another night or two at the Waldorf. I smiled and said that it wouldn't be necessary. We would continue the following evening at 11:00 P.M. Besides, there were flights to catch, and we couldn't miss those.

Michael then offered to purchase new flights for the family, but I declined. "Tomorrow evening will be doable, and I'll see you at 11 p.m. sharp."

Andrea showed me to the door and hugged me as I departed. She said nothing as I wiped a tear or two from her eyes, then hugged her, and walked into my own hotel suite at 3 a.m.

Marie was curled up on the couch by the fire in the parlor. She awoke and asked whether we were finished.

I said, "No, one more night."

Marie said that she wasn't surprised, and she seemed agreeable and as she turned over and went back to sleep.

The next day, the previous evening's snow was already being removed by the time we finished our brunch. We had afternoon tickets to *The Phantom of the Opera*, and we rode a cab over to The Majestic. We were able to enjoy the *Phantom* with its original cast, and afterwards, we walked over to Sardis's for dinner. It was Christmas, and at that time of year in New York City, more smiles abound. People are friendlier with more noticeable laissez-faire attitudes.

Two more nights and we would be back in Georgia. What a great Christmas vacation getaway it had been, but as I had promised, I would spend one more late night with Andrea and her friends. I thought that what I had yet to describe for them would leave them completely dismayed and disbelieving.

I couldn't help it; I saw what I saw, even though it would be years into the future before I was able to connect the missing dots and understand what God was showing me. I dreaded the upcoming meeting, but it would have been too much for them to comprehend at one sitting. The epiphany of Heaven was strenuous enough, but the event that I had yet to describe to them would more than likely send them away in total disbelief.

I had to tell them the story, for why else had it been divulged to me? Was I truly going to write a book—as I had been instructed to do, in a manner of speaking, at age 26? If so, then when would I write it?

Then came the two most pressing questions of all: what conclusions could be drawn from what I had seen? Then, having written the book, who would benefit from its conclusions?

As it would turn out, the answer to those questions was that the entire world would benefit.

It was a long, cold walk back to the Waldorf by way of the skating rink and the Christmas tree at Rockefeller Center, but with the spitting snow, holiday lights, and Christmas street music, we didn't complain. Jen had placed ice skating at Rockefeller Center on her life's to-do list.

We were back to our suite and our little French fireplace before we knew it.

It was almost time for my gathering, and I asked Marie one more time if she would care to join us. She said no. She understood that I had experienced a second episode or epiphany, but I had never given her the details. I didn't want her to be afraid of living in our new home. The latest epiphany was not of Heaven, even though it was as dramatic—but in a frightening way.

Marie ordered some snacks to be sent up for her and the children, and I departed for Andrea's suite and the meeting. It was 11 p.m.

I was again anxious to see Andrea, but I knew that—in all probability—this would be the last time that we would see each other. I dreaded that much worse than the information that I was about to give them.

A quiet knock at her door, and a long thirty seconds later, she was smiling at me once again. She invited me inside and took care of my coat, then again reached for a long hug. We went back to the parlor where the fire was burning, and she told me that both Phil and Michael were late, but both were en route. It gave us a chance to catch up on the missing years.

Sadly, she said that she'd had several opportunities for relationships over time, but that she had decided to stay single all those years. Her suitors were all professor types whom she said tended to be overeducated and shallow one-track liberal thinkers.

I thought: *what a tragic lost opportunity for someone to meet a beautiful mate.* Then I smiled and suggested, "Life isn't over, and you are young and incredibly beautiful."

Just then, Michael arrived. Quickly I reminded Andrea that I would like to have her email address along with her cell number, so we exchanged our business cards.

Michael walked in and apologized for being late, and Phil was just behind him. Michael shook my hand, then poured a glass of wine and had a seat by the fireplace. This time, he had a notepad.

He said, "Last evening was interesting, and I don't want to miss anything this evening."

I was amused, and I told them that I didn't think I would disappoint. I went to the kitchen and poured a cup of coffee while we waited for them to get settled.

Before I continued with the description of what I had been shown, I reminded them both that under no circumstances were they to divulge anything that I was going to say. I also asked them to be especially careful around Marie. Our home was virtually new, and I wanted to continue living there. If Marie knew what I was shown there in the second epiphany, she would remove herself from the premises permanently. I certainly did not want that to happen. What I had been shown was truly that frightening.

They all agreed, so I began to describe my second epiphany.

Also, I explained beforehand that, as frightening as the epiphany had been to view, I knew of nothing that it was connected to or for what—if any—purpose that I was allowed to see it. I had only constantly asked: *Why me, Lord?* That was my question and my concern.

So I began by explaining once again the circumstances around the construction of our cliff home in Georgia. I explained that the hole in the cliff showed indications of fires and perhaps ceremonies by others in the past. Perhaps they were either Native Americans or ancient worshipers of the Enemy.

Also, for clarification, I again explained seeing the brilliant light like a welding rod emanating from a closet in my office, only to find burn marks in a freshly painted wall. I continued, and to say that Michael, Phil, and Andrea were attentive would have been an understatement.

Finally, I explained seeing the wall of an upstairs bedroom that I was sleeping in peel back from top to bottom like an ancient parchment scroll. At this point, Michael couldn't contain himself any longer.

He asked, "What were the circumstances that would have cause you to see such as that? There had to be something to initiate the epiphany. Especially if you don't abuse substances."

I told him that I didn't disagree with him, and that the scene was what I had been shown; and I agreed that it must have been for a purpose that I did not yet understand. I was simply there to bring Andrea up to date on what was to be a continuing saga.

Michael again apologized, and I continued. I suggested that God wanted me to see what I saw. He also wanted me to see the persons that I saw.

One reason that I was anxious to speak with Andrea in person was because what I saw that early morning was unbelievable, to say the least. And I would not have been shown those things if it were not for some "greater purpose." Of all the conclusions that I could derive, "greater purpose" was the only thing that I could come up with.

During the epiphany, when the wall opened up like a scroll, I was able to view outside my house from my bed toward a unique feature that was locally called "Hole in The Rock." It is a large 6-foot by 6-foot hole that continues through the rock and exits high up on a cliff. It has seen multitudes of fires burned within its walls over thousands of years.

Michael anxiously asked, "What did you see?"

I continued and described the two men who were standing outside my house. The man on the right was shorter and was looking slightly to my right, down into the valley. However, the man who was standing slightly behind the first—to his right and to my left—was on my level of eyesight, and he was looking straight at me with a definite condescending expression.

Neither man said anything. Not a single word. They were slightly lighted by the ambience of an orange glow coming from the valley, eight hundred feet below my house.

Michael asked, "What was the glow from? It was supposed to be the middle of the night!"

I agreed and answered that it was definitely during the middle of the night. The glow was from the entire valley, which was glowing like a forest fire.

But it was not a forest fire. What I was seeing, even if only briefly, was the Lake of Fire—exactly as described in the Bible. It was like looking into the roiling caldera of a volcano. There were large sluggish waves rolling back and forth down below.

Andrea asked if I was not frightened out of my wits, and I said no! Definitely not! Although it was highly unusual, I have the utmost confidence in my belief in God's Son, Jesus, and in His promise to me. I was shocked at the scene, but not afraid! As a Christian, I know in whom I have believed, and He is able to spiritually handle anything and anybody on my behalf—even the son of Perdition himself.

What I saw that early morning was Satan and his number one minion, the Antichrist.

Andrea asked, "Why would God show you that?"

"Andrea, that is the $64,000 question. I have no idea as of yet."

Michael asked, "When did this appear to you?"

"The first epiphany was in 1983 when Jesus allowed me to see Heaven and the Crystal Sea, as I have described it to you," I answered.

"And this latest epiphany?"

"It was this very year, 1996—only this past spring after we moved into our new home. The epiphanies were thirteen years apart." I continued, "I know that the epiphanies are connected. They must be, and I didn't recognize either of the men. I just know that they were Satan and the Antichrist."

Michael asked how I knew who they were and how long the epiphanies lasted.

"The first, I have no idea except to say: who else would be standing on a cliff above the Lake of Fire? As far as the length of time, it could have been an hour or even thirty seconds for the first epiphany. The second was probably five minutes until I personally dismissed it, as I had totally observed and had seen enough."

"How did you dismiss the Devil?" Michael asked.

I did as I had been instructed as a child in church: I commanded, "Get thee behind me, Satan!" and the epiphany disappeared, and then the "scroll view" rolled up immediately as well.

I was up on my elbows again, thinking the very same thoughts as I had after the first epiphany. The Bible teaches that if you rebuke the devil, he will flee from you. He has no choice, according to Scripture. But you must be a Christian. It is the Holy Ghost, sent to Earth by Jesus Himself and acting on your behalf, who drives Satan out of our lives.

Dr. Phil said, "So that is it?"

"You must know Jesus and believe on Him as your Savior! There is NO other way but by Him!" Then I continued, "Gentlemen, I have no idea as to why I was chosen to see these two epiphanies. At this time, I do not know or recognize any of the three individuals in my two epiphanies, except for Jesus Christ Himself."

As for the identities of the other two? I am looking every time I watch the news or anything with current events. That includes the news, debates, world events, international governmental conferences—anything that may include these people whom I saw in the epiphany.

I am definitely making a concerted effort by watching and looking! I saw all three individuals clearly. I only recognized Jesus, who was also in the epiphany thirteen years ago in 1983.

I would say that what I have been allowed to see is most unusual in the overall scheme of things. Also, I know that it goes without saying that God ultimately has a purpose for it. I am more than certain, beyond any reasonable doubt, that there is a purpose still yet to be revealed. It will be one that is beyond my wildest imagination.

I have no concept as to what it may be.

CHAPTER ELEVEN:

The Prophecy Fulfilled

It was a great sendoff for our son. The only hiccup in the entire weekend was that Jen had traveled to LaGuardia without an ID. How she was able to get on the plane in the first place was a mystery; her ID had remained locked away in her dorm room at college before we made the trip. Thankfully, we were able to convince the airline: since they had permitted her fly to New York from Atlanta without one, why not let her fly back? The long stay at the Waldorf was now just a memory, and Mark was now on his way back to Texas to get married. It was fun, but also somewhat of a sad time.

I had promised Andrea that I would stay in touch. Now that I had her email, we could correspond with relative ease and I didn't have to inconvenience her with phone calls. I asked her to call me anytime, day or night, if she wanted to talk. I would wait a few weeks and let them digest the strange events I had revealed to them. I had not tried to convince them of the validity of what I said to them, focusing instead on giving a straightforward description of what I had seen. They were capable of deciding for themselves.

I had no control over either of the epiphanies, and I certainly could not help the fact that I actually saw what I saw. Whether I convinced them that the detailed descriptions were factual was highly in doubt, even in my own estimation. They were each trained to categorize such episodes as personal mental anomalies that should require the care of a trained physician.

However, during the short sessions, they all realized that I was keenly aware of the minute details. They had repeatedly asked me several questions in several different ways, but all were pertaining to the same thing. I was certain that they were as skeptical as any professional would be, and possibly more so because of the circumstances of two epiphanies. However, Andrea knew me. She knew my heart and the extent of all the gifts with which God had blessed me. She was not a doubter like a stranger might be. Before parting that morning, I gave Andrea permission to discuss the content of our meetings with several other associates and to ask them to offer an opinion.

How would anyone convince another person that they saw something that few, or possibly no one, had ever been a witness to—except perhaps two thousand years ago, in Biblical times? The simple answer is that you don't. Also, I knew full well that perhaps I wasn't the only person whom God had allowed to view the same, or similar, content of the visions. I had never made a claim to being unique, but I thought that—for whatever reason—God had looked upon me favorably in order to give me the prophecy to place before whoever would benefit.

Always I answered their questions in such detail, in an effort to confirm that I didn't create the descriptions of what had been revealed to me. I was very interested in their individual opinions, and I certainly was aware that this might not have been their first experience with interviewing similar subject matter.

I continue to see the mental images; they are with me all the time, even as I write this. They never go away! Someone asked me how I remembered all that I had seen, and I suggested that they try to imagine a person existing and walking through their daily lives with those images twenty-four-seven and for those images to be present for fifteen to twenty years and beyond. The images included detailed faces and the places that I was shown. Without consulting someone, how would I know who those people were and what they represented? Who would I consult without being thought to be unbalanced? As I divulged this information, I was risking that very thing. How would I fully reveal, and convincingly tell anyone, what I had been a witness to? How? Who would I go to? When would I see the men on the rock again? I had hoped never. I wanted it to be a bad dream that would fade in time, but it wasn't, and it would never fade from my memory.

Marie and I returned to our routines at home in North Georgia, and the children were both back in Texas. All the talk now was about the Y2K millennial end of the century in 2000. Even with all of the dire predictions that had been made, as the clock counted down to the stroke of midnight, nothing happened. As the clock struck midnight, we were amusingly waiting for something to happen! And? The clock simply kept on ticking. Crap! I was hoping for at least a dimming of the lights, but we knew that the hype was manufactured as efforts were made to profit from the uncertainty.

It was simply the year 2000. Besides Y2K, the dominant news of the day was the scandal in the International Olympic Committee in 1999, as a Mormon businessman named Mitt Romney had been asked to come in and help save the 2002 Winter Games that were scheduled to be held in Salt Lake City. I had believed, at that time, that his extraordinary organizational skills would be remembered and called upon someday as a future congressman or senator.

Meanwhile, as the world celebrated a new century and all the dire snafu predictions fell by the wayside, another *world-changing* group of individuals were planning to mark history with an indelible diabolical event in the very near future. Then came the day, and without warning. Just as in the Pearl Harbor horror, our generation was subject to a horror of our own on September 11th, 2001.

Every person who was alive that day remembers where they were, who they were with, and what they were doing while they watched in disbelief as the World Trade Center Towers were attacked for the second time in eight years. The first attack was a basement bombing in 1993. The second was more effective and ultimately successful in bringing the Towers down. Marie and I, along with the rest of the world, sat in numb shock as the widespread attacks evolved. It had seemed like only yesterday when we had been on top of the World Trade Center, viewing the city through the clouds. Our immediate thoughts went to the employees whom we had spoken with, the tour guides, the guards, and the concessionaires whom we had chatted with. Then it suddenly dawned on me that Eric's apartment was immediately behind the South Tower on Liberty Street.

I was stunned with the additional horror that the apartment may have been destroyed as the Towers fell. After the South Tower fell, it didn't take but a moment to realize that directly behind the Tower, Liberty Street, and the buildings along that street no longer existed. Eric's beautiful apartment on Liberty with the fabulous view of the South Tower surely had also been destroyed. I panicked again when I couldn't recall whether Andrea had told me that Eric and Sam had sold the Liberty Street Apartment, or if they still lived there. Constant emails and phone calls to Andrea and her office went unanswered. Then I tried calling the old number at my apartment on Beach 131st. The number no longer was in service.

Along with the thousands of horrible deaths, we were saddled with the additional prospect that our personal friends may have suffered death and destruction at the hands of these unknown idiots. Mark and Jen realized it also, and they were the first to call us, inquiring about my friends. Marie and I sat glued to the TV for days, praying but not knowing. I knew that if Andrea was safe, she would certainly give us a call to help relieve our anxiety.

I didn't know it at the time, but Andrea's friend—Rabbi Michael—had attempted to call our home and was not able to contact us. So he called a local synagogue, and their Rabbi Kitchener was able to inform us—on Andrea's behalf—that Andrea and Chris were safe. Sadly, he also had to inform us that Andrea's sister Sam was being counted among the missing. Marie and I both broke down and cried at the news. Sam was such a precious soul, as were all of the victims. We prayed for weeks, but she was never found.

The bad news kept coming in during such a short period of time. Andrea was doing support work in the NYU Hospital, mainly in the psych ward. Three days later, and even before I was ever able to speak with Andrea about the original attack and about her precious sister, Flight 587 left JFK and, only three minutes later, it fell from the sky onto my old street at Beach 131st. Again, panic set in as we didn't know whether Andrea was at the apartment or away at the hospital. We really didn't know if she still had an apartment there. It was hours before we knew that the apartment had not been harmed, and we knew that only because of a local Sky News helicopter that had shown a camera shot of my apartment. The crashing plane missed the apartment on the beach by only twelve hundred feet. Five precious people on the ground—including a young boy who was playing basketball in his backyard—died, along with all the passengers and crew aboard.

MY GOD IN HEAVEN! We asked: *what else?*

Marie and I both prayed, and we cried. My heart was aching to speak with Andrea, but I didn't interfere. I knew that she was safe and dealing with her own mental anguish. My friends at Rockaway lost over seventy resident firemen, police officers, and First Responders in the Twin Towers attacks. They received the calls and, without hesitating, they strapped on their equipment and left for the Towers. New York City, along with the entire nation, agonized over their loss.

AN EVIL LEGACY

Then, much later, came an *everlasting evil gift* to those who had survived the Tower's collapse and those who had tried to assist the

World Trade Center victims and rescue officials. For weeks, a camera was trained on the streets below the Towers. Smoke and flames were eventually extinguished. On the first few nights, the First Responders stood in long lines, awaiting the call to come forward and help in any rescues. While they stood in line, volumes of smoke and ash drifted through the air around them. I explained to Marie that the smoke was filled with asbestos and chemicals, and in all probability, many would eventually die an early death due to breathing the toxic air. The subsequent years proved my concerns to be true, and hundreds of victims and First Responders have died as a result of asbestos-related illnesses. It was an evil gift that kept on taking lives long after the Towers fell.

As the weeks passed, conspiracy theories abounded, and they would eventually prove that the terrorist plot was multifaceted with coordinated efforts from many directions. The operation was executed by persons and entities unknown—all with military precision. For a time, it created havoc in the world. As always, there had been longstanding animosity against our nation and its flag. For a vast number of other players, 9/11 was payback for various vendettas. Also, there was plenty of evidence that this wasn't just another revenge-bombing. Even though the attack was from the air, there were apparently plenty of players on the ground who were doing prep work to help the Towers fall.

Greater unsolved questions that may never be answered involved Building Seven, which was the first all-steel building in history to collapse from fire. Thousand of structural steel engineers signed a letter stating the impossibilities of that ever occurring. Even all-steel buildings in Hiroshima withstood the direct explosion of an atom bomb and never fell.

Then there was the news broadcaster who announced that Building Seven had collapsed. Six seconds later, it could be seen falling outside her NYC studio window. It fell six seconds *after* she announced that it had fallen. It appeared that something else was going on! Something else was definitely going on.

The Bible says, "The love of money is the root of all evil." Follow the money and you would find the eventual culprits. The 9/11 culprits will never be found. After 9/11, most of the topics of the day were largely concerning the End Times.

In light of the magnitude of the 9/11 tragedy, I discussed—with Marie and all of my friends—my views on the subjects as they may have related to the predictions in the Bible. I told Marie that it appeared that, over the past several years, there were many incidents falling in place that would be found to be as predicted in the Scriptures.

What did the Bible say about the Twin Towers falling? Nothing, as far as I know; but the unprecedented havoc it wrought was certainly on a Biblical scale.

THE GOSPEL HEARD UNTO EVERY NATION. A PROPHECY FULFILLED?

However, on Friday, September 14th, 2001, a special chosen God-loving Christian evangelist named Billy Graham led a one-hour service at the National Cathedral in Washington. It was broadcast to the entire nation and, miraculously, to every country in the world—including all of the Muslim nations. Reverend Graham proclaimed that God loves each and every one of us through His Son, Jesus Christ and that, by accepting His Son, we are assured eternal lives in Heaven. He explained the evil that we are dealing with on a daily basis, and he said that one day in the future, and at a time of God's own choosing, He alone will deal with the evil in the world.

The ultimate significance of this sermon was that, in the Bible's Book of Revelations, it is explained that the Gospel will be preached unto every nation on Earth—the Gospel of Jesus Christ (Matthew 24:25)—and then the End will come. When Billy Graham preached that sermon, it was heard in every nation on Earth. It was broadcast by T.V., radio, and newspaper. The entire Earth, at one time, heard the message. Bible scholars all claim that the historic sermon will be proclaimed nearer to the time of, or during, the Rapture; but it is my personal contention that Billy Graham's sermon was the one described in Scripture.

The astounding significance of this is the fact that most nations allowed the *BILLY GRAHAM* broadcast, even though they were Muslim—only because of the magnitude of the 9/11 tragedy. That express permission for Billy's broadcast of the Gospel of Jesus Christ in Islamic countries more than likely will never be granted again. I would challenge anyone to name an Islamic country that would allow a Christian sermon in today's climate. Ponder that thought!

The only reason that Muslims allowed the sermon to be broadcast in their countries on September 14th, 2001 was to show some measure of respect to our citizens and perhaps to further gloat over what they had accomplished in bringing the Towers down. Could that have been the sermon as described in Revelations? Perhaps.

Many were convinced the End Times were upon us. Jesus gave us the seven requirements Himself, beginning in Matthew 24:3 when His disciples asked, "When will this time be?" The Jews reestablishing their nation in the Middle East was the number one requirement leading to the Second Coming. The sermon that was preached unto all nations, perhaps the sermon by the Reverend Billy Graham, could have been the sixth requirement as defined in the Scriptures.

Some would argue that point, but I contend that Reverend Graham's sermon is the very one prescribed in the Bible. There was no more respected person to deliver the message than the Reverend Billy Graham, and it was definitely heard in every nation and in every corner of this planet. Also, it will likely never be heard in such a manner ever again.

Marie interrupted and asked, "What has all that got to do with us now?"

I suggested to her that we are living in the End Times as predicted in the Bible. "We go to church all of our lives and study the Scriptures. The Jews study the laws of the Old Testament, and other religions study whatever and worship whomever; but the reality is, there is a plan set forth by God Himself to bring all of this into fruition, and we are living within the timeframe of those times."

I explained to Marie that I didn't imagine what I saw, and I was more than certain that both of my visions were related to the End

Times—and most particularly to the immediate aftermath of the Rapture.

"What do you mean, aftermath?"

"God has allowed me to see. Why me? Don't ask, because I don't have a clue. Marie, sweetheart, the Bible has said that God will take all of His believers from the Earth suddenly and without warning. It's in the Bible—Daniel 9:20-27. There will be seven horrible years in which the Antichrist will reign. That is where the Mark of the Beast will come in to somehow mark and enumerate all who were not taken in the Rapture. Those who are living and remaining when God takes His Chosen in the Rapture will be required to take the Mark. The Chosen are those of us who have believed on His Son, Jesus, as their personal Savior beforehand.

"The Bible also explains that whosoever takes that Mark will be lost, and it warns against taking it. What will the Mark be? It will simply be the barcoded device or tattoo placed upon a person's body so that a scanner or satellite can read and track the individual. That man is well noted as the perfector of the barcode has six letters in each of his three names. His name is the number described in the Bible as 666.

"It's going to be a horrible time for those nonbelievers remaining. They will be existing in a world that they were totally unprepared for, and their greatest suffering will be born out of the fact that they didn't choose to believe in Jesus Christ as their Savior when they had an opportunity. They have a second chance, but not if they take the Mark."

Marie asked, "Anthony, why are you so convinced that all of this is going to occur? Why can't you just be interested in football, hunting, and golf like every other husband and ordinary guy?"

I laughed. "Marie, I love those things. I love football, skiing, fishing, and golf like any other human being likes their hobbies and avocations. I did not ask to see a vision of Heaven and of Jesus Christ! It was He who called me up! And I do mean UP! I did not ask to see a vision of the Lake of Fire, Satan, and the Antichrist! Don't you see? I had no choice in either matter. It was He who chose me, because now more than ever, it is constantly on my mind. I wasn't joking when I told you that God showed me Heaven in 1983 when I was forty-two years old. And then He allowed me to see Satan and the Antichrist years later, standing on our own cliff in front of that hole in the cliff.

"Also, in order to give me a hint at what I was seeing and to drive home the prime emphasis, God allowed me to see the valley eight hundred feet below our home right there in Georgia. In the background, the valley was a rolling lake of orange glowing smoking lava and fire!"

"Oh, Anthony!"

"Marie, I can't apologize for what God allowed me to see. *Why me, Lord*, has been my daily mantra ever since. But even though I clearly saw him, I still don't know the identity of the Antichrist, and it bothers me because I know that he is out there. I clearly saw his face. I know his every detail. I can still see his condescending smirk staring straight at me in that vision. I haven't a clue as to who he may be, but I only know that he is tall with a definite executive demeanor, and he has black hair with grey temples. As I have said before, he was dressed as if he had stepped out of GQ magazine.

"One thing is for certain: just as I immediately knew Jesus Christ, my blessed Savior, when He showed Himself and spoke to me, I will now know the Antichrist immediately when I see him elsewhere. And I am certain that I will see him in other world events or news. I am convinced of that. As I saw him, he was mature and grey in the hair of his temples. Otherwise, why was I shown his face, and for what purpose except to proclaim him to the world as a warning in any way that I know how? I assure you, I SAW HIS FACE! I will never forget that condescending stare.

"Am I a prophet? I certainly don't claim to be. You tell me! God gave me pertinent information. At twenty-six years of age, He told me that I would write a book, someday. I never imagined what I was to write about! Now, I have the subject with many details—enough, perhaps, to even draw a conclusion. I just need to find out who I saw in the vision. I am certain that he has a name, and I'm certain that he is walking the Earth as we speak. That means that he is with us today—not off into the future a hundred years from now. Today he is with us, walking among us!

"Meanwhile, my thoughts and prayers are with Andrea and Chris. I constantly pray that they will find Sam. I pray that she be found. She may even be injured and unidentified in a hospital. It bothers me to no end that I haven't been able to talk to, or even email, Andrea. I have reached out to the University, and to her maid at the beach, and I left word at the apartment house, but still I've had no response."

Finally, three weeks after the attack, I had to return to my project at Savannah. The entire nation had taken two weeks or more away from their jobs. One day, President Bush made a speech, encouraging the nation that it was time to return to work. He was correct. Even though I didn't feel like I wanted to leave Marie, I had to return to work. So I packed up and decided to drive over to Savannah late Sunday evening to start the week. I was in the South Carolina mountains when my cell phone rang. I saw the number, so I pulled over to an overlook rest area and answered it.

It was Andrea. It had been weeks since I had heard her voice. I was indescribably relieved to hear her voice and to know that she was well enough to call me. Marie and the children were as concerned as I about her wellbeing, especially in light of the fact that Sam was reported missing.

"Andrea?"

"Hi, Anthony!"

"Andrea?!"

Then a long period of total silence.

I didn't say anything. She knew that I was on the line.

I could tell that tears were pouring on her end of the call. After a while, I quietly spoke, and I told her how much we were in sympathy for her and the family and for her home.

She still said nothing, and I held on.

After what seemed like twenty minutes, Andrea began to talk with me. It was excruciatingly difficult to hear her speak through the tears and obvious pain as she struggled to regain composure and clear her voice. She tried to converse through the tears, and she travailed just to speak to me. I tried to handle most of the conversation, and I asked her just to listen if it would help and to give an affirmative or a negative to my questions. I was so very glad that she called, and I was concerned she might hang up.

I tried to find words to express how sorrowful we all were. Marie had been worried sick, not knowing what had happened to Sam and Eric and their families. I also explained that we could have this conversation at a later date, but we were so extremely concerned for her safety—and for Eric's as well—that if possible, we would certainly like to be brought up to date.

At that point, she completely broke down and began crying like a suffering child. I held on for fifteen minutes or more.

Finally, I quietly spoke. "Andrea, I'll call you back at a better time; I promise you that I will!"

"No! I'm good. I just started crying when I heard your sweet Southern voice."

"Are you back to work?"

"No. I am trying to get there, but after spending three weeks helping out in the psyche ward, I almost broke down myself. 'Horrible' is not the word to describe the psychological aftermath—much less the devastation and the event itself. It's a state of total dysfunction on half of Manhattan, and it leaches over into all the boroughs. Besides the Towers falling and all the loss of life from First Responders in Rockaway, the airliner fell on our street."

"Were you out there when it crashed? I couldn't believe that when I first heard. It was on our street, and when they first announced where it fell, I went weak—thinking that you or someone we knew may have been injured or worse. I tried calling everywhere, but I could get no reassurances."

"Yes. I was leaving the apartment when I heard the impact, and then I saw the fireball. It was scorching hot, and the concussion knocked me to the sand. I thought the fireball was going to come all the way out to the house on the beach. The heat from it scorched the paint and the roofs on houses on the street, and it set fire to the trees and houses nearby. It was directly at the intersection of our dead-end street, and if I had departed for work five minutes earlier, I might have been directly underneath it. It fell at the corner of the intersection. I didn't know any of the ground victims. It barely missed the Jordache house on the corner. It was so sad that I cried for another week, and we can't find Sam, which is totally unbearable. I know that she is gone, and I don't know how I'm going to go forward without her."

"Andrea, words can't express our sorrow. Sam is certainly precious and special. I pray you will find her. What about Eric and his family?"

"He was traveling that week, and Jill and the children were Upstate visiting their family before school started. Otherwise, he would have been back at the apartment with Sam. Thank God he was away. As far as Sam, we don't know for sure if she was in the apartment or coming or going. We can't find her, and we have pretty much accepted that she is no longer with us. Her children were with their grandparents on a trip out to Long Island. They are all moving back to the Beach at

140th at our parents' place. The renters had moved after the summer, and it's empty. That's a good thing."

"Andrea, I am so sorry. It's been a long while since we were there, and I was going to touch base with you and Rabbi Michael about our meetings, but I just never got around to it. He had an acquaintance notify us about Sam, and we are devastated. Sam was precious."

"Anthony, I do want to talk more about our meetings in the Waldorf. I have had long discussions with several well-versed individuals from the theological field and the psychiatric field, and you may very well be one for the books."

I laughed and told her that I wouldn't argue the point. "Don't concern yourself about that now."

"May I call you when I get settled back in Savannah later this week?"

"Please do. I'll be listening for your call."

We ended our conversation as I was arriving back at my apartment. It was very late, and the prospect of discussing our Waldorf meetings was something to look forward to; but it was not of great importance in light of the current tragedy.

That conversation would have to wait.

CHAPTER TWELVE:

One Phone Call And No More Doubt

A few weeks later, Andrea finally called when she found the time to talk at length. It had been several months since we'd had a conversation, and we had not spoken since the brief call after 9/11. We had much to catch up on.

I had spoken with her on several occasions in the years since our New York visit in '96, but we never discussed our meetings and my revelations. It was a difficult story for anyone to imagine, and the last time we spoke, she seemed to avoid any questions about the two meetings.

I would have drawn the same conclusions as any other person, trained or untrained, had I heard my own story.

Again, I told Andrea how deeply sorry Marie and I were about the 9/11 tragedy, and I added that she and her family would always be in our prayers. After we caught up on our recent news, Andrea told me that the reason for her call was, in fact, to finally let me know the opinions of Dr. Phil and Michael about my epiphanies.

I listened intently for the news that I already knew was coming.

She let me know that neither Dr. Phil nor Michael could give credence to what I had described seeing in the epiphanies. They were more concerned with my psychological wellbeing because, frankly, they had never been introduced to anyone or studied anyone who had ever experienced anything near the same experiences.

I can't say that I was too disappointed with the news. The consensus of negative opinions was much what I had expected. They were thumbs-down straight across the board, including even their constituents. Those who didn't know me, but were later informed in detail of the events, simply could not be convinced.

Of course, it was no surprise and I had expected it. I knew that Andrea truly wanted to tell me that Phil, Michael, and she wanted to believe. Reflecting back on the actual events, I had often thought that I wouldn't believe my own parents or siblings with such a wild tale.

Their doubting didn't help every time I tried to "un-see" what had been shown me. I was not a prophet. I refused to admit to the prospect that there was even such a thing in the modern era. Then I realized that there is no "modern era" for the Scriptures. They are unchanging, from Alpha to Omega. All predictions that were described in the Bible have either come to pass or will come to pass.

The Bible is the true and perfect word of God. And few were those in the day who believed that Jesus was the Son of God!

I went back to the Bible and studied the various prophets through the ages. My main concern was to not be a false prophet. I was very wary of that prospect.

I had seen, and I also knew in my heart, and I had been given the information. What should I do with it? Were the visual descriptions and details all that I would be allowed? Was there to be anything else? What on Earth was I to do with it? With all the self-examination, research, and soul-searching, my self-examination always led to the same conclusion: I SAW WHAT I SAW! And nothing will change what I saw for an eternity to come.

I saw what I saw and, with that being fact, I couldn't begin to deny it and I couldn't un-see it—nor could I make it so that it hadn't happened.

So I wondered what I should do with the information. The passing time was placing distance between those events and myself. The years 1983 and 1996 and their histories were fading into the past at a rapid rate, yet the details that were shown me never dimmed with age.

God's word is ageless.

I suppose that's where the conundrum was with both the theological view and the clinical view. The story was so far-fetched that it would have been dismissed out of hand at first examination from both perspectives.

I know that I myself would have shaken my head and walked off. Had my brother, the pastor at our church, or a close relative approached me with such an experience or story, I would have said, "If it isn't in the Bible, then I wouldn't give the benefit of any consideration whatsoever."

And it wasn't in the Bible! Or was it? There will be prophets in the End Times. Was God making one out of me? Surely not!

With 9/11 fresh on everyone's minds and Bush about to go find weapons of mass destruction in Iraq, it certainly felt like we were definitely well into the End Times. I was of the opinion that if we weren't already living in End Times, then we were bringing them about as quickly as possible in warring ways!

War was breaking out in all the Middle Eastern countries. By 2003, we were at war.

A friend and I went skiing for a week in Steamboat Springs, Colorado in March of 2003. We would have fun skiing moguls all day, then eat Chinese takeout in the hotel room in the evenings while watching the war in Iraq live and in living color until 4 a.m. The more we did battle in the Middle East, the more I imagined that we were smack in the midst of the End Times.

I remember the Scriptures as saying that there will be wars and rumors of war. There were both wars and rumors. They occurred for a multitude of reasons, and they eventually became the longest continuous conflict in the history of our nation. Looking back, I suppose that—in my personal opinion—the falling of the Twin Towers may have been the prelude to the End Times. Or perhaps that was the reestablishment of Jews to their country of Israel in 1948.

Jesus said that the generation that saw the reestablishment of Israel occur in 1948 "shall not pass away." How long is a generation? Seventy to one hundred years? Do the math! We are close to the end, no matter how you calculate it.

The Afghan War started in 2001 and would still be rolling strong fourteen years later.

My friend Jerry was my ski buddy. He was very intelligent, and he had been around. He was also a Vietnam veteran and a cryptanalyst who was always talking about war and the End Times. He was standing next to an intelligence officer in a secret monitoring facility on the Black Sea near Sinop, Turkey, when the Russians launched the first existing flying guided missile. The intelligence officer informed the Pentagon, saying that the missile "Cruised down range and cruised back to Russia"—thus coining the term "cruise missile" then and there on the spot.

Ever since that strange early morning in 1983, while sitting on my bedside, I suppose that the beginning of the end has been almost constantly on my mind also. I later found it unusual that I never ever mentioned my strange experiences or the things that I had seen to Jerry. I had known him since 1969 when he came home from Vietnam and went straight to Woodstock in Upstate New York.

We met on a golf course, and from then on, we struck up a friendship that would last nearly fifty years. We played golf. Lots of golf. Then we learned to ski, and we skied all over North America. We never fished or did anything besides playing golf and skiing.

Occasionally he would inquire about New York City and my time there. I never divulged much, except to tell him that my time there changed my life considerably. I never told him about Andrea or my other friends. He would have thought "affair," which it really wasn't. I never should have gotten as close to Andrea as I did because I would never have left Marie. I married for life. Marie was in my life and always would be. Andrea was a Jewish intellect and someone with whom I enjoyed having an occasional meaningful conversation. She was knowledgeable in almost any subject. She was a confidante who spoke with clarity in her reasoning. I enjoyed conversing with her and I simply adored her family.

Jerry always said that he didn't know which affected his outlook on life more, Vietnam or Woodstock. When the Towers fell, I did tell him about my former apartment and the loss of Sam, my friend's sister, whom I had known and adored.

It wasn't long afterward that I received word that Jerry himself had also died.

Over time, I had lost touch with Jerry, since I had to travel as much as I did. As far as Jerry was concerned, in the end, it may have been the substances he told me he had experimented with that caused his death. He passed away at an early age from dementia. In the end, hard drugs and LSD in one's early life sometimes can take a deadly toll on the closest of friends.

He had never been a flower child, but he was a byproduct of that age. I miss him greatly.

LIFE TAKES A CAREER TURN

I was still in Savannah during all of this, and I received word from another friend who asked if I would design a new home and possibly construct it for him. I explained that it had been a while, but that I would accept the challenge. I asked my job for vacation time and went home for a week to work on his house plans. As it turned out,

I would never return to my job. With the design and construction of my friend's home, I would start what was to be my new career.

As I was traveling home, I received pleasant surprise call from Andrea. "Are you driving?"

"Yes! How are you?"

"Please pull over and let's talk."

So I pulled off at the nearest exit. "I'm good," I said.

"I have a new email address. Are you set up?"

It was July 2012, and we had just received service on the mountain where we lived. We had previously had service, but our new home was so remote that we dropped it because we had no provider. Andrea wanted to give me her email address, so I wrote it down.

I laughed when I wrote the "andreapsycho@" on a business card, and she said factitiously, "Don't laugh, it fits." I would not argue that point!

We laughed and talked briefly, and she asked that as soon as I got set up along with an address that I should email her so we could keep in touch. I explained to her that at least she had still reached out to me despite the rest of her crew thinking that I was the one who was "psycho." She replied that I wasn't the least bit psycho, and she said they didn't think any such thing as that. She understood that something was tumbling through my life and that it had a hold on me. She wanted to keep closer tabs on me. She knew me, she knew my heart, and she was truly in my court. She just wouldn't admit to my realities in a professional way.

She did say that they could never explain away our incident on the beach long ago and all the precognizant episodes that I had experienced in my life.

"Thanks for the understanding, Andrea. As soon as I get a new computer and get online, I'll give you a call. And thanks for calling; it's great to hear your voice."

A few hours later, after the long and twisting drive through the North Georgia mountains, I was home. Marie was excited to see me, and she met me at the door.

"I have a surprise!"

"What?"

"I bought us a new computer and had internet service installed!"

"You have got to be joking!" I said. "Surely not."

That is as coincidental as it comes. I'd taken a call from Andrea earlier, and she had wanted us to set up internet service so we could exchange emails. I had previously suspected that it would take another year to get service up there in the mountains. Marie explained that she had subscribed for service months ago. They set up our email account, and we were ready to go as soon as we set up the new PC. I suggested that later in the evening, we should give Andrea a test try with her address so that we could keep in touch.

Marie had prepared a great meal, and we grilled steaks on the deck that evening. I told Marie about Andrea's call and the conclusion that all of the other "shrinks" had drawn concerning my explanations of the epiphanies.

She said, "I don't suppose you expected that they would have believed, do you?"

I just looked at her, smiled, and shook my head. "No."

The sun was low as we sat on the deck and looked eastward out into the valley eight hundred feet below. For a July evening, the air was unusually cool, and the late shadows were getting long.

I looked over my shoulder at the hole in the cliff. It was still there.

Just like the hole in the rock, all of my thoughts and memories were still present. As usual and as always, the entirety of all the events weighed on my mind. Now it had been years, and I still had no idea who the men on the rock were and what I would do with the information if I ever did learn who they were. For myself, it was a never-ending concern.

Later that evening, Marie and I sent our first email to Andrea.

THE PENINSULA, OUR NEW DEVELOPMENT

After being at home for a couple of days, I returned a call to my friend who wanted to build a new home. He asked that I meet him on the weekend to view a property that he was considering for his new home. I told Marie that I was excited about the prospect. I made the appointment, and Marie and I rode out meet Chris and his wife.

The property consisted of beautiful lakeside acreage and happened to be for sale for subdivision and development. Chris wanted to build there, but he only wanted one large lot on the water.

I looked at Marie, and she said, "It's better than driving all over the country, as you have been doing for the last twenty years."

Marie had wanted me to buy land and subdivide it. Now was our chance.

Chris and his wife gave me their ideas for their house, and we discussed subdividing a residential building lot for them. Marie and I agreed to purchase the land, and my career changed in the one afternoon that I became a developer.

Chris and his wife left the property, and Marie and I stayed behind to watch the sunset on the lake. In the meantime, I called the realtor and made preliminary arrangements to make the purchase. After that call, Marie and I found a spot to sit and watch the sun go down.

DEJA VU ALL OVER AGAIN

As the sun sank out of sight, Marie suddenly jumped up and said, "Oh my goodness!"

It shocked me because Marie didn't usually move that fast. "What's that matter?"

She pointed to a strip of land across the lake and said. "Do you remember that spot over there across the lake?"

I said, "No, what about it?"

"When we were dating, and we were only 19, we were looking over here from that point and discussing how beautiful this land is. Do you remember?"

"Yes, I do!"

"Do you remember what you said that day?"

"No, but I guess you are going to tell me!"

"I pointed this land out to you and commented on how beautiful it was, and you said, 'Yep, I'm going to build houses over there someday!' That was twenty-five years ago, and I remember that you proclaimed it as if would occur!"

I laughed and began to remotely hear "Twilight Zone" music, and then the sun went down.

There were so many odd occurrences and coincidences in my life that, over the years, Marie and I finally stopped counting. Nevertheless, it was property that we had picked out and placed on our wish list a long time ago. We felt strongly that it had been predetermined twenty years earlier that we should own it someday.

To my understanding of those little times in life such as that, and when a little Tinkerbell begins to ring from off-stage, those are the times when God has plans for you. They are there to let you know that He is in it with you.

Marie and I returned to our home, and I began making plans for a new direction in life as a builder/developer. Then it hit me.

Wait a minute! Had God sent me to New York and Trump Tower for training?

It would be another question that I would often ask myself. The career change suited me well, and Marie much happier with me at home every evening.

There was much work to be done, plus weeks and even months of planning, before even the first street could be installed. Time was critical, since Chris needed to get clearance on the lot and loans in place before construction could begin.

Both Marie and I kept in touch with Andrea as time passed. Occasionally, I would email her with personal notes, current events, or amusing local stories. Marie and Andrea would even swap old family recipes at Thanksgiving and around the holidays. Andrea had a great sense of humor, and she and Eric enjoyed laughing—especially at little stories about the Southern slant on life. Andrea even sent Marie recipes for Rosh Hashanah.

Marie asked me one evening, "What the heck is gefilte fish?"

The correspondence gave Andrea some relief from the "New York state of mind."

It was a hot July in Georgia, and we spent a great amount of time on the deck, cooking out with friends. Then came an amusing and strange phone call that changed even the minds of all my educated friends.

JAMES HOLMES' BODY SHOP

Late on the evening of July 19th, the phone rang.

I answered, "Mr. Marchant?"

"Yes, hello! Mr. Marchant, you don't know me, but my name is Franklin Wiley."

"Yes? How may I help you?"

"Are you buying that vacant property down on the lake?"

"I don't know yet. I suppose that word travels fast in these parts. Can I ask why you are asking?"

"Mr. Marchant, I own a business near there. I upholster cars and install convertible tops and vinyl tops, and I install carpet in cars and trucks, and I install vinyl beds in pickup trucks, and I been doin' it for near thirty years—"

"Mr. Franklin, that's very nice, but would you mind telling me why you are calling?"

"Well, I wanted to tell you that, first of all, I'm the one who owns that business. My sister has absolutely nothing to do with it. My daddy left it to me—lock, stock, and barrel—'cause for the thirty-nine years that he owned it, he gave my sister a brand-new car every year and didn't give me nothing! Not one damn thing!"

"Wow! Sorry to hear that, Mr. Wiley. Uh, mixed blessing, I guess. Could you tell me: why the call?"

Across the den, Marie noticed by this time that I was crying real tears at the humorous exchange, and I certainly didn't know where this conversation was going.

"Well, Mr. Marchant, I'll tell you that my daddy made up for it. He left me all that business and didn't leave my sister nothing! I'd say I got the business and she got the shaft! He got even with my bossy sister."

"Mr. Wiley, I truly appreciate the information and I enjoyed the story, but was there something you wanted from me?"

"Yes sir, there is!"

I was crying with laughter and holding my side with pain. Marie gave me a tissue to wipe the tears as I said, "Well go ahead and ask, Mr. Wiley!"

"Mr. Marchant, if I give you a good discount on a new vinyl top or seat covers, here's the deal: would you consider letting me go fishing on your property? I've fished for years out there."

"Why certainly, Mr. Wiley. Anytime you wish. And may I ask: is the fishing good out there on my property?"

"No sir, I ain't never caught nothing, but it's always been a nice pleasant place to wet a hook!"

"Mr. Wiley, fish all you want, and I'm truly sorry about your sister."

I hung up and my side was still hurting from laughing with Mr. Wiley. It was very late, and I sat there amused at the entertaining conversation with a true Southerner.

Much later in the evening, I suggested to Marie that I would send the text of that exchange to Andrea, as we had swapped amusing tidbits since we'd had the email set up.

Marie said, "If you do, please change his name and the name of his business so that it doesn't get back to him. It might be an embarrassment."

I suggested that I would wait until later or even the next day. Andrea would get a kick out of the "Southern" conversation.

It was a hot July 19th in 2012 when we went to bed that evening. I got into bed, still laughing from the call with Mr. Wiley, and I laid there forever. I couldn't seem to sleep. After an hour or more, I got up and told Marie—who was also still awake—that I was going to send an email to Andrea, describing the funny exchange with Mr. Wiley. She reminded me to be sure to change the name of his business. I agreed and set off for the office, turned on the computer, and started typing.

I was still amused as I typed the email, and I made up a fictitious name and changed the name of his business, just as Marie had suggested. I told the amusing story, signed it, and sent my regards to Andrea and Michael.

Then I pressed SEND and went to bed. I never noticed the time.

2:20 A.M. EST, JULY 20, 2012

Marie woke me up the next morning, on the 20th of July. We had much to plan and even more to do with the development project. After breakfast, the house phone rang. Marie answered it and Andrea was on the line, wanting to speak with me.

That was unusual! She never had called me in the morning. I thought that maybe she had received the email and was amused. Apparently, she wasn't amused, and she wanted to speak to me.

I thought that she might be having an emergency from the initial tone of her voice. "Andrea, good morning. How are you?"

"Anthony! I'm fine. This email that you sent—tell me about it, please!"

"Andrea, it was just a funny conversation I had with a new neighbor near my business property. I wanted to share because I thought you might find it amusing."

"Anthony, did you notice the time that you sent it?"

"Not really. I was sleepy and never noticed. Why?

"Anthony, what about the name of his business?"

I said, "Actually, Marie thought that I should change the name of his business to maintain his privacy. Why are you asking, Andrea?"

"Because as I understand it, you sent the email at 2:20 a.m. Eastern Standard Time! And you changed the name of this person's business to a name you actually just made up?"

"Yes, I did, to save him embarrassment. Is that against the law?"

"No, Anthony! You sent me an email at 2:20 a.m. EST?"

"Yes, I did. Andrea, why are you asking me all these questions?"

"I'm asking the questions because, at 2:20 a.m. EST, you sent me a message with the business name of 'JAMES HOLMES BODY SHOP.' "

"Andrea, what on Earth about it? I didn't want to call it by his business name, which is Mr. Wiley's Upholstery Shop. I just made one up! Besides, it was Marie's suggestion."

"Anthony, have you heard?"

"Heard what? Andrea—"

"In Aurora, Colorado, at 12:20 a.m. Mountain Time, a man named James Holmes was shooting and murdering twelve people. Anthony, how did you know to use that name?"

I sat there in total disbelief and silence.

"I apologize," I said finally. "I honestly didn't have any idea. Andrea, I was only changing the name of a business to protect a man's identity. I simply pulled the name out of the air as I typed you the email, which I immediately sent at 2:20 a.m. EST. Andrea, I just am that way. It is my nature, and I can't explain the process, nor can I even begin to explain why God gave me that ability. It happens often and without warning. I'm certain that it's only a strange coincidence."

"Tony, I don't believe that it was a coincidence."

"Andrea, I have been telling you the truth for years. I am terribly sorry for the event or shooting or whatever happened. I certainly didn't know. And I certainly didn't know in advance. It is just another unexplained coincidence recorded in my existence on this Earth."

"Anthony, you are weirdest person I have ever known!"

"I apologize, Andrea! Coming from a PhD in the field of psychology, that means a great deal. And there is nothing that I can do to change that, Andrea."

"Anthony! Oh, Anthony, I apologize. I'm beginning to believe, and that is a very difficult thing for me to do!"

"Andrea, I promise, I did have the two separate epiphanies that I fully described to you. They truly did happen as I described. I can't help the way God made me or what He has apparently revealed to me."

"No one can make this stuff up," she said.

"Andrea, I hate to interrupt, but may I call you later? I want to watch the news. Please give my regards to Phil and Michael when you call them about the email. You also have my permission to forward this on to them, if you care to."

Andrea hung up without replying.

Why was she upset? Was she perturbed that she hadn't committed to believing me in the first place? She had seen me flying backwards across the beach.

The email had noticeably upset her. She had never truly believed my ramblings, and now she was a firsthand witness and could not deny what had happened. It had left her at a loss for words.

I turned on the television and caught up on the news. I certainly hadn't known a thing about the shooting before I sent the email. The time stamp on the email was within seconds of the shooting, if not exactly at the same time.

Had Mr. Wiley not called with his amusing request to fish on my property, I would not have sent the email in the first place. To me, it was just the same as another story about a red '72 Ferrari Testerossa passing me on the Interstate, as it had when Mark was three years old and I suggested that he watch for one. That red Ferrari came truckin' by us five minutes later.

I cannot explain how it comes upon me—to blurt out a statement about something or someone, and then have it come true almost simultaneously. It is beyond all reason, and I consider it to be a gift from God. I didn't create myself. God created it in His mind billions of years ago. This was just my time to spend on Earth. Perhaps it was my purpose. I didn't argue, because it was a common occurrence with me.

A few weeks later, Andrea called and said, "Guess what?"

I said, "I have no earthly idea. What?"

She apologized, then informed me that Phil and Michael—as well as other constituents of hers—were beginning to believe.

I readily accepted her apology and explained that I was at a loss for an explanation, just as much as she was. She laughed and hung up.

It was late summer, and autumn was approaching with the fall debates for the 2012 presidential election. I didn't know it at the time, but I would soon be in for another life-changing revelation as the run up to the 2012 presidential elections began.

Marie and I were busy working with the engineers and surveyors who were subdividing the property for our subdivision. We already had clients lining up for building lots, and we were ecstatic about my career change and the future possibilities with the development.

Marie suggested we take a nice fall trip before we got tied up with the development to the point that we couldn't get away. She wanted to return to Jackson Hole to see the fall colors, then make a loop into Yellowstone before it closed around October the 12th.

I certainly didn't argue about the trip. It had been years since we had visited the area, so we scheduled for three weeks—from the last week in September through the middle of October. It was 2012.

As a teenage college student, I had worked in Yellowstone for two long summers. I never got over the enjoyment of the region's grandeur, and we had visited every few years with the family. Once I took Marie there for the first time, she was forever enamored with its remote and wild beauty.

This trip would be for just the two of us: no children or friends, just Marie and myself. So we prepared for a full week and packed to hike, trout fish, and play golf at Teton Village. Of course, we would tour the area as much as time would allow, but we had already seen it all and had accumulated perhaps two thousand or more photographs to prove it. I used many of the photographs professionally to create landscape scenes for my paintings.

A NAME FOR THE FACE

We would never know when it would be our last trip, and I told Marie that I wanted to forget the past months and years and pretend that we were born and raised in Wyoming and that the aspens, the eagles, the vistas, and the elk had been in our blood from birth. I imagined that my time spent in the South and in New York never happened, and for the short period of a couple of weeks, it seemed to work.

My mind was free of the clutter that was washed away by the sunrises over the Grand Tetons, mustangs under the cottonwoods, and the float trips down the Snake River. There is nothing like a good dose of the wild.

For a while, everything else was all washed away and I was re-freshed—standing in the center of one of God's greatest creations. And for a short time, I was free from all of my responsibilities, and my mind was refreshed.

One evening, near the end of our trip, we were sitting in our condo high up on the ski slopes at Teton village. I was watching the long afternoon shadows reaching southward over the golf course where Vice President Cheney's home was located. Marie turned on the TV for the first time on that trip. We had not watched it for two weeks.

Marie said that she needed to catch up, and I didn't argue the point. Had she not turned on the local TV at that time, I would have never seen the image that still shocks me to this day.

It was October 2012, and a local guy named Mitt Romney and his political opponent were debating for a seat on the city council in a little town in Wyoming. There was a point in the debate where there was a low camera angle shot on Romney just as he looked slightly downward. He had hesitated or misspoke an answer.

At that very moment, he realized that he may have just lost the debate, and the expression on his face was one of bewilderment but with a condescending glare. At that same moment, a shock that felt like a bolt of lightning went through my body. I shouted and leaped from the recliner, turning it over.

Marie screamed at the commotion at the same time and dropped cookware, bewildered by my reaction to the scene on TV.

I reacted with, "My God, my God. THAT'S HIM!"

"Who on Earth are you talking about? What's him? WHO'S HIM?"

"That is the tall second man on the rock—I saw him outside our house in the second epiphany! Marie, that is him!"

I'll never forget that epiphany and all of the details, right down to their cufflinks. THAT IS WHO I SAW. It was Mitt Romney!

"Anthony? That is too farfetched—up to the point of being crazy."

Marie, I'll take a lie detector test if I have to. Why God would allow me to have a epiphany in the first place is enough to drive a sane person to the brink!"

"Anthony, do us BOTH a favor and tell no one. Please! We are going home in a couple of days. I wish to goodness that I had never turned on the TV."

"Marie, it wouldn't matter—don't you see? I would have eventually seen him somewhere else anyway! God showed that man to me in an epiphany, and he was standing on the rock with the devil himself. God did it for a purpose! I saw what I saw sixteen years ago, in '96, in the upstairs bedroom of our new house. God has given me strange gifts that I rarely speak about, but everybody knows about them. God has purpose for me and purpose in what He has shown me. I simply have no idea why, or for what reason, but that is definitely the man

I saw in the second epiphany. I will call Andrea when we get back to Georgia."

"Oh Anthony, please don't. Please forget about this."

"Marie! Sweetheart, I can't forget it. His face has wrapped my mind up and has lived with me day and night, and now I have a name to go with it. That's him, without question. That's the man in the epiphany."

I kept asking: *why?* All I knew is that I need to go and tell people what has been shown me. I need to know why he was shown to me. The most frightening aspect of the entire matter was the identity of the man. Why did God show me a small-town Mormon politician?

I thought about calling Andrea from Jackson, but I decided to wait at least until I got to the airport.

When we arrived for our flight, I had second thoughts: *What if the plane crashed and the knowledge passed away with me? No one would have the important information or any warning.*

I broke away from Marie for a few minutes and called Andrea's office number. I was hoping to catch her in a quiet setting so that she would fully understand what I had to divulge.

No answer! It was time for our plane to depart—they were giving the last boarding call at the gate—so I just left a message on her voicemail: "Andrea, this is Anthony. This is brief, but I wanted you to know that the man in the epiphany was definitely Mitt Romney. Make no mistake. That is definitely who I saw in 1996. He is a small-town Mormon politician. I'll explain when I return home."

The gate closed behind me, and I found my seat with Marie as we left the runway.

CHAPTER THIRTEEN:

So Now We Know

The late flight home out of Jackson Hole was beautiful, and I gazed out at the Grand Tetons as we lifted off. There was fresh snow at 10,000 feet of elevation, and the yellow brilliance of the aspens and the cottonwoods made for a breathtaking contrast. The low western sunset was streaming light through the canyons of the Grand Tetons and Mount Moran. The peaks were casting long shadows across the Snake River and Jackson Lake.

My final glance at the surreal scene gave me a brief urge to go back immediately. I looked down as we circled over the Jackson Hole Terminal where, in 1963, I was fortunate to have met President John F. Kennedy. At the time, we had been surveying the airport nearby, and we gathered to watch him arrive. That was also on a September day, and President Kennedy was there on a western political tour when the Rat Pack joined him for a long weekend of rest at the Jackson Lake Lodge.

Only two months later, JFK was dead. I was crushed by the news.

Between Vietnam and the assassination, the realization that my youth had abruptly come to an end was almost more than I could bear. The negative events and the uncertainties on the horizon meant that my youthful adventures were over, and I faced a most uncertain future. What a screwed-up time it was becoming!

However, God had other plans. It was that year, when I returned home, that I met Marie, and she steadied my ship.

My dad asked me if I was certain that Marie was the right one. I told him that ever since I was nine years old, I knew that someday I would marry a girl named Marie. He smiled approvingly.

As we flew home to Atlanta, I also thought back to all the adventures that I'd had when I was only 19.

My first airplane flight was out of Jackson Hole on Frontier, and our only stewardess, Judy Blume, assured me that we wouldn't crash; but with our particular pilot, we would be in for an adventurous flight. I was on my way to Denver to buy a 62 MGA 1600 MKII. There were only eight people on the plane.

We took off in the Frontier DC3, and sure enough, the pilot flew over the top of the Grand Tetons above 13,000 feet, and then he turned south. He then flew lower, just a few hundred feet over the mesa tops—sometimes scattering herds of pronghorn antelope. As we cleared the mesas, we could see 2000-foot drops below as the cliffs were revealed. I later learned that our pilot had flown an F-86 in the Korean War. He gave us a fun ride.

When we landed in Denver at the old Stapleton Airport, there was but a single taxi waiting to pick up passengers. As I walked out of the terminal, Judy came running out behind me and rode with me into Denver. She and I spent that afternoon and the next day looking for the MGA 1600 MKII that was listed.

Sadly, someone got to it before I did. With no car, I had to pay fifteen dollars for a ticket to fly back to Jackson the next day. I was truly disappointed, except for the company of Judy!

Those were carefree days that disappeared when the Vietnam War came along. It was "The Age of Aquarius." There were times that I compared that time period to the carefree days in America that led up to the Twin Towers attack. Events such as 9/11 always bring wars. Perhaps someday, we will learn the truth about 9/11.

Suddenly, out of nowhere, America changed—with almost all of the people's attitudes changing negatively along with it. We went from happy and carefree to war mode within 24 hours. The war industry is owned by players from all nations. $100,000 bombs make politicians rich as they kill innocent people and try to adjust politics to their agendas.

As we flew home, Marie and I discussed our new adventure with the development. I asked Marie if she had sensed any change in her friends' attitudes after 9/11. She explained that her confidence in her own wellbeing had been compromised. It came from not knowing what was going to happen next after the big shock, and then having to put plans into a "wait and see" mode for the future.

We were certainly still sad about the Twin Towers and deeply saddened by the loss of Sam, but Marie reminded me that 9/11 was our new Pearl Harbor. We had recovered back then as a nation, and we will never forget. We would recover this time, and the guilty nations would pay a price; and then—again—we will never forget.

As the sun set and the horizons grew dark, I thought about the message that I had left Andrea, proclaiming Mitt Romney to be the second man in my revelation. I could only imagine the expression on her face when she heard that strange message. It would be another thing that she and her friends would probably never bring themselves to believe. For certain, they would want to hear the details about how he was revealed to me. I had not told Marie, but I was already planning a trip back to New York to meet with Andrea and Michael. With their help, I intended to try sorting out the meaning of what I had seen.

Now that I had put a name to the face, there were other hundreds of questions to be answered. The main one was: why Mitt Romney? Besides being a politician and somewhat of a local celebrity, why would Romney show up in an epiphany that God allowed—or even required—me to view?

After having seen who it was, I remained in a bit of a shock. I tried to connect him with any current event or international incidents or issues, but at that time, there were no connections that would be considered significant in my mind.

I had tried to stop calling them epiphanies—I'd only experienced two; but those two were unimaginable, to put it mildly—even though that's what they were. To my understanding, those two epiphanies represented the Beginning and the End! The Alpha and the Omega! I started calling them my "revelations." People would look at me with trepidation when I pulled out the "epiphany" word.

Regardless, Andrea was certain to have my message by now. I couldn't use my phone on the plane, and Atlanta was three more hours away. It would be the next day before I could speak with her. As frightening as the news was, I still had to smile as I imagined her learning of my message.

For sixteen years, I had been diligently visually searching for the second man, and suddenly, there he was. He was revealed to me. I immediately knew, without a doubt, who he was.

I placed the headset on as I tried to get some sleep for the remainder of the flight. As coincidence would have it, my familiar song was playing: "When You Get Caught Between the Moon and New York City..."

I was thinking, "I really did that very thing."

I turned my face toward the window and looked out into the twilight over the prairie. I couldn't help feeling a bit sad as my past rolled away below. I didn't let Marie see a grown man almost cry.

It was pouring rain as we landed in Atlanta. I dreaded the drive into the mountains and suggested to Marie that we stay in Atlanta overnight, but she wanted to get back to her home on the rock, as she called it.

I turned on my cell phone, and I had ten calls listed from Andrea and a couple of others from New York numbers. Goodness, what did I suppose that was all about? I assumed that Andrea had gotten the word. I told Marie that returning those calls could wait until tomorrow.

The entire issue was becoming an even greater lifelong mystery and headache, now that I had actually seen the living version of the tall man in my "revelation." I had resigned myself to the fact that I would never know his identity, and that it would all go away as a bad dream and total nonsense. But then he appeared in the debate. Now I knew who he was. He was even dressed the same way, just as I had seen him years earlier. My lifelong propensity to note detail assured me that he was the same person with the same condescending expression on his face that I had seen on the rock. That electric jolt of realization had struck me, jolting me out of my chair and certainly out of my comfort zone.

In short, I know who he is. As I see him in the news and in other venues, I know what he will eventually become and what he will do. As with the epiphanies that God had allowed me to view, I now live with that factual knowledge day and night. It continues to give me cold chills from just thinking about it.

We made our way to the long-term parking, picked up our SUV, and drove home. Marie said nothing until we were almost home. There was lightning and pouring rain—a perfect setting for a horror movie as we approached the house.

I asked Marie if she was feeling well.

"I will be fine once we get settled from the trip. I just hate the fact that you saw that man on the debate. That ruined the joy of the trip for me. I hope you aren't planning to go back to New York, now that you think you know who he may be."

"Well, it's not who he may be, but who he actually is," I said. "I am most certain now of who he is. Marie, we should talk about the whole saga in a couple of days. I've been privileged to have a person shown to me sixteen years ago, and apparently the reason for that revelation is coming to fruition. I can't stop or change that. But I suggest we first rest a couple of days, and let me discuss what I saw with Andrea and Michael. After that, I will find a way to lay this thing to rest. This saga has been with me now for a full one-third of my life."

Marie kissed me and told me that I was her hero, and that she had loved me with all her heart from day one—no matter what. I knew long ago that I had married the right girl.

It was great to be home, but our period of resting up from the trip didn't last long. I had much to do to plan for the project, along with servicing my current projects; and then there was the plan to visit Andrea and Michael in New York.

I had spoken at length with Andrea the day after we returned from the trip. As Marie had suggested, Andrea and Michael wanted us to fly up at their expense and discuss my possible recognition of the man from my revelation. They wanted Marie to come up with me, but Marie refused—largely because she didn't feel comfortable around "those folks."

"Why can't they just speak with you over the phone without your having to travel?" she asked.

I told her that they wanted to discuss all the possibilities. I truly did see what was revealed to me and, if it were true, I asked her to think about the implications those epiphanies would have toward our current real world.

Marie answered, "Oh Lord, why us?"

When she said that, I told her that I had been asking myself the same question since 1983. I live with it daily, and even though it is worrisome, "I have come to accept it and consider that a great blessing and a responsibility that was bestowed on me. It is a blessing that no one knows about and a situation that I must see through to the end. God showed me all that I saw for a definite reason."

"You didn't answer my question!" she cried. "When will it be over, Anthony?"

"I have no idea; I don't know!" I understood that Marie was as frustrated as I was. I smiled and finally answered, "I suppose when the Rapture occurs!" Then I added, "Andrea is going to call. Do you want to fly up to the city for a couple of days or not? The tickets are free!"

"No, you go on alone and behave yourself. I want to enjoy our deck and some solitude for a few days before we float off with the Rapture."

The following day, Michael called and asked if Marie would be traveling with me. I explained that she was not going to make the trip. Then Michael informed me that there was a round-trip ticket awaiting me at the Delta concierge at Hartsfield. I could come whenever I could arrange to get away, and he asked me to let him know the flight.

Shortly after the call, I received a text from Eric: *Anthony, we are anxiously awaiting this meeting, please be careful.*

I answered, expressing my gratitude. I told him that it might be a wild goose chase, but I didn't think so.

He replied: *No problem. We would enjoy your company, and we want hear what you have to say firsthand.*

Marie asked me when I was going. I told her that it would be a couple of weeks before I departed. The Auburn-Georgia game was eight days away, and we had great tickets. I wasn't going anywhere until after that weekend.

I made flight reservations for the following weekend and notified Andrea. For a change, I caught a noonday flight and landed at JFK in the daylight. Michael had a limo pick me up at JFK, and we took the short ride out to Rockaway. Andrea had moved back into her parents' beach house at Beach 140th, and she was waiting for me at the curb when I arrived.

I set the flight bag on the curb, and she smiled and placed her arms around my neck and shoulders and her forehead against mine. We hugged for a long time and said nothing for a time.

Finally, after several thirty-year-old flashbacks, I said, "It seems like only yesterday." It had been six years since we had last met. She never changed.

She just nodded and still didn't speak. To my pleasant surprise, Phil Landers had joined the group. He had driven down from his home in Upstate New York. It was very nice to see him again.

I asked Andrea if we could walk along the beach before we went in. She said, "Good idea."

We excused ourselves from the guys and went for a walk. And we walked for about an hour or more. The sea breeze felt great after the flight, and the smell of the salty spray cleared my mind a bit.

The last time I had been with Andrea on the beach was that last late afternoon when I watched her surf. I remembered every wave and every curl from that day. It had been six years since the Waldorf trip, and it had been over thirty years since she and I had met for the first time and flown together from Atlanta.

The beach walk was refreshing after the long flight. The Atlantic was putting on its winter green color, and the tops of the waves were covering us with light spray. I had taken off my shoes, and my feet were freezing, but it felt great. I knew that this would be perhaps my last walk on this beach. It had been a long time since the summer of '57 and the Scout Jamboree trip when I had stayed along this strip of sand.

We walked passed the big green Cape Cod summer home where the neighborhood Fourth of July party was held. Andrea asked if I recognized it.

"Tell me; I'm not sure."

"It's where we had the cookout, and you mysteriously flew backwards, sprawling across the sand," she answered.

I laughed and told her, "My being off-balance and thrown for a loop has never really stopped."

Andrea commented emphatically, "You were not off-balance that night!"

Whatever the force had been, it had kept Andrea and me apart for all those years.

It was Saturday night, and Andrea cooked out on the beach for a few friends that evening. Eric stopped by and gave me a brotherly hug. He expressed how much he missed having me around. We talked about old times until the wee hours of the morning.

The next day, Michael came over, so the original crew was gathered to listen to anything that I had to add to the mystery. The following afternoon, we gathered in Andrea's sunroom, and the questions began to pour out of Michael and Eric. Their interest was more curious about the James Holmes incident than the devil and the Antichrist epiphany and my final recognition of their identity—that is, at least the identity of the Antichrist. I suppose that the devil could be walking around in a famous person's face and body also. I do know that God only allows him to be in one place at a time anywhere on Earth. He stirs up enough messes even with those constraints, anyway.

I asked Michael and Eric why the James Holmes incident would be of more importance than the identity of the people I saw in either of the revelations. They both answered that James Holmes was more important since there was hard evidence due to the email that I had sent Andrea—with the incredible timing of an event that they had knowledge of—versus an epiphany, which they had no way of verifying. The James Holmes incident allowed them to have confidence in my descriptions of my apparitions or epiphanies.

It was hard evidence rather than an ethereal epiphany that allowed them to believe. Isn't that a juxtaposed to the way Christ wants his followers to believe? He wants us to believe by faith and not by sight. If we only have faith! Then God promises us an unimaginably wonderful eternal life.

Eric began by asking me about the timing of the James Holmes Body Shop email that I had sent to Andrea a few weeks earlier and exactly how that came about.

After a detailed explanation, Dr. Phil spoke up with a resounding, "I'm beginning to believe!"

He was being facetious as usual.

Perhaps I had two of them on my side. I smiled and shrugged my shoulders, then suggested that these sorts of coincidences were a reasonably common occurrence around our household. Had I been a stranger to them, they would have been skeptical to the point of not even giving credence to the email. However, they could not deny the incredible timing. Personally, I considered it to be serious precognition because of the exact precision of the timing.

"How did you choose the name, 'James Holmes' Body Shop'?" they wanted to know. "How did that come about? How did you do that?"

I explained that I received a call from a local businessman who owns an automotive upholstery shop near my property. He simply wanted to fish from my property. He told me so many unnecessary—and very personal—details about his life and business that they were hilarious to me. Finally, he got to the point and asked if he could fish from my property. By that time, I could barely answer, but of course I gave him permission.

I was so amused that I couldn't sleep that night, so I decided to note the details of our conversation in my journal for possible future reference. I also found it so amusing that I decided to email the story to Andrea to give her a smile.

Marie had asked what I was doing, and when I told her, she suggested that I change the name of Mr. Wiley's business so as not to cause any embarrassment to him. Out of the blue, I chose "James Holmes' Body

Shop" instead of his upholstery shop for the name. I wrote details of our conversation in the email and sent it to Andrea. The time was 2:20 a.m. EST. It was 12:20 a.m. in Colorado when I sent the email.

That is the entire story. I considered it to be extremely odd, but otherwise a coincidence and nothing more. Others have said that it was too much of a strange coincidence not to be noted. I would simply ask: *What does it prove, even though it does feel strange when that sort of thing happens?*

Andrea asked, "How many times has it happened before?"

Many times. At one time, I had kept a log with the time, date, and a description of each incident as they occurred. If they were notable enough, then I would remember and record the details.

Another example, as simple and trite as it may seem, incident that I recall was my little teenage sister-in-law asking me to guess the number of rolls of toilet paper that were required to decorate her homecoming float. I was trying to study for a college final exam and she was annoying me. Quickly told her, "136 rolls. Now go away!"

She screamed, "How did you know that?!"

Another was dreaming the serial number of a single defective relay amongst four hundred such relays in a control system. I dreamed the number of the defective equipment.

Those may be simple examples, but they are a typical occurrence in my life.

Anyway, the number of incidents is remarkable. I can't help it, nor can I shut it off. It's a natural part of being me. This I can assure you: I cannot read your mind, even if I tried; but I can watch a football game and occasionally predict a pass interception or a fumble before it happens.

Marie would slap me on the arm and say, "Stop that! You are weird." But these things just pop into my mind on occasion.

It also works as a defense mechanism, and I have learned to pay attention to it over the course of my life. I always seem to know when significant danger is around—to not turn down a certain road or venture down a particular trail. For example, I could always sense the presence of bears in Yellowstone during the years when I lived there.

Michael then asked me how I felt when I supposedly recognized Mitt Romney as being the tall man in my epiphany.

"Michael, how would you think that you would feel—knowing that a man, whom you viewed in a strange epiphany sixteen years earlier, was an actual real individual? Not only that, but he is also a man of power, and he is alive and walking the Earth as we speak? He will command great power in the end. It was frightening beyond imagination to see and recognize a person live on TV whom you had seen in a horrible scene near the gates of Hell sixteen years earlier!

"I have lived with these epiphanies for almost thirty years, and to finally realize that they are connected in some way and that they have a profound real-world significance and purpose is overwhelming. The fact that God allowed me to see that was terribly frightening. I came back up here—not just to re-describe my epiphanies, but to seek answers and logical reasoning for having experienced them. Not only that, but you are also my friends. You must take heed and believe in what I tell you. It is no insignificant thing that the Antichrist is alive as we speak! The time is here, and soon!"

Andrea then informed me that they had checked on a certain Mr. Mitt Romney. He is definitely a Mormon leader. He was noted to have survived a deadly head wound in his youth or early adulthood while he was hunting elk with a friend in Montana. A stray bullet killed his friend, and Romney was struck in the head by the same bullet. The game wardens' Search and Rescue got Romney out and noticed no pulse. They flew him out—only for him to be pronounced dead at a clinic. Then he was carried to a local hospital, and he ended up walking out of the hospital with little or no effect from the experience.

That incident alone is no light matter, in my opinion. He has already had a deadly head wound that was miraculously healed, and that is recorded knowledge. I challenge anyone to look that up.

All I can tell all of you is that this is definitely the man whom I saw in my epiphany in 1996. And this is the same man who was in the local debate.

Despite being frightened at first by what I saw, I am now beyond all of that. I asked myself: what did I see that early morning in the upstairs bedroom of our home? And how did I know for certain that it was the same man? Why would it be Mitt Romney and not some Italian priest, a Romanian, or Father Flannigan from down the street? Why couldn't it have been any person besides who I had said it was?

But it wasn't. It was Mitt Romney, a local Mormon leader! He is the Antichrist, alive and walking this Earth as we speak!

I explained again to the group about my family's trip to Jackson Hole and how Marie turned on the televised local political debates to watch. Out of boredom, I had watched the debates with her. Well into the debate and during one particular question, Romney was at a loss for a quick retort to his opponent's statement. He even stuttered a bit while trying to give his answer.

At that very second, he glared blankly into the monitor, and I was struck simultaneously with that same definite electrical static as the shock of realization that I was again staring into the face of the second man on the rock. After sixteen years, there he was, looking back at me again. Frightening? Transitioning from an epiphany to a reality can be a very frightening thing!

He is a real person! He is alive! He was standing next to Satan! He was overlooking the Lake of Fire! He was outside my house! He was on TV there before me in Jackson Hole alive and in person! And I know who he is! There is no doubt whatsoever that he is the same man from my 1996 epiphany.

Andrea spoke, and for everyone's benefit, she asked me to again describe the scene on that night of the second epiphany.

We had been living for less than two years in our new home. I went to bed upstairs because Marie had already gone to sleep in our bedroom. I simply didn't want to disturb her.

I had almost dozed off when I was awakened by a frightening low and very slow "ripping" sound, like heavy canvas being torn in two.

The wall before me had simply rolled apart vertically like a scroll. There before me, standing outside the house, were two men. One was tall, standing slightly behind and to the right of the shorter of the two. He was looking straight at me with his head cocked slightly downward, as if he were looking at me with trepidation and a condescending attitude. The other man was casting his attention out over our valley as if to look away from my visual eye-to-eye exchange with Romney.

God placed them both there so that I would be possibly an identifier of who he was. I saw him at that time, and now I know who he is—without a doubt. I know his name, and I will monitor his whereabouts until the day that I die—or until the Rapture comes!

I saw him standing on our cliff, where God placed him for me to see. I now am beginning to realize God's express purpose in my existence, and that is to give the warning that the time truly is drawing nigh and that the end will come very soon!

The light being cast up from the valley was noticeably orange from the orange glow of the valley, and that orange glow was reflected on their dark silver suits.

Michael asked again, "Anthony, describe the glow, and tell us: where was it coming from?"

I explained that the valley eight hundred feet below my home was appearing as the "Lake of Fire, rolling in waves like an ocean." That is the best and simplest way that I can describe it.

"An ocean of fire?" Eric exclaimed, "My God! As far as you could see?"

"As far as I could see. It was like the cauldron of a never-ending volcano or the surface of the sun! Eric, I don't mean to frighten anyone, but that is what my Lord wanted me to see. He allowed me to see

that—for whatever His purpose may be. I am relaying the message
to you! To this day, I have never figured out why I was one who was
allowed, or even required, to see the epiphanies—unless my telling,
and warning, you and the world is what God ultimately wants me to
do. I finally reconciled myself to the fact that I am a personal witness
to the Antichrist and to who he is!"

I continued re-describing what I saw:

After I gazed at the men and the scene for perhaps five minutes,
at the most, they said absolutely nothing to me. However, when I
had observed enough—including every detail possible—and as the
Antichrist glared back at me, I finally answered their appearance with
a determined and forceful, "GET THEE BEHIND ME, SATAN!"

I made certain that I memorized all of the details before I said that,
because I knew in my heart that I would never have another opportunity.

After saying that, the revelation disappeared immediately. I was left
staring at a blank wall. That scene is etched into my memory, now
and forever. Make no mistake, I remember every detail, and I have
since wondered—at every moment of every day—why God allowed
me to see that, along with the Lake of Fire, right below our home.
So, now that I know who he is, I finally realized that God wanted
me to know that these two were Satan and the Antichrist—and, more
importantly, they are walking the Earth as we speak!

The group sat in stunned silence, not knowing what to say or ask next.

After a few moments, I said, "This is what I know, and you may
add to or disagree as you wish.

"The Jewish people are being regathered in unbelief from all over the Earth to a State of Israel that was reestablished in 1948. The Jews reoccupied the city of Jerusalem in 1967. Then the land of Israel will be reclaimed from desolation, and that process is continuing. You will start speaking Hebrew again, and you are!

"All the nations of the world will come against you over the control of the city of Jerusalem. The Arab nations will join to attack you, and you will win, and then you will enjoy peace and prosperity. But it will not last long!

"The Russians will still have their effort to join with Muslim nations and invade Israel. They will be supernaturally destroyed by God, just as described in Ezekiel. At this point, it has been prophesied that the Antichrist will guarantee the security of Israel, allowing the Jews to rebuild your Temple.

"Here is where it becomes frightening, as I have seen the Antichrist and have recognized him as a Mormon. It would then only seem logical that, in order for him to have the authority and significant military power to protect Israel and allow them to rebuild the Temple, he would have to be in a position of great power—such as that of the President of the United States. See Dan 9:27.

"Things will go well for 42 months while the Temple is being rebuilt and finished. After it is complete, the Antichrist will walk into the Temple and declare himself to be God! See Matthew 24:15-18.

"The Jews will not stand for that, and they will reject him. Then the Antichrist will destroy over two-thirds of you Jews in an attempt to annihilate you. See Revelations 12:13-17.

"At the end of the tribulation, when the Jews have been almost defeated, they will turn to God and receive Yeshua as the Messiah. At this time, Jesus will return and regather all 'Believing' Jews to Israel. See Deuteronomy 30:1-9. Israel will be established as the prime nation of the world. Then the Lord will bless the world by fulfilling His promises made to Israel—see Isaiah 60:1 and 62:7. The blessings of God will flow out through the Jewish people during the millennial rule of Jesus. See Zechariah 8:22-23."

I used their moments of silence to strongly suggest that, even though they may believe entirely differently than those of Christian faith, they—as Jews—have their own traditional beliefs concerning the Rapture. I explained to them that, with my recognition of Mitt Romney—a man who is now in his late sixties—the ultimate realization of this prediction could not be too far off in the future.

In 1983, I saw firsthand a brief window into Heaven as I stood with the Lord. I saw firsthand the ecstatically happy multitudes, who were skipping and converging toward the gate in their ethereal bodies and dress. And then, along with them, I saw the Crystal Sea and the incredible mountains beyond. I have had the rare honor of seeing where I am privileged to be going someday—as a believer in Jesus Christ, my Savior! I have seen Heaven. Even though the epiphany lasted only a few short minutes, it would take a lifetime to describe what I was allowed to see.

Then, years later, I was allowed—or perhaps required—to see the Lake of Fire, and it was horrendously frightening. It was certainly not a place to even think about spending a single second of your existence, much less an eternity.

Jesus said, "I am the way, the truth and the life. No one comes to the Father but by Me."

I continued, "Finally, I say this to you sitting here before me: I love you as brothers and sister! I love you all, and knowing you has been a wonderful part of my life; but eternity is forever, guys! It is forever and ever!"

My friends there were all Jewish, and they were all stunned. They didn't utter a word and they didn't move. I thought they might get up and walk out, but they didn't.

I continued, "What God showed me in 1983 came at the time when I had returned from working here in New York. Nevertheless, it was as true as the sun was shining. He allowed me a short visit to the Promised Land, and He gave me brief instruction that changed my life and sent me on my way. Perhaps my being here among you as a witness at this time is it!"

I explained further. I remember that, from out of nowhere—at the age of 26 years old—I told my friend that one day I would write a book. It may be that is my ultimate purpose: to give warning that it is imminent time for His return, as He predicted. That would be the subject matter of the book.

Think of the logic of Mitt Romney being the Antichrist and having the political power to enable the Jews to rebuild the Temple, which will take three and a half years. Only 42 months! That *has* to mean that he is a leader of the United Nations or the United States of America—possibly even President!

Will this come about during the next election cycle in 2020?

Will Trump run again? May God forbid any nefarious disruption to our normal rule of government, although—with the current vitriol being fostered by those opposed to the current rule of a "Constitutional Republic"—bad things may be on the horizon that we, as a nation, have never even dreamed of.

Will Mitt Romney rise to power? It would seem that he must, if it is the Antichrist who will enable the rebuilding of the Temple by the Jews!

I predict that Mitt Romney will either run for POTUS and somehow win in the relatively near future, or he will be selected to a position of vast dictatorial power over our nation as the result of some unimaginable catastrophic event that would require an emergency government to be placed in charge of our nation. Washington DC would have to be wiped out, if that scenario were to take place.

What you also *must* understand that, for the Antichrist to be in power and build the Temple in 42 months, all of the Christians will have already vacated the Earth by way of the Rapture. *We will not be here* as the Antichrist sees to helping the Jews rebuild the Temple.

As I finished, Andrea, Eric, Phil, and Michael all sat in stark silence.

After a few moments, I explained that, for certain, I had seen both epiphanies and that I would even take a lie detector test—if necessary—to convince them and to prove the veracity of what I was shown.

Andrea interrupted and said that wasn't necessary, as she truly believed what I was telling them. She was convinced.

The Bible says that, in Him, all things are created and unto His own purpose. Was it God's will that Joseph Smith see an angel? How did Joseph Smith's description of an angel compare with what I was allowed to see when Christ called me up? I beg you to research that and compare. Joseph wrote the description on handwritten paper notes.

I believe that Jesus knew my every thought and saw to it that my observation of Him was detailed and thorough as it was taking place. In my description of Christ, I mentioned His astounding countenance that shone as if my hand would disappear within His garments: pure, glowing, without blemish, and with an incredible brilliance that was totally observable without being blinding.

When he sensed that I had adequately observed Him and His surroundings in detail, He faded upward and left me numb and shocked, sitting on my bedside. I immediately and reverently said to myself: *my Lord and Savior, what was that all about?*

That was MY Jesus that I saw—the most beautiful creation that I had ever seen or ever will see. He had thought of me before the foundations of the Earth, and He made His plans for me. Then on the day that I saw Him, I realized that—for some reason—I had been chosen simply to see Him as he is.

As I was flying to New York to meet with Andrea and her friends, I surmised that the two epiphanies that I saw had to be related—or at least similar, even though they were thirteen years apart. I had been given permission or made to see both epiphanies in absolute detail. So I later asked a few basic questions of my observations:

Why would God show me a man who was a Mormon as the Antichrist?

Why do people record ancestral family trees?

The purpose of the information-gathering is to simply record blood-linked or marriage-related individuals. By "linked," I mean all people and their relatives as far back as recordings and censuses were taken.

You and I are personally interested in where we came from and who we were, and are currently, related to. God has no absolutely no use whatsoever for historical family trees. I see the gathering of such information as foreboding as the End Times grow closer. God knows us personally, every single one—along with the number of hairs on our heads. Who then would have a use for such information? And for what ultimate purpose?

God created everything for His own purpose. Satan had only one original idea in all of his existence, and he screwed that up in the Garden of Eden. It is Satan who cannot create anything except misery and havoc in every facet of our lives if we don't defend against him through Christ!

Did you know that the registration accounts of every single living and dead soul, listed by the family trees online, are accounted for by an individual number that can be converted easily to a barcode?

Remember that, according to Scripture, the Beast's number is 666. Remember, that it is the number of a man. It explains so in the Bible.

It just so happens that the man is still living today who perfected the barcode. His three names each have six letters. Research his name!

The Scriptures warn us not to take the sign, or the mark, of the Beast if we are left behind after the Rapture! I believe that the mark or sign is actually the barcode, which can be injected under the skin in the form of a small transmitter for eventual identification by scanners and satellites. That is the ONLY way that Satan will be able to account for the nonbelievers in Christ that are left behind.

Think of it this way in simple terms. Satan needs the barcode, or mark, to keep up with those nonbelievers who are left on Earth after the Rapture. Also, an account would be needed for each individual in order to control and distribute the remaining commodities and supplies.

God, on the other hand, knows every hair on our heads from billions of years ago when He first thought of us. He needs no other means of identification for His children.

To clarify: simply give your heart to Jesus Christ and tell Him that you love and trust in Him. Trust in Him for an eternal life in an unimaginably beautiful place! No barcodes needed!

The barcode, along with the massive worldwide tracking system that is now in place around this planet, is the Beast! It will monitor and control your every move, should you partake of it.

Curiously, I asked: *what would a Mormon politician and rancher businessman who was a community leader have to do with either epiphany?*

Mitt Romney is loved and admired by most of his people, as I understand it. He was always, and is currently, a very popular man. He may even run for a national political office someday.

Why would God first allow me to view Heaven for a time and observe Jesus in all His Glory? Then, thirteen years later, why would He show me the gates of Hell with Mitt Romney standing on a cliff above a fiery maelstrom? Why?

CHAPTER FOURTEEN:

That Which Is About To Come

To say that I had a captive audience was an understatement.

I answered Andrea's questions by recapping the saga. I explained that, of all the observances presented before me, the most astounding was that of Christ and His countenance. I was below Him, and he appeared as tall as the ceilings in a house. As any mortal human would be, I was simply enamored by the purity of His being that shown through His countenance. If I could have placed my hand near the projection of his brilliance, it would have been as if my hand had disappeared within the light. The Lord brought me unto Himself, within reach of the hem of His garment, but I didn't reach out to touch it. I was overwhelmed by the representation of its pureness.

After years of remembrance and curiosity, it dawned on me that Joseph Smith claimed to have seen an angel that appeared to him on multiple occasions. I researched his writings and found Joseph's handwritten description to be a similar description of the dress or attire that I saw.

I recognized the figure in my own epiphany as Jesus Christ, without a doubt. He was holding the Book of Life in His left hand.

Most contemporary theologians think that, if Joseph Smith saw anything, it was a "being of light" conjured up by the Enemy himself. Perhaps I disagree that Joseph saw a being of light. Perhaps it was that Joseph was to establish a religion unto God's purpose, whatever that may have been. If what Joseph Smith saw was true, then our One True God allowed him to see that.

However, if my premise is true that God—knowing about and planning for the Rapture and its aftermath, which He knew would indeed occur—was doing the groundwork planning centuries in advance. In His perfect timing and way, was He laying the necessary groundwork for the final days? It would be simply a matter of conjecture, but I asked: what if this religion of well-organized people would be the ones to manage humanity in the confusion of the aftermath? Did God allow them to be founded for that purpose?

It should be noted that whatever or whomever Joseph Smith saw and perhaps communicated with at that perfect time in our nation's history, it was timed early enough in our history to establish what has currently become the largest and fastest-growing religion on the planet Earth: the Mormons.

What did their Prophet, Joseph Smith, see; and how did he describe what He saw? How did that compare with what I was allowed to see in my epiphanies? Did he see an angel? Was his "angel" epiphany an entity of light? An angel of light, as I understood it, would be an entity devised by the Enemy himself—an entity that projects "light." Or was Joseph Smith's epiphany truly an angel? An angel with a rare "countenance," sent from the Creator Himself? Research for yourselves the hand-written account of Joseph Smith's encounter with his angel.

My epiphany of Christ was an epiphany or absolute "pureness" that shone, without blemish, His grace and tender mercy.

The Scriptures state, in John 1:3: "All things were created by God, and without God, nothing was created." No matter what was seen back then, it was created unto His purpose. An entire religion was established on the basis of what Joseph Smith saw, and it is growing by leaps and bounds today.

As I recapped for Andrea: in 1983, while sitting on my bedside at the age of 40, I was allowed that startling apparition of Heaven and was admonished by Jesus Christ with those seven prophetic words: "Anthony, remain within the cleft of the rock."

He knew my future, and He thought about me and loved me exceedingly—so much so that He showed Himself to me and gave me the admonition. It was no insignificant meeting, by anyone's standards. Or did He simply use that as an opportunity—not only to gently reprimand me, but to allow me to observe and use the epiphany for future comparison?

That was Jesus' personal message to me: seven words from the Master.

Years later, I heard a pastor give the message about God telling Moses to strike the rock! Moses struck it twice—rather than once, as instructed. He disobeyed and paid a price. I can't help but wonder: did I disobey? Am I now in the midst of paying a price?

It was not lost on me—the fact that the voice that is as a two-edged sword, which I heard speak to me, was the very same voice that Moses heard when he was ordered to "Strike the rock." I realized the implications of precisely who was speaking to *me*, of all people. It was the Son of God Himself! How did I not take that very seriously?

With having later seen and realized that Mitt Romney was the man that I saw, I asked: "What on Earth would any religion or people have to do with the Antichrist?"

One evening, I came to the ultimate realization that, when all Christians who are living at the time of the Rapture on this Earth depart in one fell swoop as described in the Bible, God will have already provided for an infrastructure to manage those non-Christians who are left behind. The world will be in a state of confused panic. Instantly, and without warning, fully one-third of this Earth's population will disappear. All Christians will vacate the Earth, along with the "Dead in Christ." The Dead in Christ are all Christians who have passed for centuries, and they will be rejoined with their buried or scattered bodies from all of history.

The Scriptures describe as much in 1 Thessalonians 4:13-18 and in 1 Corinthians 15:50-44. Also, be aware that in Matthew 24:42, it lets us know that no one knows the day or the hour—certainly not me. But if the Antichrist is currently walking the Earth, I must surmise that it can't be much longer in Earth years until God calls us home. Think about the logic and the significance of the Antichrist being alive as I tell you this.

As I continued, my little audience remained spellbound and captivated by my suggestions of the Rapture. I told them that there was no mention of the word "Rapture" in the Bible, but it was described in the New Testament. With all of my friends being Jewish, they all were aware of the teachings in the Old Testament as well. For reference, they would have to crack open the New Testament and get out of the Old Law studies for a bit to know and reference what I was speaking about.

My Jewish friends are all about logic. They are masters at clarity of thought, and they are pragmatic about the old beliefs. There is no room in their beliefs for Jesus Christ. Jesus' solution to death was to conquer it on the cross, thus allowing every breathing man ever born who simply believed on Him to live forever. That was not of their belief system.

Faith in Jesus Christ was always the only solution to death, and it was rewarded with eternal life. But that has always been nonsense to nonbelievers.

So, what about the so-called Rapture? It will happen. It will affect every person who ever existed, one way or another. What if you're left behind? You still have a chance, but whatever you do, don't take the mark of the Beast.

THE MARK! CARPE DEIM!

I believe that a large, established group of some sort will remain after the Rapture and seize the day. Mitt Romney, with his vast skills at business and reorganizing, will be their senior prime choice to assume leadership. The entire world will be in utter chaos. Then at an emergency assemblage of the remnants of the United States government, along with the remnants of the governments in the United Nations and other world organizations such as NATO, a well-organized established organization will be a likely choice to reorganize the remaining governments of the world as their network of members worldwide rapidly increases.

As the initial confusion and shock caused by the disappearance of billions of believers envelops the Earth, the most logical group to reorganize those who remain would be any group who had the largest database with the most personal data about every aunt, uncle, mother, father, sibling, and child—deceased or living. Who would that be? Research for that information! The Chinese and the Koreans who remain will have much the same information.

Family tree information? What about DNA testing? Who keeps that database? Perhaps it is all just contained within, and under, the massive government storage facilities in the western mountains of the USA.

How will that information be used when, and not if, the Rapture comes?

Shortly after the confusion starts, others will be devising methods of controlling others who remain. Perhaps there will even be wars or battles to gain control of all authority of the remaining population. The final eventuality will be that individual identification will be required for practical purposes, and each person must be equipped with that simple little "barcode" personal device. It will be inserted under your skin or wherever. These devises are already perfected and have some practical uses today.

After the Rapture, those remaining must take the "mark/barcode" for identification to purchase anything. This would mean food, clothing, medicine, gas, cars, healthcare, permission to move about the country—the list goes on and on.

How will a person be monitored? How exactly will they know who and where you are?

Remember NSA? The NSA just happens to be only thirty miles down the road from Salt Lake City, Utah. It is centrally located within the United States and protected somewhat from the long reaches of enemy missiles! Coincidence? Or years of planning?

How soon will this occur (and it will occur)? As we speak, Mitt Romney is now in his late sixties. How can I be sure that he exists? God, for some reason that is unknown to me, allowed me to see him in that second epiphany.

He was standing with the Enemy, overlooking the Lake of Fire in 1996 in an epiphany near my home in Georgia. He was placed there by the Lord in order for me to see him. Now I give witness and testimony to his existence and the imminent events that he will be associated with. And to repeat, even though he is now in his sixties, I only just recognized who he actually was when I saw his face on the televised political debate. It had been thirteen years earlier in the epiphany that I saw him. His image was indelible in my memory. A person does not forget epiphanies, and Romney's face never changed from the first time that I saw it. That must mean that God showed me his current face thirteen years earlier in that epiphany. What will happen to bring about a conflagration that would destroy the existence of our world as we know it?

I believe that nuclear war is inevitable. The Earth has finally learned and equipped itself to actually destroy itself, and it will definitely attempt to destroy itself. The ability for the Earth to be destroyed is one of the seven requirements, as described by Jesus. We have arrived at that ability.

The wormwood in the water, as noted in the Bible, is—in all probability—radioactivity from nuclear fallouts. Can one imagine enough radioactivity in the waters of the world that none are safe to drink?

Think about the Chernobyl disaster, then the more recent Fukushima Daiichi Power Plant disaster in 2011. The earthquake and tsunami disaster, which is currently pouring untold amounts of radioactivity into the beautiful Pacific. It never makes the news, but great areas of the oceans are forever exposed to increasing radiation.

When will these things happen?

I am not a predictor, but logic would have it that world destruction must occur. Thirteen years ago, my epiphany allowed me to see a person who is alive as we speak—today.

As I mentioned, emergency leadership would then have to be selected by the powers that gain total Earth control. The new leaders, along with the key leader, would not be elected; they would be selected. Voting would be impossible after the great conflagration, and it wouldn't be allowed—even if the option were possible and available. The New World Order, or the Deep State, will desperately wrestle for control. Peace will eventually break out, but it will last for only 42 months. The cleanup begins, along with the reorganization of the world's remaining nations and populations.

Remember this: it is the Antichrist who assists Israel in rebuilding the Temple for a 42-month project. He will have to have gained great authority within the government of the United States in order to accomplish the funding and reconstruction.

The new leaders will be selected by the ones who hold the communication capabilities and all of the assets to protect them. The US satellites are scattered around the world, covering every continent. As for the probable post-Rapture command headquarters? They will be located in the geological center of the North American Continent near Salt Lake, situated as far from enemy provocations as possible.

There are vast caverns and world command posts in the western mountains. Then the bright ideas to save what is remaining of the planet's resources will be accomplished through mandatory rationing on a massive Socialist scale. That would require a system of secure individual identification. The identification would be that barcode, which is the only invention that can provide an infinitesimal and finite method for tracking and recording the existence of the bearer.

The perfector of the barcode is described in Revelations 13:17-18. The "Beast" would be the total controlling aspect of the system that enumerates every human being who chooses to receive it with a mark, or an attached implement with a barcode receiver inserted, so that satellites can identify you at all times and track all that you do. The Beast would be a fitting name for that system.

Do you have a barcode associated with your name? Do you think that you do not? Certainly, you do. Have you ever logged onto a website for DNA tracking or family tree searches? Yes? Did you enter any information at all? Then you, my friend, now have a barcode that is associated with your name.

Sadly, most people do not realize that that system is currently in place even as we speak. Perhaps it is a coincidence; but more than likely, it is not. The barcode is, in fact, either the mark itself or is incorporated within the mark as an identifier.

The period after the Rapture will last 42 easy months and 42 months of Hell on Earth for all who are left on Earth. That Hell begins at the completion of the Temple as the Jews deny the Antichrist's claim of being God. Altogether, those will be seven tough years. Those who take the mark will be destroyed and cast into utter darkness, according to the Bible.

Don't bet against the Word! Everything that was ever predicted in the Bible has come to fruition, and it will continue to do so until God calls us home. That certainly includes the Last Days.

My friends then asked me, "Why this Mitt Romney person?"

I answered: he is simply the man whom I saw in the epiphany in 1996. He is a prominent Mormon. To explain once more, there were two men in my second epiphany in 1996, standing on a cliff at my home and overlooking my valley. The valley was shown roiling with fire and lava like an ocean. I surmised that one man was the Enemy and the other behind him was the Antichrist. I later identified Mitt

Romney as the taller man who was standing to the slight rear of the Enemy. I was later shocked to see him alive and debating a politician.

When I saw him, I almost had a heart attack. I never in my life expected to see the man in the epiphany alive and walking around Earth. To me, I had to surmise that the "End"—as described in the Scriptures—was imminent.

For years after originally seeing him within that scene, I always expected it to be ten, twenty—perhaps even fifty years or more into the future. Never in my wildest dreams did I expect to see that man alive and walking around in 2012. It was sixteen years after my second epiphany. I was totally shocked—so much that I leapt out of my chair the moment I saw him. I never forgot that face with that downcast condescending expression.

Other than that, I understand that his skills as an organizer are unsurpassed. Who better than to lead the remnant of those who are left behind? After the Rapture, he is designated to seek and seize power—whether appointed or elected. He will run the show.

One thing Romney did argue in the debate, which is most pertinent and of great significance, was his statement proclaiming Russia as our greatest enemy. Who would know better?

Currently, Mr. Romney has recognized that he is a man whom others suspect is the Antichrist, and he has stated several times—and maintained—that he is simply an ordinary businessman and cattleman.

At that moment, I looked at Andrea and the group and told them that I, too, am only an ordinary man who has been allowed to witness extraordinary epiphanies. And those extraordinary details contained within those epiphanies may hold the "End Times" significance that I have described. I believe that God allowed me to see all that I saw in order to write a book and to give fair warning to all who read it.

Finally, I asked my friends if they truly understood the significance of the fact that the man that I saw as the Antichrist is currently alive and walking the Earth as a powerful politician. They all understood the significance completely. The "End," as they call it, is near.

Then I asked for further questions, and they had none.

So I left them with a Bible verse: John 3:1-21. "Ye MUST be born again to see the Kingdom of God." Simply accept, believe, and have faith in Jesus as your Savior to receive His promise of eternal life.

I wished them all a great abundant and spirit-blessed life as we shook hands, hugged each other and said our goodbyes. Did they believe me? It was their choice to make.

It was time to return to JFK. I asked Andrea if the limo could pick me up at my old street at Beach 131st. She agreed, as we wanted to walk the ten or so blocks along the beach one last time.

The late September dusk was chilly, and she held and squeezed my hand in silence as we walked the surf line one last time. She turned her head away from me and kept looking away out to the crashing waves. I could tell that she was crying and trying to hide her emotions. My heart was in my throat as well as we walked the half-mile up the beach.

This was truly the last time that I would ever see her, and we both realized that. As we approached my old apartment, we stopped and hugged each other one long last time. I glanced up at a dozen or so seagulls that had gathered screaming in the sunset as they flew closely overhead.

She said, "I see tears in your eyes."

I smiled and said, "I see tears in yours as well. I just remember an old saying that tears are a language that God truly understands. But I know that He understands all languages and knows full well our pain and sufferings."

She nodded, not saying anything. Then I spoke again in a serious tone.

"Andrea, after I return home, I'm going to send you a certified letter with important information. Once you receive the letter, you must tell Eric to assist you in following the enclosed instructions to the letter. It will be necessary for your survival."

Andrea looked at me quizzically. I told her that I didn't have time to explain, but I repeated that she and Eric needed to follow my exact instructions implicitly once they received the letter. As before, she simply nodded and said nothing.

We stole our last kiss and said our last goodbye and I departed, leaving behind someone wonderful and something that was never meant to be in the first place.

As the 737 cleared airspace over Rockaway, I looked down at our departing beach in the twilight and thought that, had a strange separating force between us not occurred those many years ago, I would never have gone back home. I would have started a new life that was not meant to be. I would have lost a wonderful family and would never have been allowed to see the two revealing epiphanies that God had planned for me. God has a way of protecting His own from our faults and misgivings.

Had I stayed, I would never have written a book of revelation with a warning! I would never have written the book explaining that this world, which we now live in and know and love so well, is much closer to its end than anyone realizes. I would never have lived the life that God intended and sounded the alarm that the end of the world, as we know it, is imminent.

Never has the world been more unprepared for that which is about to happen.

EPILOGUE:

The Letter

December 20, 2012

Dear Andrea,

I know that we haven't spoken since my last visit. I hope this letter finds you and the family happy and well.

The flight home was uneventful. Ever since our first flight together all those years ago, flights in and out of JFK always call for deep reflection on my part.

As I had explained before my departure, I am writing this letter out of concern for your safety and survival when the big event does occur. You must trust me: the event will occur. So you must prepare. In case you haven't given it much thought, you and the family will have to immediately leave New York City within twenty-four hours of the event. New York City will immediately become a hellhole, along with all of the other major metropolises on Earth. You must be prepared for the event well in advance in order to depart for a place of relative safety. I suggest that you would need to move south—down to the mountains of North Georgia, where I live, to have any chance. The safest way to get there will be by sea and along the Atlantic Coast.

This will require months of careful planning, and it will also require that Eric keep his Beneteau Oceanis 55 well-stocked with a year's worth of supplies—or more—and keep it moored nearby in Sheepshead Bay or out near Montauk for quick departure. Stay away from the coast as you travel south. A private courier will deliver two sealed, trunk-sized equipment cases to your home at Beach 140. Among the items packed away will be land and nautical and maps with suggested routes. Also, there will be legal documents, combinations for locked doors, and tactical gear so that you may safely and easily occupy my property in Georgia. These cases will also have ample means of self-protection with instructions to use with the items inside.

Remember, after the event occurs, there will be no active GPS anymore since all electronics will be useless or nonexistent. Suggest to Eric that he cash out funds and purchase all the gold coins that you can afford. You will need gold for barter. Your cash or bank accounts will be useless. Gold or silver will be the only valid currency. Whatever you do, do not take the "Mark" in any way, shape, or form. Your eternal soul will be at stake if you do!

The supplies and equipment will be sent to your mother's home at Beach 140. You should arrange to have only yourself, Eric, or others in your most trusted inner circle meet the shipment. I suggest locking the shipment away in your wine cellar until you can move the equipment cases to the sailboat after the event occurs.

Whatever you do, tell no one. I repeat, tell nobody! Your life, and the lives of those you love, will depend on absolute secrecy.

I will call or write in the near future to check on you, but please remember that—after the event—I will not be around to help you. Until that time, please call me anytime, as you have my number.

All my love,
Anthony

Made in the USA
Monee, IL
15 April 2020